OLD GIRLS BEHAVING BADLY

KATE GALLEY

Boldwood

First published in Great Britain in 2024 by Boldwood Books Ltd.

Copyright © Kate Galley, 2024

Cover Design by Lizzie Gardiner

Cover Photography: Shutterstock

A CIP catalogue record for this book is available from the British Library.

Paperback ISBN 978-1-83533-866-7

Large Print ISBN 978-1-83533-862-9

Hardback ISBN 978-1-83533-861-2

Ebook ISBN 978-1-83533-859-9

Kindle ISBN 978-1-83533-860-5

Audio CD ISBN 978-1-83533-874-2

MP3 CD ISBN 978-1-83533-864-3

Digital audio download ISBN 978-1-83533-858-2

Boldwood Books Ltd
23 Bowerdean Street
London SW6 3TN
www.boldwoodbooks.com

For Sarah

COMPANION WANTED FOR ELDERLY
WOMAN – NORTH NORFOLK

Temporary position
LIve-In
BOX: 765034

Job Specifications:

Live-in companion wanted for an elderly woman. You will have your own room with a private bathroom in a substantial home on a large country estate in North Norfolk.

The position is temporary – seven days in the last week of August during a family wedding party.

Your duties will be light. No personal care is involved. The woman requires, in essence, a friendly person to be her companion while the family are otherwise engaged with wedding preparations.

You must be efficient, quick-witted and happy to join the family for their very special occasion.

If the applicant is successful, there is the potential for a permanent position in the woman's London home.

Salary £750

Please apply with CV

1

GINA

'So, is that it then, no discussion; you're selling up and buggering off? What does my dad have to say about it?'

'Your father was *finding* himself on a wellness retreat in Santa Fe. He's back now and staying in a flat in Maidenhead, apparently.'

'He had a holiday, Mum! Maybe you could have gone too if you'd shown some interest.'

I held the phone a little away from my ear while my daughter vented on the other end of the line. I hadn't told Alice that two days after her father had dropped a grenade into our marriage and disappeared to the airport, a *Dear John* letter had arrived. Douglas, it seemed, had left it quite late to have his midlife crisis. He was seventy-three.

'And you don't need to sell the house. Let Dad have his moment and then he'll come back.'

'He's not coming back, Alice. He's made that very clear and I really don't have any choice; he's the one pushing the sale,' I said. 'I can't keep this place on my own. Your dad needs his half share and, frankly, I don't want to rattle around here any more. It's too big and has been for a while.'

This wasn't actually true. I didn't rattle around; the house was quite modest and we'd never pushed ourselves to extend it past a small conservatory.

'Get a lodger then,' Alice said. 'It's our family home, all our memories, and you're just going to hand them over to somebody else! Take a breath, Mother. You don't need to do everything all at once. Dad's only been gone five minutes and you've packed up the house without any conversation or consideration. This is not like you.'

I sighed. I couldn't help it. Alice just wasn't listening and contrary to what she said, this was actually the third of such conversations I'd had with my daughter; I didn't have the energy to do it all again. Alice adored her father; it was so much easier if this was all my fault.

'I haven't packed everything up, I've just been going through the loft, but I do have *your* things boxed up carefully. You can come and get them and enjoy your childhood memories in your own home.'

That was when the tears started and I moved the phone away again. Alice was forty, married with two children and behaving like one of them.

'Look, darling, this thing going on with your father is complicated. He needed to go away and he doesn't want to be with me any more. I can't stay here and look after a house of memories on my own. You wouldn't want that for me, would you?'

'I think you're being completely selfish,' Alice said, sniffed for effect and then hung up.

I took one long calming breath and placed my phone gently on the mantelpiece. The oak had been salvaged from a reclamation yard, then after it had been sanded and oiled I'd let my two children carve their names into the end of the timber. I ran my fingers over the letters: Alice and Christopher. It was just one of the many memories that Alice was talking about. Their handprints were in the concrete base now under the conservatory floor. Their heights had been recorded on the inside of the door frame between the living and dining room. Chris had been just eighteen months old when I had marked his height in ink. The lines of my careful hand tracing the growth of my children, now sun-bleached and faint with the passage of time. To be fair to Alice, these memories could not be boxed up.

I walked over to the French doors that led out onto our garden, small as gardens went, but what we could afford when we first moved to this part of Oxfordshire and it was the one thing I would take with me if I could. I'd devoted years to the garden, to careful planting and experimenting with what worked and what didn't in our soil. There were not many days in the year that I wouldn't be out there, pulling weeds, deadheading, trimming. Even in the winter months I'd find little jobs to do. It was my sanctuary.

The treehouse that Douglas had built, all those years ago, was still just about clinging to the boughs of the beech. I imagined that the new owners would pull it down. They'd sand out the names on the mantelpiece, paint over the lines on the door frame and obliterate the very existence of our family in that house. I wasn't at all sure how I felt about this. It was just a house after all, wasn't it? Memories were not things cemented into the fabric of a home, they were thoughts you could carry with you, weren't they? My own thoughts had been preoccupied with how Douglas had just left me. With a few things thrown into a suitcase, a letter absolving him of a conversation and barely a backward glance, he'd simply gone.

I opened the doors and stepped onto the patio to pull a weed out from between the slabs, then sat down in one of the garden chairs, my elbows on my knees, my chin in my hands. I watched as a butterfly flitted from one purple spearhead of buddleia to another, before coming down to land on the ground beside me. I was pretty sure it was a red admiral and I trawled my limited butterfly brain deciding that it was. Then, I noticed that one of its wings was torn at the corner; one little piece missing in an otherwise perfect symmetry.

'Hello there, are you hurt?' I said, as it rested in the full glare of the sunshine. I had a sudden urge to pick it up, to look after it, to keep it. I didn't, of course – I hadn't completely lost my mind – but as it lifted off the ground and disappeared over next door's fence it suddenly hit me, like a hefty punch in the gut, that I was very much alone.

* * *

I had celebrated my seventy-first birthday a few months previously and my son had given me a huge coffee-table book about the history of art. I knew he'd been watching me closely for my reaction, and I had managed to keep my face steady and receptive, a warm smile placed on my lips while my heart did that flip-flop of sadness that it still did from time to time.

'You know,' he'd said tentatively. 'A reminder of the good old days...'

He'd trailed off, but I was quick to reassure him with how much I loved it. And I did love it; well, I loved the idea of it, but I'd only opened it three times since my birthday. The first couple of times I'd flicked through, just admiring the pictures while it was still on the table, but the last time, I had taken it onto my lap and disappeared inside the pages before Douglas appeared and took it gently from my hands.

'You don't really want to be dragging all that up again, do you, Gina,' he'd said and wedged it onto the bottom of the bookshelf.

* * *

At the start of my working life, I had studied art history at Warwick University, focusing on Italian and Renaissance studies and then after a spell at the British Museum, had spent a whole summer with my mother, Ellen, in Venice where we had immersed ourselves in the city's art and culture. When we returned I had worked in partnership with her at a National Trust property in Richmond where she held a senior role as curator.

But, everything changed after those precious years working with her. There had been a bleak spell where I hadn't been able to do anything at all. My mother was gone and the landscape of my life had shifted.

I'd sleepwalked through the next few years and woke – as if from a coma – to find myself married to Douglas with baby Alice on my hip, Christopher toddling about and little memory of how I'd actually got there. My friends at the time urged me to go back to work, to be as independent as possible, find a way, but my heart was broken, and after what had happened to my mother I just couldn't consider it. Instead I clung onto what I regarded as my comfortable bubble of familial bliss with Douglas at the centre – my rock.

I'd never gone back.

As Douglas inched closer to retirement and we both began to slow up, I started to examine my marriage. I'd always called him my rock, and he had been. He'd steered me through the most awful time of my life and I'd become completely dependent on him. I wondered what our retirement years together would look like.

He'd often talked about his wish to travel – although we only had a Mediterranean cruise and a handful of British holiday cottages under our belt – but still, I imagined the two of us sipping cocktails in Italian bars, walking the Cornish cliff paths while we were still able, taking in a castle or two in France and trekking trails of discovery. I had an image of these future years that really didn't fit with the ones that had come before, as if we'd both sidestep into a new existence.

In reality, Douglas had his leaving party from the pharmaceutical company he'd worked at for all of his career, collected his crystal decanter and taken up golf. He'd spent the last five years on the golf course or in his armchair, or on the stool playing his prized piano and, now it seems, had been silently planning. His plans didn't involve me, though; they were all about *finding* himself, he'd told me, and it turned out he couldn't do that with something as inconvenient as a wife in tow. My marriage of forty-three years was over and Douglas had pulled the rug out from underneath my feet before he left. We'd been merrily playing this game of life, the two of us; I thought I'd been following the rules, but just as the finish line was in sight, Douglas had changed them.

My phone was ringing again inside and I got up and steeled myself for another conversation with Alice, but it wasn't my daughter on the phone, it was my son.

'Hi, Mum, do you wanna come over? We can go to the pub and talk about what an absolute prat my dad is?'

2

GINA

Chris lived in the beautiful village of Turville in the Chilterns with his husband, Gavin, and their gorgeous Labrador, Kenny. He was named after Gavin's grandfather and was, in turn, called Kenneth, Kenny and Ken. Sometimes after he'd stolen a shoe, a boot or even once Gav's cashmere scarf and discarded it in the garden, he was referred to as shithead, but never by me. After losing my own lovely dog the previous year, I was always delighted to see him and to let my fingers stroke his soft head and caress his velvet ears. He slept on the end of my bed whenever I stayed overnight in their spare room, taking up more space than was comfortable, but I really didn't mind.

Chris and Gav's house was the right-hand-side of a pair of semi-detached cottages with old red bricks and slate roofs. The cottages were turn of the century, impeccably maintained and they shared a wisteria that wound its way around their front doors and across the little porch roofs. In May, when it bloomed, the facade of the two houses was a riot of lilac with a musky fragrance that enveloped you as you arrived. Driveway space was limited, but I just managed to squeeze my Renault Clio next to Gav's Golf.

Chris greeted me at the door and folded me into a tight hug while Kenny sat patiently by my feet waiting for his turn. Not only was he the most gorgeous dog, but he was also the very best boy.

'I assumed,' I said, pointing to my overnight bag.

'Damn right you did. There are adult beverages in that pub with our names on them. Gav's just popped up to the shops for provisions. He's making us a curry later.'

I took a breath and felt myself relax into Chris's company. He always made everything so easy.

The pub was crowded inside because the landlady was having a birthday party and even though she'd made it clear we were very welcome to join, we decided to go and sit outside in the garden and we found a table under the gazebo. It served the dual purpose of shading us from the sun when it bothered to come out, but also from those occasional drops of rain that fell from passing clouds. It was early August and the weather, so far that summer, had been mixed, but the Met Office were predicting a heatwave come the end of the month and everyone was holding out for it.

'I've had Alice on the phone,' Chris said, picking up his pint and taking a sip. 'I won't play with your intelligence and repeat what she said, though.'

'She's upset about the house and her memories, but I've taken close photographs of everything I can't move and boxed up all of her special things,' I said.

'So special, she didn't take them with her when she left home,' he scoffed.

'Some people just don't like change – I do understand. She's sensitive, that's all.'

'So, what about you and Dad?' he asked. 'You know he's back, don't you?'

I picked up my Pimm's and scooped out half a strawberry as the crowd inside the pub burst into a rousing rendition of 'Happy Birthday'. I looked at my son across the table, his sunglasses hiding his brown eyes, his hair, once dark, now speckled with grey. He was the image of his father.

'Yes, I know.'

'And have you had the chance to talk? I know he disappeared off quickly, but now he's back, will you be able to, I don't know, sort things out?'

I felt very uncomfortable talking about Douglas with Chris. A child should not have to listen to tales of a failed marriage, no matter how old that child was. I opened my mouth to tell him about the *Dear John* letter, but then I remembered the contents and closed it again. Not only had Douglas told me he no longer loved me and wanted something more from life, but he'd stuck the boot in by writing that I'd become beige and unexciting. Well, he'd said his life had become those things, but I knew he really meant me.

'I haven't spoken to him since he came back. I need to, though. We've house stuff to go through,' I said, popping the fruit into my mouth. 'I don't think there is anything to sort out personally; his intentions are pretty clear.'

'Right,' Chris said slowly. 'So, he means business then.'

'It seems so,' I said. 'I've been in contact with the estate agents and they've got the paperwork ready for the house to go on the market. Douglas has booked an open week where they channel most of the viewings.'

'Don't make any rash decisions, Mum. I don't think you've really processed what's happened. It's a big thing. Did you see it coming? I mean, did he show any sign of wanting to leave? Is there someone else?'

I thought about that for a moment. I'd been so wrapped up in dealing with my situation, I'd not given much thought to why I was in it. I cast my mind back to the last ten years of our marriage and certainly the years since Douglas had been retired. If I was honest there had been less intimacy, conversation had become limited to what was for dinner and what time that would be, what we might watch on the television or when Alice might be visiting with her children – always a good reminder of our important family bond. I had assumed it was enough. I'd been wrong.

I didn't bother to ask Chris if he'd spoken to his dad, because they didn't speak much at all. Douglas hadn't exactly embraced Chris's sexuality in the same way that I had, and his relationship with his son had become more distant since Chris and Gavin had married. Douglas had said on more than one occasion that he just didn't really get it, as if there was a special something he had to understand more tricky than two people simply loving one another.

'I didn't really see it coming, although I probably should have. I don't think there's anyone else,' I said, but I wasn't sure that was true. I didn't know who owned the Maidenhead flat and I knew the anecdotal fact that men rarely left a marriage to be on their own. Women did; not men.

'And you really have to move? I'm not being sentimental about the house, I'm just thinking about you. Where will you go? Don't forget our spare room and of course it's yours if you want it.'

I took his hand across the table and gave it a squeeze. I loved him for offering, but the thought of being so desperate I'd have to move in with my child was depressing. I adored Gavin and could see how easy it would be to fit in with the two of them in their relaxed cottage with its pretty garden and a view across the Chiltern Hills. I wouldn't though. I didn't want my son to see how limited my options were. He really didn't need to know how reckless we'd been with our future.

'I think I may have found something,' I said.

'Something? Don't you mean somewhere?'

'Well, actually it's a job.'

'A job? Things aren't that bad, are they? Look, Mum, Dad can't just sell the house and leave you to it. You're entitled to part of his pension, savings and all that. You do know that don't you?'

'Yes, of course,' I said, not really knowing what I was due. At the moment I was just thinking of what I could do short term. It was all very well being told you were entitled to something, but how long would it take to resolve all the financial issues. Did Douglas want a divorce? How could we possibly live separately but still be married? Shouldn't I try to be independent and untether myself from the rock, or was it too late because the rock had untethered itself from me?

'The job is just something I've been thinking about for a while,' I lied.

I'd spent the previous day with my head in my laptop. Firstly looking for properties I could afford with my half share of the house. The problem with that was the equity release we had done. It had been primarily to pay off the student loans both Chris and Alice had accrued, but then Chris had needed help with a deposit on his house and Douglas had suggested a new and rather extravagant car and why not a cruise, while we were at it. It wouldn't matter down the line, when it needed to be paid back. Douglas had done the maths and we could easily afford a nice downsize with the remaining equity, he'd told me. Now though, dividing that into two was a bit of a joke. Douglas would be all right; his pension was larger than mine and his ninety-eight-year-old mother was still alive – just – and had pots of money squirrelled away for him. Mine was not.

I'd closed down the search for properties when my filters had taken me too many miles away and the options had become unbearable. Instead, I'd found a link to a wanted position for a companion in *The Lady* online magazine and had fallen down a new rabbit hole of possibilities. The words *live-in* had sprung out at me, also *efficient* and *quick-witted*. Surely those were skills I had. After all, hadn't I spent most of my adult life looking after others? I needed an income if I was to be independent and I had to find somewhere to live. Combining those two problems into one situation could actually be the answer. Most importantly, I really wanted to be out of the house during that open week. I'd sent off my details and was now waiting to hear back.

Chris took another gulp of his beer as I told him all about the advert.

'It sounds rather like you're running away,' he said with a sad sort of frown stretched across his forehead.

'I'm not running way.' I laughed. But actually I thought that I might be and it was possibly forty-three years too late.

3

DOROTHY

Dorothy Reed had been in the boathouse all morning sitting on the balcony, overlooking the Thames, and watching the traffic on the water, trying to feel soothed by the white noise of the weir. It was busy, as it usually was, and she took a little comfort from the many boats meandering past her. Their own boat was below her: a narrowboat painted in a beautiful chalk blue with a glossy black bottom. Her husband, Philip, had bought her nearly fifteen years previously and had her restored in a boatyard in Essex before bringing her home to Hampton. She was called the *Castillo del Mar*, which translated to Sea Castle. It was a small joke for a small vessel, her husband had told her as he proudly showed her off.

The narrowboat hadn't been out of their boathouse for the year since Philip's death, though. Dorothy's son, Miles, had asked her if he could take her out in the spring, but she had said no, as she couldn't bear to see anything else of her beloved Philip's taken away. Not yet, and possibly not ever.

Dorothy glanced at the watch on her thin wrist – it would need another link taken out of it before long, as it was perilously close to sliding off her arm. It was nearly twelve-fifteen and she had lost the entire morning up here, sitting, watching, seething. Lavinia would be here soon and she wasn't at all ready.

She closed the doors and stepped back into the living area of the boathouse. It was another space they had renovated with a kitchen, a bedroom and a bathroom. Dorothy had filled it with the art she no longer made and a collection of houseplants, books and gorgeous scented candles. She had a lovely walnut sideboard and a long velvet sofa in a rich teal with gold cushions. Her house was more traditionally decorated in creams and greys, but out here she liked a bolder look. Miles had suggested she rent it out in the summer months to make use of it, or to get a lodger for a bit of company, but Dorothy couldn't even think about that at the moment.

She walked down the steps and noticed her neighbour, Erik, relaxing on a sunlounger with a paperback book in his lap. He turned to her, shielding the sun from his eyes with his hand.

'Good afternoon, Dorothy,' he said. 'Gorgeous day, isn't it.'

Dorothy walked over to the low fence that separated the two gardens and rested a hand on the top of one of the panels. She was in the shade of the weeping willow that softened the hard edge of the lawn before it stopped at the water.

'It is,' she agreed.

Dorothy liked Erik very much. He was in his late sixties and had lived next door for the last five years. He was divorced from his wife and had a grown-up son who visited often. Erik had a narrowboat of his own and Philip and he could talk for hours about adjustments to the engines, or new latches for the windows, storage solutions or how best to fix a pump. Erik also had a penchant for crime thrillers and liked to discuss plot twists with Dorothy, but not so much recently.

'I'm about to put the kettle on if you fancy joining me,' he said, sliding a bookmark between the pages and getting up off the lounger.

'I would like that very much; however, I have my daughter-in-law coming to assist in me choosing a companion this afternoon.'

'Oh? Didn't know you were in the market for help.'

'I'm not, but we have this family wedding in Norfolk and Miles seems to think I need assistance while we're there. Also, after my little *fall* the other week, they've got it in their heads that I need watching or something. They're glossing it up as companion, but all I'm hearing is minder. I had a dizzy spell and fell over – that was all – and they want to move a carer in. It's all very frustrating.'

'Ah, I see. And you obviously don't think you need help.'

'I *know* I don't need help, but they won't listen, so I shall have to do my utmost to frighten off the applicants.'

'Can I come and watch?' Erik asked, with a grin.

Dorothy laughed for a moment and then seemed to catch herself.

'I'd better go and sharpen my teeth,' she said turning for the house, and she listened to Erik chuckling as she navigated the pathway to her kitchen door. She'd have a quick cup of tea and then prepare herself for the bustling and kind warmth of her daughter-in-law.

* * *

'Well, I suppose we'll let you know then, Clare,' Lavinia said to the girl, who was already on her feet, her phone in hand and making her way to the front door.

Dorothy could hear the two of them whispering in the hallway and then the sound of the door clicking shut. Lavinia stood for a moment in the doorway to the living room, her arms folded tightly across her chest while Dorothy sat rigid in her chair.

'Dot! What was all that about? You frightened the poor girl away. You can't ask questions like that.'

'But she did have a terrible complexion. I was only wondering what sort of skin care regime would result in such a breakout.'

'It's not like you to be cruel. We'll never find someone if you behave like that and the wedding's in only a couple of weeks.'

Dorothy set her lips into a tight line, chastened. Lavinia was right – that was probably too much. She hated to disappoint her daughter-in-law. Lavinia was a blessing and the best thing Dorothy's son, Miles, ever did was to marry her. Some considered her a little cold, but really, when you got to know her it was obvious she just liked things done properly. She quietly put in the hard work to make sure everything was perfect. Someone needed to, because if Dorothy was honest, Miles was rather lacking some-times. Oh, he worked hard enough at the office, but left all of the emotional heavy lifting to his wife.

The sound of a car on the gravel outside made both women turn to the open window. A door closed and footsteps could be heard, then voices.

'Are you here for the companion job?' said a voice that sounded like Clare, clearly still loitering outside. They couldn't hear the response, though.

'Good luck with that, then,' she said. 'She's a right miserable cow.'

Lavinia's head whipped round to Dorothy and the two women locked eyes for a moment before they both began to giggle as the doorbell rang.

'Be nice,' Lavinia whispered before going to answer it.

An older woman walked into the living room and seemed to be sizing up the place, the way her eyes darted over Dorothy's possessions.

'Dot, this is Gina Knight,' Lavinia said with a pointed look. 'Gina lives in Oxfordshire and has two grown-up children and two grand-children.'

Dorothy thought that Lavinia sounded like a game show host introducing a contestant, but decided to keep her mouth shut.

'Good afternoon, Mrs Reed,' Gina said.

'Dorothy is fine,' Dorothy said, taking in the woman standing awkwardly in the middle of her living room.

She seemed a bit mousy. She wore navy trousers and a white cotton blouse. Her shoes were sensible and flat, and her hair hung in gentle waves around her face. She could be as young as fifty-five or as old as seventy; it was hard to tell because she had the air of an older person, but her skin was luminous and had few wrinkles. At least she was considerably closer in age to Dorothy than the last girl, but then she reminded herself, she had no intention of employing her anyway.

'You have a lovely home,' Gina said, taking the seat Lavinia offered her. 'It's such a great setting with Hampton Court just over the road and the Thames behind you.'

'Thank you, dear, I'm very happy here,' Dorothy said, but she could hear how wooden her own voice sounded and she didn't smile.

Her daughter-in-law beamed, though, and Dorothy sensed that Lavinia was overcompensating.

'Isn't it lovely. It was my husband's childhood home. We love coming back to visit, well me visiting, him coming home I suppose. So, what was it that appealed to you about a job as a companion? I see you have no experience,' Lavinia said glancing at her notes. 'Not that that's a bad thing necessarily.'

Gina shifted her position on her chair and suddenly looked a little awkward.

'My circumstances have recently changed and, I suppose, I'm looking for a new challenge.'

'I don't think Dorothy is much of a challenge,' Lavinia said with a smile. 'What did you do in your working life? Did you have a job outside of the home?'

There was silence for a little longer than was comfortable and Dorothy wondered if Gina was going to lie, but when her words arrived they seemed to come naturally.

'I was an art historian many years ago and spent some time curating collections at Ham House in Richmond, actually. But then I gave it up, and we moved to Oxfordshire anyway, for my husband's job, so it didn't really work. That might be one of my biggest regrets,' she said wistfully.

'Art historian?' Dorothy spoke up, her interest piqued. 'Well, that's fascinating.'

'Yes, I worked at the British Museum for a while too. At Ham House, I worked with my mother,' she added.

Dorothy sensed a complete change in the direction of her afternoon and she homed in on Gina's expression, which clouded over for a moment at the mention of her mother.

'I do realise that art history doesn't feature in the working life of a companion,' Gina continued quickly, while blushing, 'but I'm practical and quick-witted.'

'I think it could feature, actually,' Dorothy said. 'I'm very interested in art myself.'

'I can see,' Gina said, looking around Dorothy's living room. 'Your Meissen vases are beautiful.'

'Thank you. Would you like me to give you a tour? We could walk down to the boathouse. My husband was a collector and kept a few pieces in there and some of my own too.'

'You're an artist?'

'Used to be. I worked with kiln-formed glass,' Dorothy said, suddenly keen to impress this woman.

'Are those your pieces in the borders under the windows at the front? Because they're stunning. The sunlight really catches them.'

'I made those in my friend's studio in Buckinghamshire and Jacque and I exhibited at Stourbridge.'

Dorothy tried to rein herself in as she realised she was beginning to sound boastful.

'I'm very impressed,' Gina said.

Dorothy glanced at Lavinia who looked completely surprised.

'I'll go and make a pot of coffee, Dorothy, ready for when you get back, shall I?' she said.

'That would be lovely, my dear,' Dorothy replied, easing herself up out of her chair.

* * *

After Dorothy had shown Gina some of Philip's most treasured pieces in the house while steadfastly ignoring the glaring gap on the wall above her fireplace, they walked down to the boathouse.

Dorothy had picked up the key from the dish inside her patio doors for the second time that day before they had stepped out into the garden, and once they had walked up the stairs to the side of the boathouse, she used it to open the door.

Gina was impressed, Dorothy could tell, and it gave her unexpected pleasure to see this woman pick up her things and talk about what she knew about them and listen as Dorothy filled in the gaps in her knowledge. She marvelled at the space too and said how much she loved the decor. Then she noticed that Dorothy had left a small candle lit and her expression changed at once.

'Did you know you'd left a candle alight?'

Her voice had gone up an octave and her eyes were wide. She lifted her hand suddenly and clutched at her other arm.

'I was out here earlier, must have forgotten to blow it out,' Dorothy said, stepping forward to do exactly that.

'It's very dangerous, you know – anything could happen.'

'Yes, my mistake,' Dorothy said, thinking that not much was really going to happen, other than a waste of an expensive candle with no one to admire the scent. She guessed that Gina must have had a mishap at some point; that would explain her odd reaction. Keen to get her back onto the topic of art, she got Gina's attention on the three paintings by Patsy Niven that hung along the wall above the sideboard and the candle was forgotten.

'You really do have a super place, here,' Gina said, her hands now back by her sides, her voice even.

'Miles, my son, jokes with me that he's going to move into the house and move me out here, but you know, I wouldn't mind, because I love it up here.'

Dorothy turned the lock and opened the doors, pushing them back to the balcony and watched as Gina took in a breath and admired the view.

'That's the south end of Ash Island there,' Dorothy said, pointing across. 'You can see their houseboats and boats, and all that rushing water, of course, is the weir.'

'I can see why you love it here; it's a really special spot, Dorothy.'

'I do feel guilty, though, just me in that big house, and I will move, but when the time is right and that's not quite now.'

'You shouldn't feel guilty. This is your home. Why should you give it up to please others?' she said and then added, 'I'm moving at the minute.'

'Where are you moving to? Are you staying in Oxfordshire?'

'Not sure, to be honest. I'm on my own now,' she said, pausing for a moment. 'I guess I can go anywhere I want to, but I don't really know where that is.'

Dorothy laid her hand gently on Gina's arm and offered her a sad sort of smile.

'You feel untethered,' she said. 'I know exactly how that feels.'

When Dorothy had locked up and they'd walked back down the steps, she took Gina round to see the boat.

'It belonged to my late husband, Philip,' Dorothy said.

'I honestly know nothing about boats, but I can see she's a beauty,' Gina said. 'I love that chalky blue colour.'

'We used to go out quite a lot, but not any more. Honestly, she's become just an expensive place to sit and have a coffee. It's really rather sad.'

* * *

Lavinia's coffee was always strong and Dorothy took the sugar bowl and gave it to Gina with a sidelong glance and a conspiratorial smile.

'Do you have any questions about the job?' Lavinia asked.

Dorothy watched as Gina racked her brain to think of one. She liked this woman who seemed interested in art with a history of expertise under her belt, and an audacious plan started to form in Dorothy's head. She wondered if Gina was up to the task, but she could hardly ask her with Lavinia here, and besides, she didn't want to scare her off just yet by telling her what that task was. She wondered how biddable Gina was, how persuadable. She certainly wasn't young, but Dorothy had noticed that she seemed like a quiet and compliant type. Then she silently chided herself for her thoughts.

'How about we just work it out as we go along,' she interrupted before Gina could come up with a legitimate question that Dorothy probably wouldn't have an answer for.

'We do have five other candidates, Dot,' Lavinia said.

'Cancel them. I think Gina is perfect, if you'd like the position, that is?'

'I'd be delighted,' Gina said, although Dorothy couldn't tell from her expression if this were true.

'Well, I very much look forward to seeing you in Norfolk then,' Dorothy said, and despite herself she beamed at Gina.

4

GINA

I folded myself into the back seat of the taxi outside Norwich station, my sunglasses pulled down low over my eyes, my enormous suitcase squeezed into the boot. Chris had borrowed my car while his was stuck in the garage having extensive bodywork repairs after a collision with a tractor, but I was happy to get the train. It was quite a trek to Norfolk, after all.

'Not travelling light then,' the driver had said. 'Got the kitchen sink in there?'

He'd laughed, but I just offered him a tight smile.

We headed north out of the city, the air con making me feel chilly on what was really a fairly hot day. I looked out across the flat fields, an endless sea of golden grasses flashing past, parched from the recent drought – the Met Office had been absolutely right with their prediction.

My journey had only started three hours ago, but still I was beginning to feel weary. It wasn't the train journey, it was the month leading up to it.

'Are you here for the wedding then?' the driver asked, keen to engage me in conversation. His eyes appeared in the rear-view mirror, his penetrating gaze taking me in as I tried to keep my own eyes open. 'I hear it's to be quite the *do*.'

I rallied and sat further up in my seat. I was being rude, I knew, but my heart wasn't really in small talk at that moment. My mind was engaged with thoughts of all the potential buyers trailing through my house, opening my cupboard doors and passing judgement on my decor, sizing up my garden that they had no intention of maintaining. Douglas's plan for an open-house week had been embraced by the agents who had lots of viewings lined up. At least he'd let me pick which week and when Dorothy had told me I had the position it had all fallen into place. I couldn't bear the thought of camping out in my own house, trying to keep it show-home ready and couldn't possibly afford to stay in a hotel.

The house no longer really felt like mine anyway and I was beginning to feel hopeful that this week with Dorothy could possibly turn into more. The advert had said there was potential for a permanent position after the wedding. In fact, since meeting her and seeing how uncomplicated she was, how nice and unassuming, how lovely her home was, I had a lot of my hopes pinned on this working out.

Douglas had been round to collect the rest of his things, and I had psyched myself up for the meeting. I'd had the word *divorce* rolling around my head all that morning, waiting for it to land into the middle of our conversation and was going to make Douglas explain his position. But he'd been full of his trip and merrily showing me photos on his phone like we were old friends, rather than a couple with a collapsed marriage. Not a man talking to the woman he considered *unexciting* and *beige*. I'd dutifully looked, but really I was quickly scanning the faces of those in shot to see if there were any women, colourful and exciting women. In the end I'd lost the nerve to say very much at all and he left rather like an acquaintance would, with an *I'll be in touch*.

I took a short breath now, and answered the taxi driver anyway. I was going to have to pull something out of the bag of conversation if I was to survive the week.

'Something like that,' I said. 'To be honest, I'm more... staff.'

'Oh, right,' he said, watching me for a little longer until he assumed he wasn't going to get anything further and returned his eyes to the road.

'Are you a friend of the family then?' I asked him.

'No,' he snorted. 'I don't move in those circles.'

'But you know about the wedding?'

'It may be a big house, Mrs Knight, but it's a very small village.'

'Do you know much about the owner, Leonard Price?' I said.

Dorothy had told me he was the uncle of the bride and that was why the wedding was to be held at his home. Lavinia had said that Leonard was an old family friend and former business partner to Dorothy's late husband and that was how the bride and groom had met. I had switched off a bit at the time, to be honest, but now I realised I was to be among this family for the week and perhaps I should have paid more attention.

'He's rich and arrogant according to my wife's sister, Violet, who cleaned there for a short time a few years back. I'll bet no more arrogant than any other rich man, though. The house is something else, very grand, but Vi said she wasn't sorry to lose her job, as she was always terrified of breaking one of his precious art pieces. I've never been in there myself.

'He's done a little for the village: new planting for the green, a project with a local children's charity for a fun run around his estate, that sort of stuff. He's not married and hasn't got any kids of his own, though. There's not many that know him well.'

He sounded eccentric, like a nice, kindly old man, but then as uncle to the bride, he couldn't be that old, I thought. I relaxed a bit then. A week at a country estate in Norfolk for the wedding of

Dorothy's grandson didn't seem like much of a challenge. A house full of art – I won't pretend that didn't interest me. Dorothy Reed herself, who seemed like a person I could get along with. Of course I was to be paid for my services too, which was a huge motivator in this set-up. I settled back in my seat and tried to tell myself not to expect too much, but the truth was, with my life in a state of limbo, I was actually expecting quite a lot.

* * *

The red-brick mansion was bathed in a warm apricot glow from the rays of the late-afternoon sun. The white cornerstones of the building shone and the gilt face of the clock on the bell tower glowed. Perfectly clipped yew hedges flanked the wide driveway and the lawns appeared to have been cut with a precision laser.

The taxi driver pulled up at the front and I shook myself awake.

Walstone Hall was a jewel in the crown of all the Norfolk country estates, Lavinia had told me, and my first instinct was to agree. The driver left me and my suitcase at the main entrance and I took a settling breath before I rang the bell.

It was Lavinia herself who greeted me – the woman who had made me so welcome in Dorothy's home. She was a tall, willowy woman in her fifties with hair the colour of golden sand. She was wearing white trousers and a striped Breton top, and looked perfectly at home on the doorstep of this house that wasn't hers. I imagined she would look stunning in an evening gown, and my thoughts went to my own clothes and what I might have to wear if I was to dine with the family and perhaps expected to attend the wedding. That hadn't really been made clear at our first meeting. In fact, nothing had really been made clear.

Lavinia invited me in and gave my huge suitcase a brief glance, her eyebrows heading towards her hairline, before she quickly rearranged her expression.

'It is so lovely to see you again, Gina. Dorothy is delighted that you could join her this week. She's been a bit up and down since my father-in-law died last year, and my husband, Miles, and I have been worried about her, but this wedding party seems to have perked her up a bit. It's just what we all need, fun and games with some good food, music and of course the wedding itself.'

'I'm very happy to be here,' I said, beginning to take in the entrance hall. 'Goodness!'

The room was dominated by a beautifully carved wooden staircase that split into two, before continuing up another short flight to a galleried landing. A stained-glass window threw a kaleidoscope of colours across the stone floor at my feet from its twelve individual panes, but I didn't spend too much time deciphering its depictions. My eyes were drawn immediately to the paintings that adorned the wall either side.

'Goodness,' I said again.

'Yes, I know,' Lavinia said, closing the door behind me. 'It is unexpected, isn't it.'

The space really warranted Gainsborough or Constable, Van Dyck or Holbein. Instead, it had huge canvases slashed through with bright colours of paint; angry and livid, but somehow striking in their own way. On a table in an alcove was an unusual-looking antique carriage clock and then, next to it, a strange, ugly ceramic urn sitting on a wooden pedestal. There was an oddly placed, gilt-framed mirror that was hanging so low on the wall I wondered if it was for a small child, or for someone to view their own knees. Further round towards a doorway stood the most magnificent grandfather clock, which on cue, chimed the hour. My eyes darted around at the decor and I couldn't find an immediate link. It was like an expensive jumble sale, I thought, perhaps a little unkindly.

'Leonard is a collector of, well, whatever he fancies. Not exactly John Lewis, is it,' Lavinia said. 'Why don't I show you to your room and then you can see Dorothy? Leonard isn't here this afternoon; he'll be back later, for dinner. He likes to make an entrance.' She said that with what could have been a wry smile, but with a hard edge to it. 'I should have asked, do you have any allergies or dietary requirements? I can tell the cook.'

'No, none at all,' I said, following Lavinia up the stairs, my suit-case bumping behind me. I stopped on the landing to look at a small fan-shaped vase on the windowsill. It looked discarded, not placed in the centre or a perfect third of the way along as I would have done, but seemingly plonked down in haste. I picked it up and looked closely at the soft peach colours of the stylised tree painted on the front. 'This is Coral Firs, circa 1934,' I said, and Lavinia stopped and turned back to me. 'It's Clarice Cliff. This design is quite rare.'

'Oh, something Leonard picked up somewhere I expect. This whole place is like an Aladdin's cave. I forgot, you're an expert, aren't you?'

'A passing interest now,' I said, gently placing the vase back, but in the centre of the windowsill this time. Then I reminded myself I wasn't here to catalogue the contents of the house; that was from another life. I would need to keep my thoughts to myself.

We carried on along the long landing past the many mullioned windows with enticing views over the parterre gardens and on to the lake, and I noticed a peacock strutting across the lawn, his tail in full fan like the vase. Lavinia came to a stop outside a bedroom door.

'This is you,' she said opening it onto a bright and pretty room with chintzy curtains and matching bedspread, antique mahogany furniture and, thankfully, a door onto a small and promised private bathroom.

'Lovely,' I said, 'very conformable.'

I abandoned my suitcase by the side of the bed and walked over to one of the windows to look out. I could see a lake and the edge of what looked like a parterre garden. The other window offered a perfect view over to the spire of the resident church just visible between the leaves of the oak that sat in the grounds.

'That's where the wedding will be on Saturday, not too far to walk. The weather looks good during the day. There's talk of a storm in the evening, but I don't see it myself. The reception will be in the orangery, anyway, so we'll be perfectly fine in there. Toby, my son, and his bride, Caroline, want to set up a floral arbour with a red carpet at the front of the house for photos. Bit over the top, to my mind, but then...' Lavinia spread her arms wide. 'In for a penny and all that. I'll let you get settled in and then perhaps we can have a drink with Dorothy before dinner.'

'Thank you so much, Lavinia. You've made me feel very welcome. Oh, what should I wear and may I ask? What precisely does Dorothy need me to do for her? She wasn't exactly explicit when we met.'

'She'll let know you what she needs, but I imagine some help with dressing, perhaps some make-up and hair? I think her toileting requirements she can attend to herself. She does usually live alone.'

Hair and make-up was not something I did well, even for myself. I was firmly in the moisturiser and a lick of lipstick camp with mascara only coming out for special occasions, whenever they were. My hair, once a dark shade of auburn, was now several shades lighter with a smattering of white and it hung in waves and did best, left well alone. That word popped up in my mind again – *beige*. I shook it off.

'I'm happy to get stuck in with anything that needs doing,' I said.

'That's great. We'll all be pretty busy with the wedding activities and preparations so, mostly she'll just need a companion. The thing is, the other week she had a fall and was a little confused after. She doesn't seem to want to admit to being eighty-nine and we would like to have someone to keep an eye on her, because she won't allow us to.' She turned to leave and then thought of something else. 'Oh, of course, wear whatever you are most comfortable in. Certainly for the next few days when it's just us immediate family. We'll all be casual. The main party won't be arriving until Friday. Things will get a little more formal then, but really with fun being foremost. So, shall we say an hour?' She glanced at her watch, moving a pretty gold chain along her slender, tanned arm and then left the room without waiting for a response.

I sat down on the edge of the bed and wondered what on earth I was doing. The house was beautiful, that was for sure, but I didn't really belong here. Dorothy was perfectly pleasant, Lavinia seemed nice enough and had made me welcome, yet I felt a little out of my depth, suddenly. There had been other wanted ads for live-in companions, but I hadn't been asked for any other interviews. My lack of experience obviously bothered them more than it did Dorothy.

I hauled my suitcase up onto the bed. Because of the open house, I'd packed more than just what I needed for the week. I had those very precious and salvaged things I always carried with me in my handbag close and safe: the only remaining photograph of my mother, the last birthday card she had given me and the key to her beloved MG that sat in my rented garage and would never be driven again. But, because strangers would be in the house, I'd decided to take more. Looking now, it struck me that if I never returned home, I wouldn't miss anything still there. I wouldn't hanker for the kitchenware or soft furnishings, for the table lamps and rugs.

Chris took everything that belonged to him when he moved out years ago and Alice's box of memories was ready for her to collect. I had a few books, photos and personal things in my suitcase and it wasn't much, but it was mine. I had learned many years ago that it really was possible to carry with you what meant most to you. Everything else was just excess.

5

DOROTHY

The evening sun hadn't lost any of its warmth and Dorothy wiped her forehead with her handkerchief. It came away with a smear of warm ivory, which reminded her she'd rather overdone her make-up. She'd considered it warpaint really, a shield to hide behind. Being in Leonard's house was proving more difficult than she thought it would. The fact that he wasn't even here yet was making her feel twitchy and she was anxious for Gina to arrive.

Her grandson, Toby, was playing the piano and the gentle sound of his music came through the open French doors to the patio where Dorothy and some of the family were beginning to gather. There was a large oak table and chairs with a parasol open to keep the sun from the ice bucket, full of champagne. This had been provided by Harry, Leonard's chef. Harry also seemed to be a right-hand man, as he'd shown them to their rooms, helped them with their bags and offered afternoon tea – all with a small amount of conversation and an even smaller amount of eye contact. Dorothy thought it incredibly rude that Leonard hadn't been there to greet them himself, but then he always did like to make an entrance and, frankly, that was the least of his crimes.

Dorothy's daughter, Sophie, poured her a glass of champagne and sat down beside her with a glass of her own.

'This place is actually amazing, isn't it, Mum,' she said. 'Can't believe we have the whole week here.'

Sophie was right; Leonard's home was amazing. Dorothy had never actually been here before. She'd only heard about it and seen a few photos of the outside. Leonard had said in the past how she and Philip really must come and stay, but he'd never actually invited them. It always seemed odd to her that for a man so happy to brag, he hadn't ever given Philip the grand tour. The house didn't make her feel as impressed as it did her daughter, though; it made her feel a bit sick. It was huge. Where would you even start?

She glanced at her daughter, seemingly relaxed in this opulent setting. Dorothy was glad. She'd been worried about Sophie recently. She'd appeared tense and snappy, which could be the pressure of work. Sophie was the head of a girls' school in Surrey and unsurprisingly the most efficient, bossy and organised person Dorothy knew. Nothing like herself, she often mused. Dorothy tended to be impulsive and held a grudge like a drowning person would hold on to a life belt.

Sophie was Dorothy's long-awaited second child. After Miles had been appointed the title of the honeymoon baby, to the family's great delight and Dorothy's mortification – the mere thought of them all discussing their sex life – Dorothy assumed she'd have another child as easily as her first, but it took years – ten to be precise. Sophie was fifty-seven now, which could be another indicator of her change in mood; Dorothy remembered it very well.

'Granny?'

Sophie's daughter, Juliet, glanced up from her phone for the first time in a good hour. She was thirteen and probably also factored in her mother's irritability. Sophie had had her own struggles conceiving and she'd been a resigned forty-four when Juliet had made a surprising appearance. A teenager and the menopause was surely a heady combination. In fact, both of Dorothy's children had been late bloomers, in the child-rearing department, which meant she'd most likely never see any great-grandchildren, but she was grateful for what she had.

'Do you think I could have some champagne?' Juliet asked.

'I think you should ask your mother,' Dorothy said, glancing at her daughter.

'I'm right here,' Sophie said with both of her eyebrows raised in Juliet's direction.

'Yes, but you'd say no and Granny might say yes. She did let me have some of her sherry at Christmas even though it was disgusting; no offence, Granny.'

'None taken,' Dorothy said. 'Although you are dropping me in it.'

'Sorry, but no,' came Sophie's response. 'You're only thirteen; get back to me when you're an adult.'

'Gah!' Juliet exhaled, theatrically sliding down further into her seat and tucking her chin into her chest. 'There is literally nothing for me to do here. At least a glass of booze might perk things up a bit.'

'I find it usually has the opposite effect, actually,' Dorothy said with a wry smile.

Sophie glanced at her mother with a thoughtful look.

'How about I pop inside to see if Dad needs any help with the unpacking and I won't know if Granny accidentally allows you a *small* sip,' Sophie said, getting to her feet, offering her mother a little shrug and disappearing back inside the house.

Dorothy grinned at Juliet and slid her glass across the table, pleased that her daughter was prepared to ease up a little bit this week.

'A *small* sip,' Dorothy said.

The music stopped then and Toby appeared in the doorway with his wife-to-be, Caroline. She was a bright and beautiful young woman. She had a sunny disposition and even though Dorothy had only met her a few times, she could see how much love she offered Toby. Toby just needed to step up a bit to meet her, Dorothy thought. As much as she loved her grandson, he did appear a little undeserving at times. Perhaps it was because he'd always been a bit spoiled, and she had hopes that once married and away from his mother's clucking, he would blossom.

Lavinia and Miles appeared behind them and then a couple that Dorothy had only met once before, at the engagement dinner.

'Mum, you remember Leonard's brother, Paul.'

'I do, hello,' she said beginning to rise from her seat.

'Please don't get up,' Paul said walking over to her and bending down to kiss her cheek.

There had been a celebratory engagement meal eighteen months ago when Dorothy's husband, Philip, had still been alive and Leonard had announced he wanted the wedding of his niece to be at his 'manor' as he'd put it. Dorothy wondered at the time what the father of the bride thought about that, but Paul had seemed keen and she'd been pleased to see he was nothing like his odious brother. He'd been warm and interesting with a genuine smile, although he did have a whiff of whisky on his breath when he'd greeted her and there it was again, now, that sour smell of alcohol. But then, weren't they all drinking? His wife, Sandra, hadn't been all that memorable from that time before and now, she stood back and offered Dorothy only a thin smile.

'Rufus, our son, is around here somewhere,' Paul continued. 'But I've no idea where.'

'He's in the gardens,' Juliet said. 'I saw him earlier.'

Dorothy looked across the perfectly planted parterre and could see the man wandering among the clipped hedging. He wasn't admiring the vista though, he had his head down, his attention firmly on the screen of his phone. Sandra scurried off to join him.

'Hello, everyone,' said a quiet voice behind them and Dorothy turned to see that Gina had arrived. Her relief was immediate and she could feel it flooding her body.

'Gina! Wonderful to see you,' Dorothy said and then struggled to her feet as Gina looked a little overwhelmed at being thrust into someone else's family gathering. 'This is my friend Gina,' she announced to the assembled party. 'Gina, this is everyone else. Right, that's done. I'd love to take a turn about the garden with you,' she said to Gina, keen to get her alone.

'That would be lovely,' Gina said.

'No time now,' said Miles, 'Leonard's just arrived.'

As he said this, Dorothy could detect a throaty roar from the front of the house. It sounded as if Leonard had arrived on a very noisy motorbike. She took a breath to settle her nerves.

There was a scuffle at the table then, and the group were up. Drinks were abandoned as they moved towards the house. Rufus, still walking in the garden, began jogging in their direction, his mother at a hurried pace behind him.

Juliet hadn't moved. She still had her face turned down into her own phone, her thumbs moving quickly across the screen, Dorothy's now empty glass in front of her.

'Hello there,' Gina said to her, but she didn't respond or even look at Gina.

'Juliet, please don't spend the whole week on your telephone. The rest of us have to socialise and it's not fair,' Dorothy said, and then Juliet looked up, a half smirk on her lips. 'Come on, let's go and get this party started, shall we.'

'If we have to,' Juliet said in a sulky tone. 'Not sure why *I'm* needed to watch you all get drunk and play stupid games.'

'Believe me, I feel exactly the same. Now, this is Gina, my

friend,' Dorothy said, pointedly, and it was enough to make the girl turn Gina's way.

'Hello,' Juliet said in the smallest voice possible and Gina lifted her hand in a little wave, which seemed a bit pathetic to Dorothy, but Juliet just looked through her anyway before walking into the house.

'Juliet doesn't want to be here. A week is an awfully long time when you're thirteen. Let's take that walk in the garden after dinner, shall we. We have lots to discuss,' Dorothy said to Gina.

6

GINA

Leonard was an oddity – that was clear from the moment I saw him in the hallway in black leathers, a motorbike helmet tucked under his arm, those garish paintings a perfect backdrop to his style. But, like bees on a bloom or moths to a flame, the whole family seemed drawn towards him. Even Dorothy made an effort to talk to him, but I thought it may be an act, because I noticed the way she lost the bright look from her eyes when she engaged with him.

I guessed he was in his late fifties or early sixties and that sort of tallied with what I knew about him being the bride's uncle. He had black hair stuck up at all angles, making him look a little deranged, which could have happened when he removed his helmet, to be fair. It looked as if it had come from a bottle though, because it didn't match his eyebrows and was very solid in colour. He wasn't unattractive, but had a swagger that was unappealing, as if he were on the stage. I held back while he greeted everyone and tucked myself into the corner of the hallway, my arms firmly around myself for support.

'Welcome to Walstone Hall,' he said with a large dose of self-assurance. 'My gorgeous niece is to be married on Saturday and I have a week of activities, games and fun planned for you all. Caroline,' he said, holding out his arms to the petite blonde woman. 'Toby,' he said to the man who had been playing the piano when I'd first walked into the music room, and the two stepped forward into his embrace. 'It will be a very proud day for me – uncle of the bride,' he said, theatrically and as if that were a prestigious role. I looked across at the rest of the group that I hadn't been properly introduced to and guessed at Caroline's parents. An older, blonder version of her daughter had hold of the arm of a man who didn't dye his hair or look ridiculous, but was still clearly Leonard's brother. He was the only one of the group who looked at Leonard with genuine affection in his expression. His wife looked somewhat wary, and Lavinia and Miles just smiled indulgently.

One other couple were present and looked to be Juliet's parents – Miles's sister, who I would describe as neat, with her fair hair pulled back into a perfect ponytail, and her husband. Juliet shared the colour of her hair with her father; it was a bright shade of turmeric, although his was cropped short and hers, she wore in a sharp bob with a blunt fringe. There was a lone young man too, the chap who was hanging around the garden and I tried to remember back to the potted family history that Lavinia had given me. I guessed the man had to be Caroline's unattached brother.

They all took it in turns to hug or shake hands with Leonard and there was a general ripple of gratefulness for his hospitality. He didn't even look in my direction and that was the moment I remembered I was staff. What I really wanted to do was eat my meal in the kitchen, perhaps with the cook, but Dorothy stepped my way to take my arm and pull me from my hiding place, and it was decided, I would be dining with the family.

* * *

The dining room was decorated in a style reminiscent of the 1988 film *Beetlejuice* – one of Chris and Alice's favourites from their early teens – and I half expected the langoustines from my plate to leap up and attack me. In contrast to the classic, soft pastel tones of the music room there were black velvet drapes here and purple flocked wallpaper. The lighting was low, perhaps to create a cosy atmosphere, but as someone had closed the curtains on the bright evening sun, it was a little dark.

The artwork that hung on the walls could be considered *kitsch*. Not a term that I really liked as it sometimes had derogatory connotations. It referred, in my mind, to a piece that was quirky, witty and, perhaps, sentimental, but originally it was considered banal and showing a lack of depth when compared to those works produced under the umbrella of *fine art*. A little like the snobbery surrounding genre fiction compared to, so-called, literary. I had always kept my mind firmly open.

Leonard had several pieces displayed in clip frames reminding me of my children's bedroom walls. There was *A Friend in Need* – the classic Cassius Marcellus Coolidge image of the dogs at the poker table – a couple of works by the American artist LeRoy Neiman, a Thomas Kinkade that my mother-in-law had on a jigsaw puzzle and *Chinese Girl* – Tretchikoff's very familiar oil on canvas now rendered in glossy ink on poster paper. Leonard was making a point in this space, but I had no idea what it was.

I was tucked away at the end of the table next to Dorothy and trying to engage with the woman, but Leonard was holding court at the other end and seemed determined to involve the entire group in his conversation. He'd disappeared briefly and returned with his hair tamed. It was now slicked back with some sort of oily product and he'd changed out of his leathers into a white shirt with a simple black jacket and tight-fitting trousers.

'So, Rufus, what have you been up to?'

He directed his question at Caroline's brother and Rufus seemed to jump in his seat.

'Um, a bit of this and that,' he said quietly. 'You know.'

'I certainly do know, young man,' Leonard said.

'Rufus has been very busy working at the law firm,' his mother said, throwing a dangerous look at Leonard. The expression *if looks could kill* sprung to my mind. But then the woman seemed to catch herself and her face transformed into the picture of serenity. She reminded me of a woman I used to work with many years ago. A mercurial person who was quietly known as Worzel Gummidge among some of the staff because no one would ever know which head she would have on when she arrived in the morning. I made a mental note to try and avoid Rufus's mother and perhaps Leonard too. I'd just stick to looking after Dorothy and keep my head down. With that thought in mind, I refilled Dorothy's glass of water.

Leonard nodded and smiled before turning his attention to the whole group. There was a small glass of champagne in front of each of us and Leonard picked up his and pushed his chair back. 'This is a very special occasion,' he said. 'I haven't had the pleasure of your collective company since the engagement party. To see all those I hold dear to me under my roof is marvellous.' He paused for a moment and turned his attention toward Dorothy. 'Sadly, not everyone could be here, though. How missed dear Philip is to us, myself especially. And it's with this thought that I'd like you all to raise a glass: to absent friends.'

Everyone did exactly that, mumbling the names Philip, Dad and Grandad too, but I noticed that Dorothy put her glass to her lips and didn't drink. When Leonard sat back down and resumed eating, Dorothy turned to me and began to explain the family dynamics in a whisper. She'd only just managed to say that Sandra and Paul were Rufus's parents and that Paul and Leonard were brothers when Leonard's voice boomed out again, making me jump.

'And who is this beguiling creature at the other end of the table?' he asked.

For the first time, Leonard looked directly at me and I felt a chill rush through me. He was smiling broadly, but I couldn't help feel a sense of menace.

'This is Gina, a friend who's come to help me in my decrepit old age,' Dorothy said, with a tinkly laugh.

'Ah, a carer,' Leonard said and I could feel Dorothy bristle beside me.

'A companion, actually, but yes, I do need a bit of help these days. I am eighty-nine after all.' Then, as if to prove her point, her knife slipped off the side of her plate and onto the carpet. 'Oh, dear,' she said, flustered and I quickly bent down to pick it up. When I brought it back up to the table I noticed Leonard's eyes were still on me and I busied myself by taking a clean knife, laid out for the next course, and offered it to Dorothy.

'Well, you are as welcome as any of the guests here, Gina,' he said, seeming to drop the edginess and becoming the perfect host again. I wasn't sure I could handle a whole week of Leonard and decided to see if Dorothy was amenable to me slinking off at mealtimes.

The rest of the meal was a blur of family banter, most of which went over the top of my head, but I did glean a little information about the group. Juliet's parents were called Sophie and Luke. Their dynamic was instantly clear; Sophie was the boss and Luke was happy to play second fiddle. Her opinions were clear and loud and his were neither, but they both seemed likeable. Rufus tried to keep his head down despite his sister, one side of him, and his mother the other, both encouraging him into conversation. Toby and Caroline were clearly in love and it was so heartwarming to see the two of them at the start of their journey. Nostalgia flooded me as I watched them gaze at each other the same way that I'm sure Douglas and I must have done many years before. Leonard, at the head of the table watched over everyone and intermittently interrupted to add his twopence worth.

I had nothing to contribute, as usual, and I was immensely grateful to the moment that we all put our spoons down after dessert and began to vacate the dining room.

'Shall we take that turn now, Gina?' Dorothy asked and, without waiting for an answer, she took my arm and steered me out of the room and back towards the door to the garden.

'Leonard seems a very interesting character,' I said as we stepped out onto the patio and Dorothy made a beeline for the parterre garden.

'Yes,' Dorothy said brightly, glancing back over her shoulder as she spoke. She seemed quite sprightly for her age, especially with me on one side of her and her stick on the other. We passed some rounded box hedging and the pretty herbaceous planting before the older woman had guided me towards some steps. Our pace slowed to a crawl as we navigated them and then I found myself in a wooded area, the ground covered in ferns and with what looked like a little stone folly nestled into the trees.

Dorothy led me inside and she immediately sat down on a stone bench to catch her breath.

'Are you okay?' I asked her and she took a long look at me before answering.

'Can I trust you, dear? It's so important that I can, because there isn't much time, you see.'

I wasn't expecting that and I went for an air of joviality in my reply.

'Of course you can, unless you're going to tell me you're a criminal.'

I laughed a little, but Dorothy's expression was grim.

'Hmm, well *I'm* not. What do you think of Leonard's art collection?' she asked, surprising me for a second time.

'Eclectic?' I suggested, because it really was.

'I believe that Leonard has stolen a painting belonging to my late husband, Philip.'

'Oh, dear, that's not good. And you've seen it in the house, have you?'

'Well, no, of course Leonard wouldn't be stupid enough to have it hanging above the fireplace. I think he's hidden it somewhere; somewhere in plain sight.'

I contemplated this, but really it made no sense.

'What makes you think it's likely he's stolen from you?' I asked, and Dorothy took a long, ragged breath and began to tell me.

'Just over a year ago I suffered the most awful night of my life. There was a burglary at our home. Actually, it makes more sense to take you back a little further.'

She got up suddenly, poked her head out of the doorway, glanced around and then sat back down again. I wondered if she might be a little mad, but sat down beside her on the bench anyway, because I was supposed to be her companion after all.

'My husband first met Leonard when he began working for Philip's firm. At the time, Leonard was just twenty-five; that was thirty-five years ago. My Philip took an instant liking to the man and took him under his wing, so to speak – mentored him. I didn't see the same thing that Philip did. I thought he was a little arrogant for such a young person, but Philip liked his verve and always seemed to see good in people. I'm afraid I'm much more of a realist.

'Anyway, years later Leonard invested heavily in Philip's business and they became partners. It was only at that time we knew there was family money that went back some way. Later, he inherited this place from his late uncle. So, everything was quite rosy for a while and Philip and I also enjoyed a very good quality of life. Philip loved art and began collecting. It started out as a harmless enough pursuit, but Leonard took it up as well and then became a bit fanatical about it, and if Philip mentioned an auction or a piece he was interested in, then Leonard would try and outbid him, or buy the piece behind his back. *Friendly competition* Leonard saw it as, but I knew Philip was beginning to get a bit fed up with him.

'Then Philip wanted to retire and sold his share of the business to Leonard, and he left the company. He tried to distance himself from the man too, but still, he'd turn up like an art-collecting stalker. We both went out of our way to try and avoid him, but he was persistent and seemingly thick-skinned. Then, Leonard seemed to go quiet for a while and Philip wasn't really collecting much anyway. He was getting older, more frail and didn't have the passion for it so much.

'But then there was a competition, a treasure hunt of sorts. It was a thing set up by an art organisation that Philip had been associated with and involved clues from locations around the country, very complicated and far too academic for my mind. It wasn't out and about, you know; they weren't all flying around in helicopters. It was mostly online, but with some clues hidden in a couple of locations. Well, Philip won. I was amazed and so proud of my husband for outwitting all the others, and quickly too. The prize was a painting. It wasn't hugely valuable, but quite an attractive coastal landscape. We didn't know at that point that Leonard was also trying to win the competition, but he turned up unannounced the day Philip picked up the painting to congratulate him. He couldn't stop looking at it.'

Dorothy stopped talking for a moment, seemingly back at that time with her husband, and Leonard, the increasingly unappealing character, and I waited for her to continue. In fact, I got up and walked to the doorway to look out. This tale seemed to be getting darker and I wasn't sure where it was going to end. No one was in sight, though, and we were quite tucked away here. Dorothy began again as I sat back down.

'Last year, six months after Philip won the painting, we were burgled. A man broke in while we were supposed to be at the theatre, but Philip wasn't well, so we'd offered our tickets to friends. We were in bed early, but woke to the sound of smashed glass downstairs. I will always regret not trying harder to stop Philip, but he was determined to see what was going on. The thief took several small things of no consequence and also the winning landscape that was hanging on the living room wall. Philip had a number of quite valuable things – you've seen some of them – but none were taken. It was as if the thief didn't know what he had near his grasp and just took random items. I know it was the painting he was really there for. Other works of art with far more provenance were left behind. Philip was weak, but outraged and he chased after the thief onto our front steps where he tripped and fell, broke his arm and hip and smashed his head on the ground. He never recovered from his injuries in hospital.'

'Dorothy!' I said, taking the woman's hand. 'That's terrible.'

'Yes, it was terrible – poor Philip.'

'And you really think it was Leonard who took it?'

'Yes, I do. He obviously wasn't the masked thief. I caught a quick glimpse before he fled. Leonard is tall; the thief was not. Leonard was good at getting others to do things for him – he had a reputation in the office a long time before he was in charge, but he must have planned it. Who else would want the painting?'

'I assume you've told the police.'

'Of course. They investigated all of the people who entered the competition, including Leonard, but there was no evidence at all. Leonard made all the right noises about how devastated he was to have lost his dearest friend – you heard him in there tonight: *to absent friends*. But I know deep in my bones that he has it in that house somewhere, somewhere clever. Like I said, hidden in plain sight. He's so egotistical that he probably would have loved to have got one over on Philip that last time.'

Dorothy was quiet then for a moment, and I began to contemplate the reason why she'd told me this sorry tale.

'Gina,' she said, then. 'The reason I asked *you* particularly to join me for this week wasn't because I needed a companion. My daughter-in-law arranged the advertisement even though I told her I'm very happy looking after myself. I was humouring her by talking to the applicants, but had little intention of taking anyone on. But then I spoke to you and you told me about your previous role as a curator. I won't get another opportunity to be in this house, I doubt, and so it is vitally important that we move quickly. If Leonard gets wind, he'll move the painting, I'm sure.'

'Move quickly in what way?' I asked, although I was pretty sure I already knew.

'We need to brush aside the fact that Leonard is unhinged and actually in light of what I believe he has done, is pretty dangerous too. He mustn't know you are anything other than a companion and I will keep smiling at him even though I would ideally love to plunge a knife in his heart.'

'And...?' I asked, tentatively.

'And, you will search the house from top to bottom until you find the painting.'

7

GINA

The sun came up over the lake at seven-thirty and I watched it from my bedroom window. The sky went from a dark shade of indigo to a warm magenta and then just before the sun itself came into view it turned to a rose-gold and then pink. The magnificent oaks were bathed in a glorious golden light and the dragonflies began to dance across the shimmering surface of the water. The stone mullion was cool under my elbows as I leaned towards the glass. It was criss-crossed with lead-work that fractured the view, making it appear as individual vignettes.

I had not slept well, which was hardly surprising after Dorothy's bombshell. I sincerely wished my position *had* been all about hair and make-up now. How easy that would be in comparison. I'd made no promise to Dorothy, only that I'd use the day to decide whether I could possibly take on the task. In truth my mind was already assessing what I'd seen so far in Leonard's eclectic taste in art, but what Dorothy was asking was impossible, wasn't it? To creep around Leonard's house and go through his things? I couldn't do that. If he *was* responsible for stealing the painting then he showed no sort of remorse or any concern about Dorothy being in his house. Perhaps she was mistaken and if I was caught snooping I wasn't keen to think about the repercussions of that.

I decided to go down and see if I could get some coffee from the kitchen and as I left my room I became very aware of every painting, ornament, clock and piece of art. The house was stuffed full and that was just in the few rooms I had been in so far. Nothing came to me; there was no obvious sign that pointed to a hidden painting. It was just an odd mix of things Leonard liked, it seemed.

The kitchen was on the west side of the house and down a flight of stone steps. The rich burgundy carpet had stopped at the bottom of the last flight and now the sound of my footsteps echoed. There didn't seem to be anyone around. The air became cooler and was a relief from the warmth that penetrated the rest of the house.

The property was at least three hundred years old and not really conducive with modern living. There was no open-plan kitchen-diner where guests could chat to the person preparing the meals. The kitchen was in the bowels of the house and all the food would have to be brought up via the servants' staircase, into the serving room and then the dining room. The one exception to the lack of modernity was the patio and the French doors from the music room. That looked to be a new appendage, but sympathetically done.

I was surprised to see a very sleek and contemporary set-up once I had navigated the last of the steps. There were black granite worktops and glossy white doors to all the cupboards and drawers. Where I had been expecting an antique Welsh dresser there were glass shelves with chrome edges. Instead of a family heirloom dinner service there was a modern set in crisp white and when I picked up a side plate and turned it over I read *John Lewis*. I smiled, thinking about Lavinia's comment the previous afternoon.

'Morning, can I make you some coffee?'

I jumped at the unexpected sound of another person and

turned to see a young man of less than thirty in chef whites with a sharp knife clutched in his fist. My eyes went straight to the weapon, then his followed a second later and he smirked before placing it back on the counter next to the mushrooms he was slicing, seemingly in silence. It looked less threatening there in the setting it was to be used for.

'Sorry,' he said. 'That probably looked a bit menacing.' He wiped his hand on the tea towel tucked into his pocket and held it out to me. 'I'm Harry. Are you with the bride or groom?'

'I'm companion to Dorothy, the groom's grandmother, and a coffee would be lovely, thank you,' I said, shaking his hand.

I could see him assessing me with a cool stare, no doubt wondering why Dorothy would employ a woman as old as me for a companion. I could see that same thought flickering in Leonard's eyes at dinner the night before. The truth was that I was perfectly fit for my age and other than an occasional grumble in my lower back, I was just as capable as I had been when I was sixty; well, almost. I stepped back and took another look around the room.

'This is a great space to cook in. Have you been here long?' I asked, suddenly feeling that small talk was needed and perhaps it wouldn't hurt to ask a few innocuous questions.

'Just a year,' he said, and began to make me a coffee from the large chrome device on the counter by the window.

I glanced out, up the bank of grass to a wooden fence and on to the roofs of greenhouses in the distance. The view was nothing like the other side of the house with its beautiful parterre garden, but that was how these grand houses were designed in the 1700s. Stunning views from the upper floors for the residents and their many guests, and functional downstairs for the staff. I could see stone steps leading up from the kitchen door and, to the side at the bottom of a bank of grass, a small plastic table and chairs tucked away near some bins, a plant pot on top overflowing with cigarette ends.

Harry handed me the coffee and I took it gratefully, declining his offer of sugar.

'Mr Price has quite the collection upstairs, doesn't he,' I prompted, as Harry returned to preparing breakfast. 'Nice to see an old house chock-full of artwork. Are you interested in art?'

'Not particularly. I mean, I like what I like and I really like those paintings in the entrance hall. Great colours and not all dingy like some of the other stuff he's got.'

'I suppose such an avid collector would be bringing things into the house all the time. I guess you see a lot of comings and goings?' I asked and then began furiously sipping at my drink as Harry gave me a sidelong glance.

'What?' he said, clearly surprised.

'Oh, I just wondered about Mr Price's art collection, that was all.'

'Right,' he said, halfway between looking uncomfortable and bemused. 'Did you say you were a companion?'

'Yes,' I said quickly, wishing I hadn't asked such a ridiculous question and that I'd just made some harmless comment about the weather instead.

'Well, it's not my thing really,' he said, and dismissed me with his back as he continued with his task.

'Thanks so much for the coffee. Shall I take some up for Mrs Reed?' I asked, my fingers trembling around my cup.

'No need – tea's already gone up,' he said.

He must have done that in near silence too, because I hadn't heard anything since I'd been awake.

'I'll let you get on, then,' I said and, spying a large bowl of fruit, I asked him if I could take a banana. He told me to help myself in a quiet, dismissive voice and I quickly left the room. At the doorway, I glanced back to see his head turned and that cool stare on me. I offered a smile, which wasn't returned.

So much for slipping around unnoticed. The first person I'd talked to and I'd rendered myself as a bit of a noticeable idiot. I wasn't going to be able to do this. I was completely out of any sort of comfort zone. I probably wasn't in the right frame of mind to be solving a mystery. My marriage was over, my house was being sold from under me and I was about to embark on a solitary life, no doubt until I died. As if on cue, that grumble began in my lower back.

I made my way back up the stone steps and onto the carpeted stairs to find Dorothy. I had helped her back to her room last night and was pleased to see she'd been given a wonderful bedroom with some of the best views. You could just see the folly where we'd had our conversation, and then beyond a wall covered in a vibrant Virginia creeper there was a sort of temple at the end of a long expanse of lawn, flanked by huge rhododendron bushes in a riot of purple. Her room was on the corner of the house, like mine and through her second window you could see all the way to the end of the driveway and onto the fields of cattle beyond. It seemed odd to think that the man responsible for the death of her husband could have offered her such lovely accommodation. Maybe Dorothy was entirely wrong about the whole thing, or perhaps Leonard had a large guilt complex.

I knocked on the door and left my coffee cup and fruit on the windowsill at the end of the long landing, catching sight of a gardener on a ride-on mower, cutting the grass on the stretch of lawn down by the lake. Dorothy called out for me to go in. The words were lined up on my tongue; I wouldn't be able to help her and I had to be as honest as possible. I might be well versed in identifying a particular piece of art for a collection and know where it would have been found originally in that home, how best to look after it for generations to come and which major collectors would give their right arm to own it, or certainly I would have done many years ago, but this here was a possible crime and I surely couldn't and shouldn't get involved. Besides that, Dorothy hadn't been at all honest with me and I felt a little annoyed at the deception. The promise of a permanent position was slipping away.

'Gina, good morning,' Dorothy said from an armchair by her window. She was just sipping from a cup and looked animated. When she put the cup down on the table, next to her newspaper, her smile was broad. 'I have to say that for the first time in a year I feel hopeful. You being here is like balm on a wound, a real tonic and I'm very grateful. I know you said you needed the day to think about it and I respect that, but I would urge you to take a good look at Leonard and you'll see what sort of man he is, what he's capable of.'

I leaned against the door frame and folded my arms, the words I had practised in my head now dying on my lips.

'Is there anything I can do for you?' I asked, thinking that regardless of a missing painting, I'd quite like to be paid for the week.

'If you wouldn't mind solving this damn crossword for me, I'd be delighted,' she said.

* * *

By eleven-thirty the whole group were collected on that same stretch of lawn and I could see why it was necessary for it to have had a fresh cut. Leonard was rummaging through a huge wooden box and pulling out mallets and balls. He was organising a game of croquet.

Dorothy was sitting on a chair under a small gazebo and I

walked over to join her. Assuming it was unlikely that Dorothy would be playing I would have the perfect excuse to sit it out also.

'Let me tell you who's who,' Dorothy said as I sat down on the chair next to her. 'You didn't really get much of an introduction last night, did you?'

'No, not really, but I sort of gathered who was who from the conversation around the table. I don't really need an introduction, though. I am here to do a job,' I said and Dorothy gave me a sharp look.

'Yes, and your job will be made easier by knowing the family. They might have information they don't realise is relevant. They might say something about Leonard to you that they wouldn't think to say to me.'

I thought this was unlikely, but I nodded anyway. I had a strong feeling that I wanted to please Dorothy.

'My job,' I repeated.

'Should you choose to accept it,' Dorothy said, her eyes sparkling.

'Mission impossible. I was thinking more of my job as your companion.'

'Ah, well, I'm afraid that position is now obsolete.'

I could feel myself being talked into this task I didn't want to attempt. I really couldn't see how I could get out of it and the expectation in Dorothy's expression was vast.

She sat back and gave me a brief round-up of her family and extended family in bullet points.

- She adored her daughter-in-law because she was an excellent wife and kept Miles on track.
- Miles wasn't good with money, but was micromanaged under his wife's beady eye.
- Toby was an excellent musician, but a bit pompous.

- Caroline was simply a sweetheart.
- Sandra had nothing to say for herself and seemed incredibly boring.
- Paul was a decent sort and couldn't help being related to a monster.
- Rufus was a closed book, but seemed likeable when he bothered to converse.
- Sophie was bossy, but great fun and loyal.
- Luke did as he was told, which in Dorothy's opinion was the best course of action.
- Juliet had great potential once she had moved on from being a tiresome teenager.

'So, Miles and Sophie are your children, and Toby and Juliet are your grandchildren. Sandra and Paul are Caroline and Rufus's parents, and Paul and Leonard are siblings,' I clarified.

'Absolutely spot on.'

'Why does Leonard have this house and not his brother? Is it because he's older than Paul?'

'Well that, my dear, is a very good question and one I don't have the answer for.'

I pondered this while I watched the players thwacking their balls across the lawn under the watchful eye of the master of the house, most missing the hoops and becoming increasingly annoyed. My phone began ringing in my pocket and I pulled it out to see Douglas's name on the screen, so I put it back, unanswered.

'Please take the call if you need to,' Dorothy said, but I shook my head.

'My husband,' I said. 'Really no need.'

'Oh, when you said you were on your own, I thought you meant he'd died.'

'No, not dead, just buggered off.'

'I'm sorry, Gina. That's hard, at your time of life.'

I turned to look at her, to tell her I was only seventy-one, but then I thought about that number and realised that it was actually quite old. Not as old as Dorothy herself, but old enough to be considered old.

'Why did he leave you?'

'Because I'm beige and unexciting,' I said, without thinking. 'And now, I have to move and our finances don't stretch to make that easy. I might be able to afford a very small, damp flat a million miles away from everything I know.'

I could feel my throat thicken and then Dorothy reached her hand out and took mine.

'Gina, you are not beige and unexciting. Look what you're about to do for me. Imagine telling your husband that you found a lost painting and put a criminal behind bars. That is very exciting.'

I turned to look at her again and thought she should really have ten out of ten for powers of persuasion. I imagined her in her house in Hampton with her rich and full life, her boat, her boathouse and up until that fateful day when her husband died, leading a very exciting life. One to aspire to, one like my mother used to have.

'I grew up in Bushy Park, in front of your house,' I said, suddenly. It was an odd thought that swooped into my head, seemingly from nowhere.

'In the park itself?'

'Yes, my front garden was full of deer.'

Dorothy was eyeing me as if I'd lost the plot.

'It's a long story, but a true one,' I said.

'Perhaps you can tell me later,' she said and then leaned in closer to me. 'You know, this would be a good time for you to get inside and start to have a look around,' she said.

'Dorothy, I understand how important this is to you and I'm

terribly sorry about Philip, but I don't think I can poke around someone's house. What if he were to come in and find me?'

'He won't. He's going to be very busy out here showboating around. I have your mobile phone number and can message you if he makes a move towards the house. Just have a rummage and see what you think might be off or out of place. Just a start and then if it doesn't feel right, we can forget it.'

'Do you even know how to message?' I asked her dubiously and Dorothy looked aghast.

'Of course I can! I like to play the decrepit old lady when it suits me, but I'm more than capable of most things.'

I looked over to see that Leonard had moved closer to us and was also setting up a game of boule. I made a quick decision.

'Dorothy,' I said with a raised voice. 'I'm a bit worried about you not having your hat. If you're going to play, you'll need it in this sun.'

Dorothy fixed me with a sharp look at my rather pathetic attempt to sound natural, but quickly rearranged her features.

'Oh, you're right,' she said as Leonard looked in our direction. 'Would you be so kind as to fetch it for me please. I think it's on the top shelf in my wardrobe.'

I didn't dare look at Leonard, but got up out of my chair and before I could change my mind I made for the house.

'Won't be long,' I said.

Only when I had reached the safety of the patio doors did I dare look back, but everyone seemed fully absorbed in their games – Leonard included.

I rushed through the music room and into the entrance hall with my phone out, snapping photos of anything and everything as I went. Then I paused in front of the twelve-panelled stained-glass window to catch my breath and take stock. It wouldn't do to run around like a headless chicken; I needed to be methodical. I suddenly thought of the principles of art history operations: description, analysis, interpretation and judgement.

I took another breath and turned slowly on my heel, my discerning eye taking in the contents of the hallway. It kept coming back to that oddly placed mirror, so I held my phone down low and took a photo. It seemed relevant somehow, but I didn't know why at that moment, so I tucked the info away and set off up the stairs. If I was to be discovered snooping I'd need to be in possession of Dorothy's hat.

With a guilty conscience I told three people that I was just there to get Dorothy's hat. One was Harry, who had gravitated upstairs for some reason, but he looked just as bemused by me as he had before and scurried away, probably worried he was going to get into some sort of conversation he didn't want to have. The second was a young woman I came across as I returned to the ground floor to navigate the rooms leading from the entrance hall. Her job, apparently, was to decorate the orangery for the wedding reception and she was looking for Leonard. She clearly wasn't interested in Dorothy's hat, and the third person was vacuuming the carpet with an industrial-looking cleaner. I waved the hat in his direction and began to explain what I was doing in the house, but the man had earbuds in and he wouldn't have heard me anyway over the noise of the machine. I felt ridiculous as he turned away from me to carry on with his work.

I found my way into Leonard's library, which was accessed from the hall by a small dark corridor with some dusty-looking curtains covering the window which, if I had my bearings right, would look out onto the inner courtyard.

The library took my breath away. The showroom of the house,

elaborately decorated with beautiful wallpaper of trailing honey-suckle in pinks and greens. Five huge bay windows, all with cushioned seats, lined one side of the room, while a bank of dark mahogany bookcases ran along the other. The fireplace in the centre was surrounded in marble with a tapestry hanging above it. The leather settees looked worn but comfortable. I could smell the old leather and imagined how many people had sat there over the years, a small glass of port or sherry on the side table and a large leather-bound tome in their hands.

The most remarkable thing about this room was the ceiling, though. It was in bright-white intricately carved plaster. My first thought was that it was old and perhaps restored, and I tucked Dorothy's hat under my arm so I could take my phone out of my pocket again. When I took a photo and enlarged the image I could see the emblems were actually modern portraits of authors. I recognised Arthur Conan Doyle, C. S. Lewis, Roald Dahl, then Ian Rankin and that made me laugh at the unexpectedness of a contemporary writer. I walked across to the other side of the room and took more pictures: Agatha Christie, Mary Shelley, Charlotte Brontë, Kate Mosse. It was a wonderful idea and something I had never seen before. I walked further down the room completely lost in the faces above my head.

As I crooked my neck for a better look to see who else I recognised, I failed to hear the light footsteps coming across the Persian rugs that ran down the centre of the room, and it was only when he spoke that I realised I wasn't alone.

8

DOROTHY

Dorothy watched Leonard with narrow eyes as he paraded around the lawn, swinging his mallet as if he owned the place. It made her angry to think of him so alive and in so much splendour while her beloved Philip sat in an urn on her dressing table at home.

She hadn't scattered the ashes yet, despite Miles and Sophie occasionally suggesting that she'd feel better if she did. The problem was that the only thing that would make her feel better was Leonard behind bars. Or dead, she wasn't fussy which.

Once either of those had occurred then she did feel as if she might be able to move on and her plan was to take Philip to their most treasured holiday destination. They had honeymooned in Venice in 1956 as Dorothy was keen to see the island of Murano and the glass produced there. They'd taken the children when they were younger for a holiday too, so it was somewhere that meant something to all of them. And once Leonard was incarcerated or incinerated, she'd be taking Philip back there for the last time.

She hoped Gina was going to be successful, but there was a tug on her conscience. She'd railroaded Gina into looking, she knew. The woman wasn't in a good place and Dorothy was taking advantage of her. But, if she was to find it, then surely it would make it all worthwhile. What a boost it would give Gina if she was victorious. Dorothy grimaced knowing she couldn't take the moral high ground here and hating Leonard all the more for it.

Juliet came over and sat down next to her, a large glass of lemonade in her hand.

'Want one?' she asked and when Dorothy nodded, she hopped up and went to fetch one from the table that Harry had left in the shade.

It was as Juliet was returning that Dorothy noticed Leonard was walking towards the house. She pulled her handbag up from the ground onto her lap and rummaged for her phone. Leonard was at the door now and then he disappeared inside.

'Oh God,' she said, flustered, which made finding her phone all the harder.

'Juliet, can you find my phone in my bag, please, quickly.'

'Sure,' Juliet said and pulled it out in seconds.

She handed it to Dorothy, who took it with fumbling fingers and pressed the button on the side, waiting for the screen to light up. It didn't. She handed it back to Juliet.

'Can you make this work?'

Juliet pressed the same button and then handed it back.

'It's dead, Granny. You forgot to charge it up. Do wanna borrow mine?' she said holding out her phone with the most reluctant expression on her face.

'No, thank you, I need to...'

Dorothy got up out of her seat and began to make her way to the door that Leonard had disappeared through, her stick scattering the gravel as she went.

'Are you okay?' asked Juliet.

'Fine, just need a wee.'

'Put your phone on charge while you're in there.'

Dorothy walked as briskly across the hallway as she could, which wasn't brisk at all, and poked her head around the dining room and the music room doorways to find absolutely no one. Please don't let her be upstairs in Leonard's bedroom, she thought as a sick dread swept through her for putting Gina in this position. She made it to the library and then heard Leonard's voice.

'Ah, Gina, there you are. Dorothy was getting rather worried you'd run off. Aren't you supposed to be her companion? While you're in here she's out there, all alone.'

Leonard's words came out like rapid fire making Dorothy jump. Goodness knows how it was for Gina. Dorothy hovered in the doorway and could just see the back of Leonard's checked shirt.

'Mr Price, you surprised me,' said Gina's voice from inside the room. 'I came in for her hat and then managed to take the wrong door from your hallway. May I just take this opportunity to say what a beautiful house you have? And when I found this room I couldn't help but stop and marvel at the ceiling. I don't think I've ever seen anything like it before. It's wonderful.'

She sounded very natural, Dorothy thought, walking into the room.

'Thank you, most kind,' Leonard said.

'Gina, did you find my hat?' Dorothy said, making her presence known. Her puff was short from the exertion of getting here so quickly, but she took quick breaths and tried not to sound as if she'd been rushing.

'Yes,' she said, waving it in the air in a ridiculous gesture. 'Managed to get lost too – typical me. I was just telling Leonard how much I admired his things.'

Yes, Dorothy thought, compliment him; he'll love that.

'This,' Gina said, turning and pointing to a vase on the table next to her. 'This is very nice.'

'Yes, it's um, from the Far East. Made in about the, um, 1700s,' Leonard said.

'Gosh, how interesting. Well, I think you have some lovely stuff,' Gina said and gave him a patronising smile, which seemed to go over the top of his head.

'It is a passion of mine,' he said pompously. 'I've been known to stop at nothing to get what I want. Woe betide the man who stands between me and my treasured possessions.'

Dorothy shrank at his words. How could he possibly say that after being responsible for Philip's death?

'We'd better get back outside, Dorothy,' Gina said taking hold of Dorothy's arm. 'We're missing all that lovely sunshine.'

'I think that's best,' Leonard said, and continued to stand there staring at them as they left the room, Dorothy on incredibly wobbly legs.

* * *

'I'm so sorry, Gina, I took my phone out to message you, but it just had a blank screen. I showed it quickly to Juliet, but she said it was dead.'

'No harm done,' Gina said slipping into the seat next to her. 'I made all the right noises and he thinks I'm a bit of an idiot, I think, I hope. Really, he doesn't know what he has. That supposed Far Eastern vase was a piece of Martinware made by the brothers in their Fulham studio. Not the 1700s, but rather the late 1800s. I think *he* may be the idiot.'

'Do not underestimate him,' Dorothy said, pointedly.

'Are you trying to put me off? Because I'm teetering, to be honest. I'd like to help you, I really would, but...'

'Then do, please do.'

'The thing is, it's been many years since I worked in that world. I'm not sure I know that much, any more.'

'You know a lot more than me; in fact, you seem quite the professional. The fact that you're a stranger is on your side too, and if I may say, because you're an older woman, you could more easily slip around unnoticed. Before you get offended, tell me after the age of fifty if you became more invisible.'

'I understand what you're saying, but I've always been invisible,' Gina said.

'Well, that's wonderful then – you're a step ahead already,' Dorothy said clapping her hands together.

Gina gave her a long look before she spoke again and it afforded Dorothy the time to reflect on what she'd just said. She realised she ought to tread a little more carefully.

'I think you should talk to your family and get them to look. If they knew or even suspected, they would surely take on the task,' Gina said.

'Like I said last night, if Leonard got wind he would move the painting and that would be the end of it. I wouldn't get another opportunity. We have the element of surprise at the moment and if my family were to start hunting, that would be over.'

Dorothy could see that Gina was contemplating her words and then she nodded.

'What he said about no man getting in his way was very chilling,' Gina said.

The two women stopped talking for a moment as Leonard reappeared, seemingly from thin air, or more likely a small servants' door tucked away somewhere. He strode back across the lawn towards the group who had clearly had enough of the games and were beginning to take silly shots and argue.

'What's the plan for this afternoon?' Gina asked Dorothy.

'A walk around the lake and then lunch on the patio. I would strongly urge *you* to do the former, but I'll be having a nap, and then, apparently Leonard has organised a game in his maze.'

'Right,' Gina said.

'Ask questions, dig about a bit, but subtly, mind. They don't know you – you can use that to your advantage. If I start asking questions out of the blue, they'll be suspicious or think I'm losing my mind, and however well intended, it may get back to Leonard. And that's another thing: as much as I want you to poke about, you need to try and stay away from him.'

'Right,' Gina said again. 'So, I'm doing this, am I?'

9

GINA

The afternoon was glorious and I almost forgot what I was there to do – almost. The family were all very welcoming and I fell into step with Caroline as we set off for the walk around the lake.

We'd left through the main entrance and down the gravel drive before Leonard instructed us to go left and through an archway cut into the yew hedge. We were out onto a path that I noticed led down to the church, but we kept to the left and were into a copse of trees.

'Important to take this path,' Leonard boomed from the front. 'If you leave from the other side of the house and through the gardens you end up at the ha-ha.'

Of course I knew exactly what this was, but decided to play up my stupid persona.

'What's that, Leonard?' I asked and his face lit up. He was delighted to be able to explain. I resisted the urge to roll my eyes and turned to him, all ears.

'Well,' he began. 'It's a type of sunken fence commonly used in landscaped gardens and parks in the eighteenth century.'

'But what does it do?' This came from Caroline and I kept my mouth firmly clammed shut.

'The point of the ha-ha is to give the viewer of the garden the illusion of a continuous rolling lawn, whilst providing boundaries for livestock,' Leonard said.

'Such a silly name though,' Caroline said. 'Why is it called that, Uncle Len?'

'Um, because it sounds funny and unexpected,' he said, suddenly flustered. 'Right, everyone head round to the left and you'll see some fine examples of the wonderful English oak,' Leonard blustered and then began striding forward.

Caroline looked round at me and shrugged.

'You dig a deep, dry ditch, the inner side of which would be built up to the level of the surrounding turf with either a dry-stone or a brick wall. The other side was designed to slope steeply upwards before levelling out to turf again. It was originally a feature of French formal gardens in the eighteenth century. Goodness I've forgotten the name of the chap who first wrote about it, but the idea was that the name derived from the optical illusion created on the viewers of the garden from a distance. They would come closer and be hugely surprised and cry "Ah! Ah!"'

I had pretty much whispered this to Caroline, but I realised my mistake when she snorted out a bark of laughter. Dorothy had expressly asked me to make sure everyone saw me as a companion only. She also asked me to chat to the family and draw out anything relevant. I was going to be walking a thin line.

'I think I remember reading that in a National Trust leaflet,' I added quickly.

'I wonder,' Caroline said, lowering her own voice, 'if Uncle Leonard always knows what he's talking about.'

There was no annoyance in her tone and, actually, she spoke with a lot of affection.

'Are you close to your uncle?' I asked, capitalising on the moment.

Caroline looked surprised by the question, but then seemed to contemplate her response.

'Uncle Len is a sweetheart,' she said simply. 'He's so generous to have let us use his house for the week. Not many people can brag about being married in such a beautiful setting. The reception is going to be in the orangery. Have you seen it?'

'No, I haven't.'

'It's got the most gorgeous lemon trees and vines. Some of the trees will have to be taken outside to fit in all of the tables, but it will still look lovely. I've got the florist to entwine her displays of cream lilies and pale-yellow roses all over the place. There's going to be low-hung chandeliers above each table and the linen is all in crisp lemon to complement the trees. I can't wait!'

'It all sounds wonderful, and you're right, your uncle is indeed a very generous man.'

'Well, I think sometimes he can be a bit ruthless,' Caroline continued.

'Oh? How so?' I asked as casually as I could, although my fists clenched in anticipation.

'Well, the thing is,' Caroline said, lowering her voice, 'I heard a rumour about him.'

I glanced up to see how far Leonard was ahead of us. He was at a substantial distance and it was unlikely he'd be able to hear us. Caroline must have thought the same because she slowed her pace before she continued.

'He had a cook who worked for him for years, I mean, like many years. And then, just over a year ago there was some nonsense about her stealing from him. She was a really nice woman and had known Uncle Leonard and our family really well. The thought of her taking anything from him was abhorrent, but Uncle Len decided she had to go, and so she did and then Harry turned up pretty quickly after that. I suppose you can't have dishonest staff working for you, but it did seem very unlikely and as I say a bit ruthless somehow. I wondered if he made it up so he could get rid of her and he's so friendly with Harry that I guess he just wanted to give him the job.'

A heron stood in the middle of the lake surveying its surroundings. I thought it might be a statue for a moment as we walked closer, but then it turned its head, fixed its black eye on us and took flight, its huge wingspan clear as it glided over our heads. I digested what Caroline had said. I was building a picture about the man and didn't like what I was seeing. Caroline, of course, had no idea of the bigger picture and could be forgiven for misunderstanding, but my impression was coalescing into a dark image.

There was little shade on the left-hand side of the lake and we walked into the sun as we headed back to the house. I pulled the brim of my hat a little lower, although it was mostly just making my head hot. Rufus was ahead of me and as Caroline had caught up with Juliet and linked arms with her I decided to see what I could gather from a conversation with him if he was willing. His slim shoulders were hunched over and his hands were pushed down low in the pockets of his black shorts. His demeanour wasn't unlike Juliet's, in a sulky teenager way, even though Rufus looked to be in his twenties. He bore an uncanny resemblance to his uncle Leonard with his black hair, but I assumed it was his own and not from the same bottle.

'Hi there,' I said as I drew level with him.

'Hello,' he said. 'You're Dot's friend, aren't you?'

'Yes, just here to give her a helping hand.'

'That's nice. She looks capable, but I suppose she's elderly and could do with someone to lean on.'

He said this with a tilted, sad smile and I assumed he was referring to the loss of her husband rather than her faculties.

'Did you ever meet her husband, Philip?' I asked.

'Only once, at the engagement party,' Rufus said, quickly. 'He seemed to be a nice man, very sad what happened to him. It was a terrible accident apparently.'

'I'm not aware of the particulars,' I lied.

'Oh, he had a fall outside his home and hit his head.'

'That is very sad,' I said, wondering why he didn't mention the burglary, but then this was supposed to be a special occasion and perhaps not the time to be dragging up unpleasant things. I decided to change the subject and get to safer territory. 'Doesn't the house look glorious from this position by the lake? I think I'd have a bench right here to admire the aspect if it were mine.'

Rufus laughed, but it was a dark sound, as if there was something hiding behind that smile.

'Uncle Leonard is a very lucky man for sure. Whatever is going on he always seems to land on his feet. Not sure that others are so lucky, though. Excuse me,' he said as he picked up his pace and then walked away.

* * *

When we got back to the house everyone disappeared off for lunch, but I took a croissant from a plate on the counter, a chunk of cheese from the fridge in the kitchen and decided to do a little research in the safety of my room. I couldn't just go around asking questions; I needed to look at the crime itself.

It didn't take much of a search on my phone before I found the news article about the robbery, dated a year ago.

An elderly man succumbed to his injuries last night, following an incident at his home over a week ago.

Philip Reed of Hampton Court Road, Hampton, was chasing an intruder from his riverside house when he fell down his front steps and suffered hip and head injuries. The 89-year-old pensioner was being treated at The Royal Free Hospital where he arrived in a coma and never regained consciousness. His widow, 88-year-old Dorothy Reed, is said to be being looked after by family members after what she described as the most devastating day of her life.

Detective Inspector Collinson of the Met Police has issued a statement saying that they are looking for a person of slight build and average height who used the victim's phone to call for an ambulance. They have been looking at CCTV footage from the neighbouring houses and the area, and are appealing for anyone with any information to come forward.

There was a link to a Facebook post where Miles had appealed on behalf of the family for everyone to keep an eye out for the stolen items. And there was a picture of the painting along with snapshots of the other things that had been taken. Dorothy was right; they were just inexpensive trinkets, perhaps taken to disguise the fact that the painting was what the thief was really after, as she had suggested.

I sat and looked at the painting for a moment, scrutinising the strokes of paint across the canvas and trying to understand the motivation for its theft. At best it was a pretty little watercolour of a coastal scene. It was fairly accomplished, but nothing particularly special. It would be a top raffle prize rather than a coveted piece of art. Perfectly nice to hang on the wall, especially if you had won it in a competition. What a terrible outcome for a mediocre piece of artwork, I thought.

So, this was the picture I had to find, but I knew it wasn't about the painting itself; it was all about proving Leonard to be at the heart of it. I went back to the Facebook post and screenshot a picture of the missing artwork.

I was about to search for the original competition where Philip had won the painting when I could hear muffled voices outside on the landing. I got up off the bed and opened the door, but the voices had gone and only Juliet was there, walking past, her phone in her hand.

'Hi,' I said to her and she turned around. 'Is lunch finished now?'

'Yeah,' she said. 'Leonard said that we all have to meet at the entrance to the maze at four-thirty for some lame treasure hunt.'

'You don't fancy a treasure hunt? What would you rather be doing?'

'Be with my mates. I was allowed to bring one friend here, but obviously they're all on holiday somewhere brilliant, not waiting around for an invite to a *boring* wedding.' Juliet suddenly let out a big yawn and tried to disguise it with the back of her hand, her phone still clutched tightly in her grip. It looked as if she had something flashing across the screen, but I couldn't make out what it was before she took her hand away and plunged the device into her pocket.

'Dorothy said there's going to be horse riding tomorrow, and quad biking the day after. Is that something you'd like to do?' I asked her.

'Spose,' she said, sulkily. 'So, four-thirty at the maze, yeah?'

'Oh, me too?'

'If you can get out of it then do. I won't tell them I've told you.'

I smiled at the girl. 'I'll come, but thanks. If I can get you out of something later in the week I will, okay?'

'Okay,' she said and there was the merest hint of a smile on her lips.

I turned back to my room as Juliet walked away, but the sound of voices was unmistakable again. Perhaps she was watching something on her phone. I closed my door and opened my wardrobe to find an outfit suitable to wear for a game in a maze.

* * *

I found Dorothy in the music room, sitting on a sofa by the open doorway with a book in her hands. She glanced up when I walked in and smiled.

'Ready to get lost in Leonard's maze?' she asked me.

'I feel like I already am,' I replied, in a whisper, looking about for the man in question.

'Don't worry – he's already down there, preparing, apparently. Have you managed to find anything out yet?'

'Only that he's not a very likeable person, but don't be downcast,' I said, sitting down next to her. 'I do feel that there's something going on with him and I will do my best to find out what that might be.'

I didn't want to start repeating what Caroline had told me until I could see it was relevant. And also it sounded very much like Rufus had some dirt on Leonard that he wasn't prepared to divulge. It wouldn't be right to start speculating; this was Dorothy's extended family after all, and I needed to tread quickly, but carefully.

'I have decided that I will look for the painting, but only while I feel comfortable about it. If I think I'm in any danger, I will stop.'

'Of course, but you won't be in any danger,' she said, smiling and going back on everything she'd said previously. She'd definitely used the words *unhinged* and *dangerous* yesterday. 'I have every faith in you.'

'Shall we take a slow walk down to the maze? I assume you're up for the challenge,' I asked, and Dorothy rolled her eyes.

'After this wedding is over and whether the painting is found or not, I will never set foot in this house again, so I may as well take a look at that loathsome man's maze.'

I laughed and took her arm and then we walked out onto the patio and slowly down towards the garden.

The maze was behind the orangery on the other side of the house to the walk that I had taken earlier and Dorothy wanted to stop and see where the wedding breakfast was going to be held. It was a white-painted building with huge floor-to-ceiling windows. Some of the citrus trees that would normally be grown inside had been removed and now lined the outside of the building, the lemons and limes looking luscious in the sunshine, just as Caroline had envisaged. The place was a hive of activity, with a team of people lifting tables and chairs out from the back of a truck and carrying them inside the vast space. The ceilings were high and I noticed, as I poked my head around the door frame, that the back wall hosted a number of trailing passionflowers in full bloom – a riot of white and pink and lilac.

The chandeliers that Caroline had talked about were in position and the florist, whom I had encountered in the house earlier, was walking around with a book and taking notes.

'It's going to be lovely,' I said.

'It is a reminder of why we're really here,' Dorothy replied with a grim smile. 'Not that I will let my grandson's wedding distract me from the other matter in hand. They will be married, it will be lovely and we will be victorious.'

Dorothy stepped back outside and I followed her, wondering how she could be so confident. Then I remembered that all that confidence hinged on my own performance and my stomach rolled at the thought. I had told Dorothy that I would do my best, but I realised I hadn't had that conversation with myself.

We met the others at the entrance to the maze and Leonard was already holding court. He was wearing a costume that I assumed was supposed to be the white rabbit from the book *Alice in Wonderland*. He had an odd combination of maroon trousers and a white waistcoat. His top hat had rabbit ears sticking out from either side and he had an oversized pocket watch in his hand.

'Come along, you're late,' he said, tapping the watch with a smug smile.

I noticed there was a fake rose tree next to him with bright red plastic roses stuck into the foliage. He was clearly setting a scene, but with his own very beautiful rose garden in view over to the right, it did rather fall short.

He began explaining that there was a list of riddles and that not only would we have to work out the answers we would also have to navigate the maze itself, but that the answers would show us the way to the middle and the winners would find a prize there – namely dinner.

A couple of the group were looking restless and Juliet rolled her eyes.

'Dinner is the treasure?' she said in a scathing voice. 'Hardly worth the bother.'

'If you would like to fend for yourself and cook your own meal, then I will congratulate you on your resourcefulness, Juliet,' Leonard said and even I had to smile at that.

Caroline and Toby rallied, then, and encouraged the others out of their afternoon slump.

'God, it's only the first day. I'll be dead by the end of the week at this rate,' Miles said to Lavinia, and she gave him a playful but warning slap on his arm.

'Not the man we want dead,' Dorothy breathed, and I looked up to see if anyone had heard. Luckily the group had all surged forward for the first clue.

'Dorothy, you cannot give yourself away,' I whispered and she gave me a grudging nod of acknowledgement. 'Do you want to go in the maze?' I asked more loudly.

'Just for a slow wander maybe. I don't really fancy worrying about those clues. We can just have a chat as we go, if you like.'

I quite liked the idea of going back to the house and curling up in an armchair with a book, and wondered if I wasn't cut out for being a companion, certainly not one that required a particular set of skills.

'That sounds perfect,' I said, anyway, and we followed the others.

'Not clueing, ladies?' asked Leonard as we attempted to walk past him without taking the outstretched piece of card with the first clue.

'We were just going to have a wander, if that's okay,' Dorothy said. 'I'm feeling a bit tired to be honest, but don't want to be a complete party pooper.'

'No problem at all. Have a wander, enjoy the sunshine, and don't forget your hat,' he said, looking directly at me. 'Perhaps you'd like to have a go at solving the first clue, at least.'

He handed the card to me and I took it reluctantly.

'I'll give it a try, but I'm not great at puzzles,' I said.

'Well, I don't believe that for a moment,' he said, with a sinister smile.

We left Leonard at the entrance and disappeared into the bowels of the maze.

10

GINA

'What does it say?' Dorothy whispered urgently, dropping her nonchalance as soon as she was out of sight of the master of the house.

I looked down at the piece of card and read the words on the front. It was a riddle and there was a code on the bottom with directions relating to the letters of the alphabet. It was the sort of thing I would have concocted with my brother when we were kids on those very wet Sunday afternoons that seemed to go on forever. I could feel Leonard listening on the other side of the hedge as I read out the clue.

'I am an odd number. Take away a letter and I become even. What number am I?'

It was an obvious conundrum that I understood immediately, but I kept it firmly to myself.

'No idea,' I said to Dorothy. 'Let's go for a walk and if we get lost I'm sure someone will come and rescue us.'

I took us a short way along the first stretch of hedging and then stopped to show Dorothy.

'If you take away the letter S from the front of the word seven you have the word even. Do you get it? Seven: an odd number,' I whispered.

'Oh, I suppose I get it,' Dorothy said with a raised eyebrow. 'Not my sort of thing really.'

'Dorothy, you do the crossword; you must have some idea.'

'I buy the newspaper and I *try* to do the crossword, but in truth I'm much happier with a gritty thriller,' she said with a smile.

'Right, well the answer to this is seven and if you look at the code at the bottom, the letter S means go right, then the letters E and V take you left, so that's left three times and then N takes you right again. You see?'

Dorothy frowned and then shrugged.

'Can *you* see now why I chose you as my companion?' she said with a grin, and then linked her arm through mine as we set off and I steered her confidently into the maze.

The others had clearly worked out the answer quickly and had long disappeared, although their chatter and laughter could be heard at various points as we traversed the hedgerows back and forth.

Our pace was quite slow as Dorothy couldn't walk very quickly and soon the excited voices of the others seemed to have grown softer and more distant.

'Hang on, here's another clue.'

I pulled out a card that was stuck into the edge of the hedge and read it out.

'*If two's company and three's a crowd what are four and five?* God, he's not very imaginative, is he,' I said. 'So, it's another right, then a left and then a right, then a left again.'

'What was the answer?' Dorothy asked. 'I'm honestly not very good at quizzes.'

'Nine,' I said. 'He asks the question *what are four and five?* Four plus five equals nine.'

'Oh, I see!' Dorothy said, delighted.

'Please don't be impressed.'

'No, you're right. So, Gina,' she said after a moment. 'You were saying about growing up in Bushy Park. How did that happen?'

'My parents were living in a grotty flat in Teddington with me and my brother. I was five at the time. They'd heard about an old prefab the Americans had left after the war and it was in the parkland. So we and two other families took it over and made it home for a few short years. It was a happy time,' I said and almost wish she hadn't asked. It had been a happy time, but it all went wrong shortly after.

'That sounds wonderful,' Dorothy said. 'Idyllic, but does that mean officially you were squatters?'

'Yes.' I laughed. 'I suppose we were – not that I would have understood that at the time. They made it such a lovely home and with the deer park as my front garden, it was great.'

'And you mentioned your marriage earlier. If it's not being pushy, can I ask what happened?'

'You, pushy? Perish the thought,' I said and she laughed.

'Touché.'

'After forty-five years of marriage, two children and two grand-children, he decided I wasn't the one for him. He said he couldn't understand what had brought him to this place in his life and if this was all there was, then what was the point. He also said he needed to find himself.'

I began my statement with a matter-of-fact tone, but as I got to the last few words I had to swallow, hard.

'My goodness, how very disappointing of him,' Dorothy said. 'I'm generalising here, I do realise, but women tend to find themselves through friendships and activity, through reading and learning. I think men tend to need some sort of justification for existing through sex.'

There was a beat of silence while we digested those words before Dorothy added her caveat: 'Not all men, of course.'

'My son asked me if I thought there was someone else and I suppose it's entirely possible. His letter suggested that I was beige and unexciting, like I said earlier, so it would make sense.'

'And like I said earlier, you are neither of those things,' Dorothy said. .

'I think there is some truth in it, though. I'm not being self-deprecating,' I added quickly as Dorothy opened her mouth to speak. 'I've let myself go a bit. I don't worry about my clothes much; I rarely buy anything new. I don't colour my hair any more or wear much make-up. I can't remember the last time I looked at myself in the mirror and felt pleased with what I saw.'

'Oh, Gina, that makes me so sad to hear you say that. It's not all about looks, but you do have wonderful skin. You are very attractive.'

As she said this, my left hand reached involuntarily to my right arm and to the damaged skin under my sleeve, and I suppressed a shudder.

'One assumes he was happy with how you looked for the majority of your marriage?'

'Yes, I suppose,' I said. 'He did used to compliment me. He used to say how lucky he was to have such a lovely wife who doted on him. God! How pathetic that sounds. The thing is for the first time in my life I will be living alone and can please myself, but...' I paused while I tried to get to the heart of what I really wanted to say. 'I've only ever looked after other people. It sounds lovely doesn't it, to please oneself, but I don't really know how.'

'There are different ways to deal with that situation. You can decide to be unhappy and abandoned or you can embrace an opportunity, shake off the shackles of marriage, because that is really what it is to be married and raise children, as a woman, to constantly look after those you love.'

'But you were happy with Philip, weren't you?' I asked her, surprised at her views.

'Yes, of course, but I didn't know that marriage, for a woman, equated to signing up to a lifetime of servitude,' she said with a smile, as if in full acceptance of her role. 'What did you expect when you said yes to your husband?'

I thought about that for a moment and felt a bit embarrassed by my answer.

'I don't really remember much about that time, to be honest.'

'Ah, young love; I remember it well,' she said.

I opened my mouth to tell her that it wasn't like that, but she'd started talking about my new-found freedom again.

'Anyway, you can take off whenever and wherever you like, start a new hobby or pick up an old one. You could write a book, take up a dance class or find a new bloke; lucky you.'

'Dorothy, you could do the same, you know.'

'Ah, well, you see it's different for me at the moment. I was lost when Philip went. I couldn't produce the art that I'd always loved so much. I could barely be bothered to pull a pan out of the cupboard and cook myself a proper meal. It wasn't just about his death; it was because of Leonard. The thought of him orchestrating what he did, to have what he wanted at any cost, eats away at me. What I'm suggesting for you, is what I'd be suggesting for myself – possibly not the dancing or the bloke, though. And I will, once I have justice for Philip. It consumes me, you know, this need for the truth. But, when it's over, and I do have faith that we will be successful this week, then I will allow myself to become a woman content on her own. I know I can do it once I've shaken off this anger. And, Gina, I know you can do it too.'

'Dorothy, my friend, you are so insightful and offer up such an impassioned speech with a great argument for independence without shackles and yet, somehow I'm feeling myself even more compelled than ever to do your bidding and find this painting for you. Bravo.'

'I meant every word, you know. I think we can help each other,' she said.

I was about to ask her how she planned to help me, but some of the others' voices were within earshot again, so I took her hand, gave it a squeeze, and tried not to think about the task before me that was far greater than getting us out of this maze.

I then pulled my phone from my pocket and opened my maps app, zoomed in on our location and, watching the flashing blue dot move, I pulled Dorothy gently to the left.

'Here,' I said. 'We don't need Leonard's terrible clues to reach the middle; we have technology!'

* * *

The middle of the maze was surprisingly large, and the entire group were already there, proving that Leonard's clues were hardly tricky at all. His staff had managed to navigate the labyrinth of hedging and deliver a table laden with food and drinks. There were more plastic rose trees and I remembered the game of croquet earlier. Leonard liked a theme; that was for sure.

A huge glass bowl of something that looked like punch sat on one end of the table with a sign next to it – *Drink me!* Platters of meat and cheese, bread, cakes and fruit covered the rest with the obligatory sign – *Eat me!* Juliet was crowing over the fact that she had worked out all the clues and wanted to know what her prize was because it couldn't possibly just be dinner. Leonard smiled, indulgently, and handed her a twenty-pound note from his wallet.

She looked surprised at his change in attitude, but then pocketed the money.

This was going to be a meal that I couldn't get out of, I realised as everyone took their seats. Some jazz music began to fill the air around us from hidden speakers and mingled with the sounds of people piling food onto their plates and glasses being filled. If it hadn't been for what Dorothy had planned for me, this all might be a lovely thing to do on a warm summer evening, but instead my mind was twitchy and preoccupied. I opened my photos on my phone and began to scroll through the pictures I'd taken earlier while Leonard was safely at the other end of the table. There was so much of the house I had yet to see and probably many places that would be completely out of bounds to me. He could have it hanging up in the attic rooms or hidden in a shed or storeroom somewhere; he may have even destroyed it.

I glanced across at Dorothy who was sitting opposite me on the other side of the table. She had helped herself to some food and was nibbling on a chunk of cheese with slices of apple. She looked like she didn't want to be there much either and I wondered what would happen if I didn't find the painting. Dorothy had already said she wouldn't be able to let it go and move on. She would be consumed with anger when she should really be grieving the death of her husband, but then, wasn't anger one of the many stages?

When my beloved mother Ellen died, I had eventually been angry. Firstly, though, I'd wandered aimlessly through my days in a haze as dark as the smoke that had filled our house on that terrible night. There was a numbness to my existence with the occasional awakening to grief and guilt.

Ellen was a gentle woman, kind and funny, smart and serious when seriousness was needed. She was appreciated for her work, loved by many, admired by more than just my father and, ultimately, fallible.

It had been eighteen months after her death that I met Douglas. The year was 1980 and I was twenty-eight. My friends had dragged me out in some odd celebration after the successful court case, but I couldn't feel any sort of victory over the man who had started the fire. How could I possibly? Douglas had been drinking with a few of his own friends and as the pub filled and we had to start sharing tables, I found myself talking to him. To this day I can't remember what was said – I don't recall much about that time at all – but I must have thought him nice and friendly, because I married him and had his children. I wouldn't have guessed that a man who would see me through that terrible time with care and compassion would be able to discard me so easily over forty years later.

I felt a determination settle over me. I would find the painting or certainly find out if Leonard was responsible; then Dorothy could move on with her life.

* * *

Harry had arrived and was spooning ladles of the punch into glasses and they were being passed around the table. I declined his offer as he handed one to me, but Leonard had other ideas.

'Gina, you are more than Dot's carer here and I'd very much like you to enjoy your time the same as everyone else.'

With all eyes expectantly on me, I took the glass. Then I took a breath and a sip of the drink that Harry handed me, unfortunately at the same time, and as the liquid hit the back of my throat I coughed.

'Bit strong for you?' said a voice and I looked up into the eyes of Harry, who wasn't smiling, but actually, at that moment as the sun made me blink, he looked a little intimidating.

'A bit strong for everyone, I would imagine,' I said, attempting a laugh, once I'd stopped coughing. Instinctively I took another mouthful to soothe the tickle that remained in my throat and this time, as the cool liquid flowed down to my stomach and began to flood my system, I got a taste for how potent it really was. Not just fruit punch then. Harry was hovering and put out his hand to take the glass away, but I held it firmly. Everyone else was drinking, apart from Juliet, and I would just have this one. It might help me to relax a bit and perhaps I may have some sort of epiphany about where that painting might be.

For the next couple of hours Leonard held court at the end of the table with stories of his trips abroad. He'd travelled the Trans-Siberian Express and the Orient Express, stayed in lavish hotels and dined in the best restaurants around the world. He'd skied in first-class resorts and sailed on exclusive boats. Everyone was rapt by his tales and, despite myself, even my attention was caught. I'd usually find this sort of bragging incredibly tedious, but for some reason, that evening I didn't. I drank and ate along with the rest, joined in animated conversations and felt completely relaxed and safe.

As the sun went down and we finally vacated the middle of the maze, Leonard escorted us back towards the house. I stumbled on a tree root poking out onto the path as we walked past the orangery and realised that I must be a little drunk, but no one seemed to notice. I thought back to all that had been discussed that evening, feeling as if I'd missed something vitally important, but my brain couldn't seem to remember anything that had been spoken about. My relaxed state had evaporated and now I just felt disconcerted.

I saw Dorothy up to her room, but as I headed back to my own, I couldn't remember whether I'd even said goodnight. One thing I did see before I closed my door, though, was Harry watching me from the far end of the landing where he raised a hand in a funny sort of farewell gesture and then disappeared behind his own bedroom door.

11

DOROTHY

Dorothy opened her newspaper and turned straight to the crossword, her hand poised, pen clutched, ready to storm the first clue. She read it once, twice and then a third time before she folded the paper back and laid the pen down on top. She reached for her library book and read four pages, not really taking in a word before she closed that too and leaned back in her chair. She was thinking about Gina.

She sensed that Gina was holding on to some deep-rooted pain that went further than an imminent divorce. Dorothy was trying to convince herself that by asking Gina to find the painting, she was giving her some sort of validation of her stronger self, but really, she knew she was using her and it wasn't sitting very well this morning. The trouble was, this meant so much to Dorothy, she was probably going to keep persuading her regardless. What she needed to do was find a way to help the woman and that had to go further than payment for a week of companionship. She liked her, she liked her a lot, and she'd like her even more if she could find that blessed painting.

There was a knock at the door then and Gina appeared with a tray of breakfast things.

'Morning,' Gina said brightly.

This surprised Dorothy because if she wasn't mistaken Gina had been a bit drunk the night before. She walked across the room and Dorothy moved the newspaper and library book so that Gina could lay the tray on the table.

'You don't look well at all,' Dorothy told her as Gina sat down heavily in the chair opposite.

'I'm not feeling that wonderful to be honest. Whatever was in that drink hit me quite hard. I should never have drunk it. It was very unprofessional of me. God knows what your family thought of the help getting tipsy.'

Dorothy laughed and began pouring the tea from the pot into the two cups. Then she added a lump of sugar to Gina's and handed it to her.

'Who cares what they think; in fact, it's genius really. You said that Leonard thinks you're an idiot, well, now he thinks you're a lush too.'

Gina did not return Dorothy's laughter; instead she buried her face into her hands.

'Mine wasn't strong at all,' Dorothy continued. 'I had three and I feel fine.'

'I don't really remember getting back to the house. Did I see you upstairs?' said Gina.

'Yes, but you weren't making an awful lot of sense and you did stumble outside on the steps.'

'There's a huge blank space between the dinner in the maze and me waking up this morning. I think that I must have been topped up and hadn't realised,' Gina said. 'I'm not a big drinker.'

'Neither am I. It's very odd,' Dorothy said, narrowing her eyes.

Gina drank some of her tea and grimaced at the sugar.

'You may not usually take your tea sweet, but I think this morning should be an exception.'

Gina nodded and drained her sugary drink, then sat staring into the bottom of the cup.

'I've just remembered that Harry was watching me as I went into my bedroom last night,' she said.

'Perhaps he was concerned that you were wobbly and decided to make sure you got back to your room safely.'

'I might have thought the same, except he'd been the one pouring the drinks,' Gina said.

'Did you see him when you got the breakfast tray?' Dorothy asked, lifting the lid on her bacon and eggs and offering it over to Gina, while she started on the yogurt and fruit.

'No, it was just there in the kitchen with your name next to it. I think I must have just missed him because it was still hot. Perhaps he was coming back to bring it up to you, but I got there first,' Gina said and then her phone began ringing in her pocket.

'Douglas again,' she said, but she didn't answer it.

'I was thinking, what you said about your husband last night and what he wrote in his letter. I was rather quick to dismiss him as another flaky man keen to revisit his youth and abandon his responsibilities, but you said he'd needed to find himself and that he wondered what was the point. Do you think he could be having some sort of breakdown?'

Dorothy watched Gina as her expression changed from one of surprise to one of contemplation.

'I don't honestly know. I haven't really had much of a conversation with him since he packed up and went on his retreat. He popped in to get some of his things and left before I'd plucked up the courage to ask questions.'

'You needed to pluck up the courage to ask why your marriage was over?' Dorothy asked in surprise and Gina shrugged, looking a little embarrassed.

'He's left a message,' Gina said glancing down at her phone and then she pressed play, seemingly not bothered that Dorothy could hear it too because the sound of a man's voice suddenly filled the room.

'Georgina, it's me. I realised I don't know where you are. You didn't actually say; I'm not sure why. You need to phone me to let me know. There might also be some news on the house. So, I'll speak to you soon then.'

'Perhaps he's bored of Little Miss Maidenhead already,' Gina said quietly, turning the phone over in her hand.

'Sorry?' Dorothy said, amused and confused.

'Oh, it doesn't matter. I'm just being silly, probably. I should phone him back and let him know where I am. He doesn't like being in the dark about things.'

'Did he let you know where he was going when he went off to his spa thingy?' Dorothy asked, suddenly feeling a little less generous towards the man.

'Well, no he didn't but...'

'We should probably get ready for the day, don't you think? I'm not horse riding – I can tell you that for nothing. You won't get this nearly-ninety-year-old carcass up onto a horse,' Dorothy said, looking pointedly at Gina until she slid her phone back into her pocket.

'I did wonder,' Gina said, 'if we could both get out of it and with Leonard out of the house, I could have a little search?'

'That, my dear,' Dorothy said, 'is music to my ears.'

* * *

Dorothy wasn't at all surprised to learn that Leonard had stables in the grounds of Walstone Hall. It wouldn't have come as a huge shock to find he had a theme park hiding in a grove somewhere too. He had everything, it seemed, but not a special person to share it with. Dorothy wondered about that as she and Gina took a slow walk through the kitchen garden towards the stables.

'He's never been married, you know,' Dorothy said, nodding towards Leonard who was striding ahead of them with the others scurrying in his wake.

'He'd have to find someone to tolerate him, perhaps he hasn't yet,' Gina said.

'I can see you're on board with my way of thinking; good girl,' Dorothy said, with a grin. 'The thing is he can be quite charming when you first meet him. Philip was very taken with him at the start. You might not think so now with all his showboating and bluster, but when he was younger, or even now, when you take away all of this, he can capture you. I've fallen for it in the past, I don't mind saying.'

'Dorothy, you're very close to complimenting him,' Gina said.

'Please don't misunderstand – the fault lies with me for being taken in and anyway, it's been many years now that I've considered him the most deceitful man I've ever met.'

'How did Caroline and Toby meet?' Gina asked.

'At a party, at my house, actually,' Dorothy said. 'It was our sixty-fifth wedding anniversary, a couple of years ago, and Philip arranged a group of our friends and family to come. We had a lovely time, with wonderful food, music and were able to spread out into the garden, the weather was so nice.'

'Your house would be a fabulous place for a party,' Gina agreed.

'We have had many parties over the years; we've been very lucky,' Dorothy said as they turned onto a lane leading to the stables. Even though the others were out of sight now, the distinctive scent of hay, leather and manure reached her and told her they were heading in the right direction. 'Leonard turned up out of the blue with Caroline. We thought we'd finally shaken him off, but he arrived uninvited with his niece in tow and a magnum of the finest champagne in his hand. He said he was passing and wanted to congratulate us both, that Caroline was staying with him for a week and she wanted to accompany him.'

'So, an unlikely Norfolk to Hampton drive-by?' Gina said.

'Yes, exactly. Philip and I hadn't discussed with anyone how irritating Leonard had become at that point. I think Philip was a bit embarrassed to have lost a couple of art pieces at auction to Leonard's outbidding and didn't want to talk about it, so everyone still thought of him as Philip's old mentee, his trusted ex-partner. Well, Toby and Caroline hit it off and became inseparable, pretty much straight away. Then it was only a month after, that the art competition started. I did wonder if someone at that party mentioned it to Leonard and once he knew Philip was involved, he decided to enter it himself. It does seem such a shame that Caroline was with him that day. I can't see another time when Toby would have met her. I mean, she is lovely and they are so well suited, but we will forever have to be associated with Leonard Price.'

'Have you thought about the repercussions of him being found guilty, the ripples through the family?' Gina said, her voice suddenly so low and controlled that Dorothy turned to her in surprise. 'It can have devastating consequences.'

'Are you saying that I should let a criminal go unchecked so we can all continue to play happy families?'

'Absolutely not. I'm just saying, prepare yourself for the inevitable fallout.'

Gina looked so stony-faced all of a sudden that Dorothy wanted to find out what was behind that expression and what had motivated her to ask the question, but they were at the stables and in earshot of the others, so she stored it away to ask later.

'Ready to saddle up, ladies?' Leonard asked in a bright and cheerful voice, which made Dorothy grind her teeth.

'Dorothy isn't riding and as her companion I will stay with her, and I think we're going to take a walk in your lovely garden,' Gina said.

'Well, you're missing out,' he said, bluntly.

'Our loss, then,' Gina replied and walked past him into the stables.

Leonard was standing with Paul and they began discussing who was to have which horse. Paul was dressed simply in jeans and a navy T-shirt with a pair of old trainers on his feet, but Leonard had full-on riding gear. He looked like someone who was about to go on a hunt with white riding jodhpurs and a long-tailed red jacket. Dorothy wondered if he knew he looked ridiculous, but judging by the way he conducted himself, she imagined he was actually very happy with his appearance. She bit down on her tongue to stop herself from telling him and followed Gina.

The smell of hay and hoof oil, of leather and horses hit her more intensely as she walked inside the stables. The building was huge with space for several horses, but most of the animals were tied up outside their stalls while stable hands tacked them up. Gina had walked across to a chestnut mare and asked if it was okay to stroke it. The young lad looked up at her from where he was buckling up the saddle.

'Yeah, she's very friendly,' he said and Dorothy watched as Gina extended her arm cautiously until she made contact with the horse's soft nose.

'Such beautiful, gentle creatures,' she said and the stable lad laughed.

'She is gentle, but she's called Lawnmower.'

'Lawnmower?' Dorothy said, thinking that this horse deserved a more fitting name for her majestic frame.

'Yeah, because with the wrong rider, she'll spend the whole time with her head down munching the grass.'

'Ah, she needs a firm hand then. Maybe Juliet could handle her,' Gina said, as Juliet herself walked their way. 'Think we may have the horse for you.'

Juliet ran her hand along Lawnmower's side and then patted her.

'I think we'll get along fine,' she said.

'Do you know much about horses?' Dorothy asked Gina as they stood together watching as riders were allocated animals and the group organised themselves.

'I used to ride with my brother. Our neighbour had two horses and we would help look after them and in turn were allowed to take them out. It was a great arrangement for us all.'

'Does your brother live near you?'

'No,' Gina said, seemingly surprised by the question. 'He still lives in America. I don't see him very much.'

'Oh, you lived in the States?' Dorothy said.

'After we left Bushy Park, we moved to Seattle when I was nine until I was fifteen. My father was American.'

'How interesting. What made you move back?'

'I moved back with my mother only. My brother was older and wanted to stay. It's a bit complicated and I'd rather not talk about it, if you don't mind,' Gina said, quietly.

'Of course, I don't mind at all,' said Dorothy, who minded very much indeed.

Dorothy followed Gina back outside and then noticed that Harry was with Leonard while he prepared himself to ride. She was sure he hadn't been walking with the group. He was saying something to Leonard, which made the man raise his eyebrows in response.

'Harry turning up when you least expect him again,' Dorothy said quietly in Gina's ear. 'I've never seen a chef so often out of the kitchen.'

The horses looked a little restless by the time they were all ready and then they were off in convoy. Dorothy saw that Leonard looked back at them a couple of times before the group rounded the corner and disappeared out of sight. His expression was dark.

'Can I offer you both a lift back to the house?' Harry said, walking over to them.

Dorothy opened her mouth to say that they would be fine to walk, but Gina got in there first.

'That would be kind,' she said. 'I have an awful headache.'

They didn't talk in the car even though Dorothy kept forming questions in her head that she wanted to ask Harry. He was the closest person to Leonard, it seemed, and would perhaps know a lot about the goings-on in Walstone Hall. The trouble was, all of her questions seemed too obvious and she could hardly ask him straight out where the painting was. Then they were back at the house anyway and the opportunity was gone. Harry dropped them off at the side door and both women thanked him before climbing out and watching him drive away. Dorothy turned to Gina, her eyes alight.

'Right,' she said. 'I think we have a good couple of hours, so let's get to it.'

'Do you really think this is a good idea? I think I've lost my nerve,' Gina said, and it wasn't lost on Dorothy that she looked a bit pale.

'If I could do it myself, I promise you, I would, but your mind is sharper. It won't seem odd that you're scurrying around on errands for me and to be honest, the stairs are a bugger. We may not get another opportunity like this. He's out, everyone is out and it's a great chance to have a look in his bedroom.'

Dorothy suppressed a shudder at that thought. She didn't want Gina to know how abhorrent the idea of being in Leonard's bedroom was to her. Hopefully it would be hanging directly above his bed and Gina could just hook it off the wall, job done.

'His bedroom! You didn't say anything about his bedroom. I'm not going in there.'

'You only have to pop your head around the door. He won't be in there. Please, Gina. You can be in and out in seconds. We may not get another opportunity.'

She watched as Gina mentally tried to talk herself into it and recognised the moment she succeeded when her face hardened. At that point, Dorothy knew how much she was asking of this quiet woman and felt another stab of guilt.

'Right, well, I think that I'd prefer it if you positioned yourself somewhere with a good view for anyone coming back early and with a fully charged phone this time.' Gina looked at her pointedly.

'You're right – we don't need a repeat of last time,' Dorothy said, smiling gratefully.

'Perhaps if you sit in the drawing room, you'll be able to see across the kitchen gardens, towards the stables. This is assuming they'll all take the same route back. I'll start upstairs and have a poke about, then I'll come and check in with you. Hopefully the staff will be thin on the ground this morning, but I'll have to come up with a convincing story if I come across anyone. Harry seems to get about the house quite a bit and the grounds too. Not quite sure why that would be.'

'I think that Leonard has a team working for him and I don't just mean to run this house. I think that he has a team supporting all of his criminal endeavours,' Dorothy said.

'Do you think that he's committed more than the crime against your husband?'

'I think he's a criminal mastermind,' Dorothy said.

'I'd not stretch to mastermind, personally, but like you said, he's not to be underestimated,' Gina said. 'What's the expression? Believe someone the first time they reveal themselves to you. The first time I saw Leonard, I have to be honest, I felt quite a chill with just one of his looks.'

'Exactly! Keep hold of that thought.'

'Keep hold of that thought while I'm going through his bedroom?'

'Yes,' Dorothy said uncertainly as they made their way to the drawing room.

'I do know this is a lot to ask,' she said as she settled herself into the window seat. She could see out across the kitchen gardens, along the sheds and greenhouses, where they'd not long ago walked.

'As I said before, I'll do this as long as I feel comfortable, but if that changes then I'll have to stop.'

'Absolutely,' Dorothy said and watched as Gina took a long breath in and then left the room. She took her phone out of her handbag, checked it was on and that it had some life in it and then left it on the seat next to her where she took furtive glances at it before settling to her post as lookout. She crossed her fingers that Gina would be successful.

12

GINA

I made my way up the second flight of stairs to the third floor. I knew I was on thin ice here. I could easily have said I was lost on the lower floors, but up here, in Leonard's very private territory, his bedroom and possibly his office, I could have nothing to offer in the way of an excuse. There was absolutely no reason for me to be here. If I was caught, the police would be called. In pursuit of doing the right thing and finding the culprit to a serious crime, I could well be the one in trouble.

Unwittingly, I found my thoughts drifting back all those years to the court case after the fire and remembered how hard it was to do the right thing and make sure that justice was served, whatever the repercussions. Talking about it with Dorothy had brought it to the forefront of my mind and it would hang around there until I could get rid of it again for a while.

The oak staircase was just as beautifully carved as it was in the entrance vestibule. No expense had been spared for this private part of the house. I ran my hand along the turned spindles as I went quietly and carefully up, but each step came with the horrible knowledge that I was closer to doing something I really shouldn't, and instead of rushing to get it over and done with, I found myself slowing down.

'Come on, Gina,' I said to myself. 'You're either doing this, or you're not, but if you are, you need to get your backside moving.'

At the top I had two options: straight ahead or a turn round to the right and along a dark corridor. There were curtains pulled closed on high windows, I assumed to stop the sunlight from bleaching the artwork hung along the walls, but could it be something else? Could Philip's painting be hanging here in plain sight as Dorothy suggested? Surely it couldn't be that easy. Not wanting to turn on the light and draw attention to my presence, I pulled out my phone and switched on the torch instead, shielding the majority of the light with my hand.

There were several paintings along this part of the landing and all were landscapes, but none were of the coastal scene and I couldn't help feel a stab of disappointment that it wasn't going to be an easy find. The light from my phone cast shadows across the works and made them appear Gothic and atmospheric. There were windswept moors and bleak mountainsides, lonely stretches of river and one was a field of corn, but because the sky was a threatening mass of dark clouds it had a sombre quality. Maybe that was why Leonard had them here, for exactly that reason. With a thrumming heart I turned the handle on the only door and opened it onto Leonard's bedroom.

What I was expecting to find, I wasn't entirely sure, but the bright, hotel-like modern decor of the room was a surprise. Leonard's drapes at the windows were swathes of sheer, silver silk in perfect folds and the carpet was almost the same shade. His furniture was mostly white, but inlaid with silver leaf, which gleamed in the light coming from the four windows. His bed was like a huge silver marshmallow, the kind that, as a child, I would have liked to have taken a running jump at before face-planting on the covers. I had no such urge now.

There was a Chinese cabinet at the end of his bed and, unusually, it wasn't facing out into the room, but instead was facing the bed itself. Almost as if it could be a TV cabinet. Again, it was mostly white with marquetry in the palest of wood. I leaned across the covers and tried the door, thinking it was big enough to house a small painting if not a television, but it was locked.

The only splash of colour in the room, although muted, was from the beautiful crewel embroidery work hanging behind the bed. Flowers and leaves with birds decorated the fabric and, on closer inspection, I could see it was old. Exactly how old I couldn't guess at first glance and I really didn't have time to dwell on it. Instead, I carefully pulled the corner away from the wall, to see if there was anything hiding behind, but the wall was blank.

I took out my phone to check it and that was when I saw a missed message from Dorothy. I'd forgotten to take my phone off silent. My heart was in my mouth and my feet were already on their way to the bedroom door as I opened the message.

All quiet here.

I let out a long breath and walked towards the window to make sure that Dorothy was right about the coast being clear. From here, I could see across to the lake and further towards the woods. The other window had a perfect view of the parterre garden and across to the folly where Dorothy had first told me of the plan. It made me uneasy to think that if Leonard had been up here he would easily have seen the two of us sitting and talking inside the building. But, obviously, he would never have heard us and it should have looked quite innocent. Well, apart from the two of us popping our heads out to make sure no one was watching.

Keen to leave Leonard's bedroom, I opened my camera app and began snapping every aspect of the room. I hoped that all these pictures I was taking would enlighten me somehow, but it felt like a fruitless search at the moment. I couldn't bring myself to open any drawers, but I did glance into his bathroom and was unsurprised to see a continuation of the white and silver theme.

Back on the landing I hesitated before opening one of the two doors at the far end. It was a sitting room, dark and gloomy with blinds pulled closed on both windows. I closed the door and tried the other and, as I suspected, it was Leonard's office: a huge room with bookcases, a desk, a fireplace with a perfectly placed chair, a side table with his current read and no obvious sign of the missing painting. It was a lot to take in and I snapped a couple of images. Really, though this was not enough and I thought briefly about what I was about to do and then stepped inside, because after all, by being in his bedroom I'd already crossed the line of no return and it was time to dig a bit deeper.

I turned my phone to record my voice exactly the same way that I used to do when investigating a new piece, or indeed an old piece, for a collection. Of course that had been with an old-fashioned Dictaphone, and what felt like a million years ago. I began to whisper and was surprised to realise how natural it felt to me.

'I'm standing in the middle of the study and there is a mild smell of tobacco in the air. I haven't noticed Leonard smoking, but that means nothing, of course. Perhaps he comes up here to fill his lungs. His desk is cluttered and unfortunately the drawers are all locked. The tall, free-standing cupboard by the window is not locked and I can see as I open it that it is stuffed full of papers.'

I stopped to take a photograph and then began to record again.

'Not much of interest. Old bank statements and documents – nothing for me here.'

I closed the cupboard and turned my attention to the shelves on the far wall. His collection of books here was as eclectic as his art and I skimmed my eyes over the spines feeling both the trepidation of being here and also the anticipation of finding something ebbing away from me.

'This is pointless. The painting is clearly not here,' I said into the phone, knowing that I was very much wasting my time.

I was about to click off the recording when my eyes fell on a small booklet sticking out between his other books. It had a grainy image of a painting on the thin spine and if I wasn't mistaken it was the coastal scene. I carefully took a photo before pulling it out. It was important to make sure I put it back exactly where I'd found it.

2021 Art Enthusiasts' Treasure Hunt
Sponsored by The Art Association Trust

I read the words into my phone from the front of the booklet and just below them was a picture of the coastal scene: the prize! I took a photo and flicked through the pages, reading out a little of what I could see there. It was a list of the clues and pinpoints to locations, hints and tips of how to get the most out of the competition. The questions were actually more simple than I would have thought. They weren't riddles; they were proper quiz questions relating to music and theatre, sport, art and literature. I didn't know all the answers immediately but most people who were good at general knowledge would. Anyone on a pub quiz team would ace it. Once you had a collection of answers in each section it led you to a location where you could pick up extra clues. A lot of fun, I imagined, but not quite the high-brow competition I'd been led to believe by Dorothy. Perhaps poor Philip had made more of it to make his wife proud of his win. When I flicked through to the rules I could see that all the names of the contestants with correct answers to the last question in the last location would be put into a hat. That was how Philip had won.

I closed the book and replaced it on the shelf in its exact position and took a moment to wonder what I was doing. Was this what it was all about? A basic but fun treasure hunt and a prize that you could honestly buy for a couple of hundred quid or possibly less? I sighed and retraced my steps to the door, but really I knew this wasn't it. For Dorothy it was all about Philip's death and if Leonard was responsible for hiring someone to take the watercolour, then he was directly implicated. Finding the painting was the only way to prove his involvement. By finding this booklet, though, I wasn't really any closer. My phone pinged with another message.

Harry is serving me tea so he's out and about. Might be an idea to come down.

I tapped out a quick response.

On my way.

I made sure my voice recording app was switched off and took one last picture of the room, even though I felt there was nothing more to find there, but as I closed the door I suddenly wondered about other cameras, those hidden in the corners of the rooms, watching my every move.

I decided to forget the sitting room for now and go and find Dorothy, check what she knew about the security arrangements in the house. Leonard was a man who seemed to like old-fashioned and formal dinners, games that involved wooden mallets and balls, basic quiz questions in a hedged maze. However, that didn't mean he didn't have a level of security rigged up in his home that would cover any potential theft of his own property. I contemplated a hurried departure to the station. I suddenly felt very sick.

* * *

Dorothy was exactly where I had left her, in position in the bay window, now with a cup of tea in her hand. She glanced up when I entered the room and gave me a very direct look before moving her eyes across to the left where Harry was busy putting something into a cupboard built into the wall.

'Ah, Gina, there you are. Did you get some rest?' she asked me. 'How's your head now?'

Harry looked up at Dorothy's words and I smiled at him.

'Would you like a cup of tea?' he asked me and I noted a hint of something close to uncertainty in his expression. I hesitated, because I wasn't sure that Harry liked me for some reason and I remembered that he'd been in charge of drinks last night. It suddenly hit me quite clearly that I would never have been that drunk to have lost an evening's memories from one, two or – if I were honest – even three drinks. Had Harry been topping me up without me noticing, or had he slipped some extra shots of alcohol in mine? As I thought it, though, it seemed silly and I felt as if I was being paranoid. Why on earth would he do that?

'No, thank you,' I said, to be on the safe side.

'Do you need something for your headache?' he asked me.

'Oh, I'm fine now, thank you. I had some of that punch you made last night in the maze and it knocked me sideways. I shouldn't have let Leonard talk me into it,' I said, smiling at him again, but his expression was fixed. Then for a horrible moment I wondered if he was in charge of those security cameras that I'd convinced myself were hiding in the corners of every room in the house and that he'd just watched me poking around in his master's bedroom. I tried to quell my thoughts and keep calm while my stomach did a nasty roiling motion.

I joined Dorothy by the window, my hand shaking a little as I poured myself a glass of water from a carafe that was on the table. We both waited until Harry had left the room and then Dorothy spoke, her voice soft, low and urgent.

'Anything?'

'I haven't found the painting if that's what you mean. I'm photographing everything and I've been in Leonard's bedroom and study, but Dorothy, I'm worried about security cameras. It's possible he has them and I'm scuppered if that's the case. In fact, if he does then he'll already have seen me poking about. I can't believe I didn't think about it.'

'Honest people don't usually think about these things and I'm sorry to say that the thought hadn't crossed my mind either.'

Harry came back in then carrying a plate of biscuits, which he put down on the table between us.

'Thought you might like these,' he said.

'Lovely,' Dorothy said, taking a cookie and pausing before it got to her mouth. 'Oh, Harry, this might seem like the musings of a silly old woman, but I was thinking with all the art and antiques that Leonard has, I'd hope he has tight security. I was very unlucky to have fallen foul of a nasty person who stole from me and I just wished we had installed security cameras. Leonard is probably smarter than me, though.'

'Well, no actually, he doesn't. I did ask when I first started work here, because, you know, I'd want to know if my every working hour was being watched, even though I'm only ever doing what Leonard asks me to do.'

As he said this, I noticed he seemed despondent, or maybe resigned. Harry, it appeared, didn't like his job all that much.

'The gardener told me that although Leonard has CCTV

installed to monitor the outside of the property, he doesn't have anything inside,' he continued.

'So, the poor gardener has his every working hour monitored,' I said with a laugh that I hoped didn't sound as full of relief as it actually was.

'Yeah, I suppose you're right. Well, I'll leave you in peace,' he said and then left.

'That's a relief, I suppose,' Dorothy said.

I opened the camera roll and began scrolling through my photos. Back and forth I went, trying to make some connection between what I could see and what I hoped to discover. I kept coming back to the picture of the mirror in the hallway and turned my phone around to show Dorothy.

'What do you make of that oddly placed mirror?' I asked her. 'I can't understand why he would hang it so low. I want to take another look.'

'I actually asked him about that and he said it was for his dog to look at itself,' she said.

'I didn't know he had a dog. Where is he hiding that?'

'Apparently he no longer has it.'

'Oh, it died?'

'He didn't say dead, he said gone, but I don't think he seems like the sort for pets.'

'I would have to agree, but if he did have a dog and put the mirror there for it, that would make him a bit more human, don't you think?' I suggested.

'Yes, well, that's why I don't believe he had a dog at all,' Dorothy said.

* * *

When Dorothy had finished her tea we wandered back down and through to the entrance hall and stood in front of the mirror staring at our lower legs. Then I crouched down into a squat, which took some effort, and when I got my bearings on the odd reflected angle I noticed that from where I was, I could see the fan vase on the windowsill above and it had been moved back to its original, odd position. I was about to tell Dorothy when there was a commotion and the house guests all suddenly appeared in the hallway. 'Leonard's bust his knee,' said Juliet with a face that suggested *that* was the most interesting thing that had happened all afternoon.

13

GINA

Leonard had been brought back on the golf buggy and carried into the house between Rufus and Paul, complaining that his saddle hadn't been fitted properly. He really did look as if he was in immense pain as they lowered him onto a chair.

'You need an ice-pack and to elevate your leg,' suggested Paul.

'What I need is a large whisky and to find the person responsible for saddling my horse!' Leonard barked.

'I'm sure it was a mistake. No one would have deliberately sabotaged your tack.'

There was a hushed silence for a moment and I could feel Dorothy bristle beside me, then Caroline appeared, pushed up Leonard's trouser leg and began to check over his knee.

'She's a nurse,' Dorothy explained.

'It doesn't seem too serious, but you have bruised it. I think if you keep off it for a couple of days then you'll be fine for the wedding, if you take it easy of course,' Caroline said.

I listened with a heavy heart. Leonard keeping off his knee meant my ability to search was lessened. I was relying on him being out of the house so I could continue. With him upstairs resting in his bedroom I could hardly scour his sitting room and I could kick myself now for not taking the opportunity while I had it. Maybe I'd just have to be patient and wait for the other guests to arrive on Friday. With a lot more people in the house I might just be able to go about my task without detection. Surely Leonard would be very busy with a house full of guests. I had a feeling that I was committed now and that just maybe I could handle a challenge.

'I fully intend to go quad biking tomorrow. You can hardly all go off on your own. I've got some knee supports somewhere from my days of tennis injuries. That will be fine.'

'This week is turning into an outward-bound course,' Dorothy muttered under her breath, and I stifled my laughter.

'Uncle Leonard, I'm not sure that's very sensible,' Caroline said, but he waved her away.

'I promised you a full week of activities and that is what you shall have. I'd love to take you all around the park, to see the full extent of my land here. There are deer and I have some alpaca too. We can't miss out on that and it wouldn't be the same without me to show you around.'

I was beginning to feel better thinking that Leonard intended to go regardless of his knee, but then he spoke again.

'And we are *all* going – no stragglers left behind on this one. Even you, Dorothy,' he continued as she began to protest. 'You can ride pillion to Gina, if she thinks she can handle it.'

He gave me a penetrating stare and I felt both intimidated and challenged.

'Of course I can handle it,' I said, only just remembering that I'd never actually driven a quad bike in my life and had very little wish to do so now.

'That's settled then. Now, you have a free afternoon and then we meet at six on the patio for a special meal. Six sharp because I have something planned.'

Leonard started barking orders at Paul for strong pain relief and then both Rufus and Paul manhandled him away up the stairs. As I watched them go I realised I had so much of the house left to search. It would have to wait for another time and time wasn't something we had an awful lot of.

'Would you like to escort me up to the temple?' Dorothy said. 'I've asked Harry to make us up a picnic lunch and I thought we could have that in the shade and then, perhaps we could have a walk around the rose garden.'

'That sounds lovely,' I said.

Harry had actually produced picnic baskets for everyone and we all scattered off in different directions with our lunch.

The temple was a large stone structure at the far end of a gravel path, which ran from the back of the formal garden and offered a wonderful view of the east side of the house. Because the house was longer than it was wide, this position really did show off its best aspect. I carried the basket and Dorothy held on to my arm while using her stick in her other hand for extra support. Once at the temple, Dorothy sat on one of the iron benches and I put the basket down next to her.

Standing on the steps and looking back to the house, I felt awed by its magnificence. I was interested to know the history of the house before Leonard came to inherit and live here.

'What do you know about Walstone Hall?' I asked Dorothy.

'Not a lot, to be honest. It belonged to Leonard's unmarried uncle who'd inherited it from his own father. Apparently they're a very small family.'

'It must be very hard for Paul to see Leonard take it all. Is it just because he's older? I assume he's older.'

'Yes he is, but I don't know the family dynamics. I don't know what they did to warrant owning such a huge estate. Lords and ladies back in the day, perhaps, or criminals more likely.'

I lifted my hand to shield the sun from my eyes. I could see Paul and Sandra walking in the gardens down by the lake and Lavinia and Miles sitting on the chairs by the edge of the croquet lawn. Sophie and Luke were talking to Juliet, but then she turned and stalked away from them. Sophie raised both of her arms in a defeated gesture before slapping them down by her sides. No sign of Caroline and Toby, but if they had any sense they had tucked themselves away for a quiet and private lunch. I opened our own basket to find smoked salmon and cucumber sandwiches, pots of crab salad with chunks of homemade sourdough and large slices of Victoria sponge cake. There was also a half bottle of Prosecco and two tins of cloudy lemonade.

'God, I shall be the size of this house by the end of the week,' I said.

'I really don't want to enjoy myself in Leonard's company, but he does make it very difficult when faced with all this delicious food,' Dorothy said.

Just then there was a rustling in the bushes beside the temple and the sound of muffled conversation before an odd silence. It reminded me of Juliet on the landing outside my bedroom door yesterday.

'Juliet, you can come out. It's only Gina and your grandmother here,' I said.

The silence continued for a moment and Dorothy and I glanced at each other, her eyebrows raised in question. Then another rustling and Juliet appeared.

'Juliet! What are you doing in a bush?' Dorothy asked her, but she wasn't cross, because she was laughing. 'You really must be bored.'

'I'm recording for my Instagram channel,' she said.

'Well, if I knew what one of those was, I'd probably be impressed,' Dorothy said. 'Have you had any lunch?'

'No, Mum and Dad have mine in their basket and there's no way I'm picnicking with them.'

'Have some of ours,' I offered. 'You'd be doing my waistline a huge favour if you'd take that cake off my hands.'

Juliet took a slice and sat down on the steps next to us.

'Tell me about your channel,' I said, and Juliet finished her mouthful of sponge before she answered.

'It's called *My Mad Family and the Week from Hell*,' she said, her expression deadpan.

Dorothy spluttered on her lemonade, but once she'd finished coughing it was clear she was laughing again.

'Oh, sweetheart, I know this week isn't easy for you, but I do hope this channel of yours is a real thing because it sounds brilliant,' Dorothy said, wiping her eyes.

Juliet got her phone out of her pocket and swiped her finger across the screen, then turned the screen towards us, so we could see a grainy image of Paul and Sandra standing in what looked like one end of the library. Their body language suggested they were in the middle of an argument.

'I'm trying my best you know, Paul, but your brother is pushing my buttons with his constant lord of the manor act,' said Sandra.

'He is lord of the bloody manor. Look, it's Caroline's big week and she's so happy you'll just have to find a way to get—— Hello, Juliet, I didn't see you there.'

Juliet tapped again on her phone and then turned it until we could see the back of Sophie and Luke sitting on a bench by the lake. I glanced at Dorothy, but she seemed transfixed by her granddaughter. Juliet pressed again and Sophie's voice could be heard.

'But who is she and why is she here? Mum doesn't even really need a

carer. It was a minor fall, a small lapse in memory. This will be Lavinia sticking her oar in again. I should really have been consulted.'

Dorothy glanced at me with an apologetic smile.

'I think that's enough now, Juliet,' she said.

'But, Granny, you haven't heard the best one yet,' she said and tapped on the screen again.

Juliet was clearly in a bush again because the screen was full of leaves.

'We need to brush aside the fact that Leonard is unhinged and actually in light of what I believe he has done, is pretty dangerous too. He mustn't know you are anything other than a companion and I will keep smiling at him even though I would ideally love to plunge a knife in his heart.'

'Juliet! Turn that off!' Dorothy said, but our voices continued.

'And…?'

'And, you will search the house from top to bottom until you find the painting.'

'Oh, God!' I said.

'And this is for a channel is it?' Dorothy said, her voice low and stern. 'Sneaking about and recording private conversations?'

'I want to help,' said Juliet.

'Nothing to help with,' her grandmother replied. 'It's just an old joke about a painting, that's all.'

'I'm not stupid, Granny. There is something clearly going on and if you need to find a painting I can help.'

'No.'

'You just said it yourself, I'm sneaking around, and *you* didn't know that I was. Surely that makes me a better sleuth than her,' she said, shaking her thumb in my direction. 'No offence, Gina.'

'None taken,' I said.

'Juliet, this is really nothing to do with you,' Dorothy said, looking a little flustered, but I knew it was too late for that – Juliet had made it everything to do with her.

'Is it to do with Grandpa? Is it *that* painting?'

'So, you've been listening for quite a while then!'

'When no one ever tells you what is going on, I find it's best to quietly listen, otherwise you'll always be in the dark. That's not a smart place to be.'

'Can't really argue with that,' I said.

'I can,' Dorothy said.

'I want to help you. Please let me. I can be really useful.'

Dorothy opened her mouth and judging by her expression it was to argue with her granddaughter, so I decided to step in. This was only going to go one way.

'Juliet, can we trust you, implicitly?'

'Of course,' Juliet replied earnestly.

'Your grandmother and I need to discuss what's best. Can you trust us to do that and to talk to you later just before dinner when we have a plan, a plan that will involve you?'

'Yes,' she said, her face brightening.

'In that case I can trust you not to breathe a word to *anyone* during that time; that's really important. I would never usually ask a young person to keep a secret, but with your grandmother present I hope that's okay in this case.'

'Yes, it's fine,' Juliet said again and more seriously this time.

'Okay, well, leave us now and do as we ask, and we'll meet at five-thirty before whatever Leonard has planned for this evening.'

'Thanks, you won't regret it,' she said and then kissed her grand-mother on the cheek, choosing to ignore Dorothy's words that followed her down the steps.

'I already do.'

'Whoop!' Juliet leaped from the bottom step onto the grass.

'This week just got a whole lot better,' she said and then ran down the lawn towards the house.

'I do not like this at all,' Dorothy said, watching her grand-daughter's retreating figure.

'I know. Neither do I, but surely you can see that to not include her would be a mistake. That conversation she's got on her phone is problematic. Isn't it better if she's onside? Wouldn't that keep her safer? There's no point telling her to forget about it, is there, because she won't. Then, a wrong word from her, here or there, and Leonard will get wind. We can tell her the bare minimum and get her to help in a small way. But however you look at it, we're a group of three now.'

14

GINA

I decided to phone my daughter when I got back to my room. Alice answered after only a couple of rings.

'Mum!'

She always did that, sounded surprised when I phoned her even though I made sure never to leave it too long between calls and my name was in Alice's phonebook and clearly displayed on the screen. I smiled at that small familiarity. After a few odd days in a house full of strangers, my daughter's voice was welcome.

'Hello, love, how are you? How are the girls?'

'All good, although we've had a dose of head lice, which is disgusting and very inconvenient. Dad was trying to get hold of you. Have you spoken to him?'

Alice was Douglas's favourite, a daddy's girl. They adored each other, which did make them blind to each other's failings and a bit dismissive of me, but I was very close to Chris, so it all worked out. Every family had its dynamics and that was ours.

'He left me a message to see where I was. I haven't got back to him yet, though.'

'Bit mean. Are you punishing him? Because I think he's reaching out to you.'

'I'm not punishing him – I just haven't had the chance. I'm working this week, in Norfolk, like I told you.'

'It's not really work, though, is it. Being a friend to an old lady – sounds like fun to me.'

'You might be surprised.' I laughed. 'Would you like to meet for lunch next week when this job is up?'

It sounded odd to me, the thought that this was a job that had a finite point. I was so involved with the situation and the family now that I couldn't see the end. Whatever the outcome, though, it would be over on Sunday.

'Come to the house or meet somewhere out?'

'Can I let you know? I'm not sure if I'm going back to the house to be honest.'

'What do you mean you're not going back? Where are you going?'

'I'll look to rent somewhere and I've got my eye on other companion jobs.'

This wasn't actually true at the moment, but I did have it in the back of my head. Also, I did wonder about the possibility of a permanent position with Dorothy. The wanted ad had hinted there was a chance, but I was getting mixed messages from both Dorothy and her family. Dorothy didn't feel she needed help, but at least Lavinia and Miles did.

'Will you bring the girls with you? I'd love to see them.'

'I'll leave them with Jim. He's working from home at the moment. We can have a proper chat if I come on my own.'

'A proper chat – that sounds ominous. Is everything okay?'

'Everything's fine with me; it's you I'm worried about. We can talk about what you plan to do. You obviously need some help organising your life, Mum. I mean, you won't look after old people forever. Frankly it's a bit weird starting work at your age.'

I didn't know what to say to that, so I said nothing.

'Well, I look forward to seeing you next week then. I'll call you on Monday and we can arrange when and where.'

'Bye, Mum,' Alice said, and then she hung up.

How was it that my daughter always managed to turn our roles around? Alice had been trying to mother me since she was a teenager. I mentioned it to Chris once, but he'd rolled his eyes at me.

'Alice doesn't mother you, she smothers you,' he'd said.

* * *

I met Dorothy and Juliet at five-thirty in the folly, as we'd planned. Juliet looked wired and I realised I was going to have to damp down her emotion and underplay what was needed.

'So, what's the plan then?' Juliet asked, her eyes alight.

'Firstly, can you be cool? This won't work if you're going to look excited all the time.'

Juliet gave me a long hard stare.

'Have you met me? I'm a teenager. I can do cool, aloof, pissed off and bored as hell. Pick which one you want.'

'Okay,' I said. 'Fair enough.'

'But you do have a plan?' she asked.

'Your grandmother would like us to find a painting she feels may be hidden in this house.'

'The painting the thief stole from Grandpa, you mean, the ugly little one of the sea.'

'I wouldn't call it ugly; it's quite a pretty watercolour.'

'And you should know, being an expert.'

'That's another thing that won't get mentioned,' I said, expecting Juliet to question this.

'Noted,' was actually her quick reply. 'So you are acknowledging that you think Leonard stole the painting?'

'We can't know for sure, and it wasn't actually him in Dorothy's house that night,' I said.

'I couldn't have been,' Dorothy said. 'I'd know his overpowering aftershave anywhere.'

Juliet giggled and I smiled, thankful to Dorothy for lightening the moment.

'We were wondering if you could accompany me when I search. It gives me more of an excuse to be wandering around the house,' I said.

'But, it doesn't really. I'm not Leonard's family, but I am a teenager and a nosy one, so *me* wandering around the house and poking about wouldn't really be a problem.'

'It would be a problem for me, though,' Dorothy said. 'We don't really know what Leonard's state of mind is.'

'Freakish and weird, I'd say.'

'He is certainly an oddity, but let's keep on topic. We have only a few days to find the painting and if you know any hiding places in this house that you've already stumbled across then please let us know,' I said.

'But this house is huge, and you're talking about a small painting that could be anywhere. It could be in a box, down the back of a sofa, stuffed up a chimney.'

I couldn't disagree with Juliet's logic, but Dorothy had other ideas.

'I think he's the sort of man who would have it hanging somewhere, but not obviously so. It was much coveted by him and I doubt he'd box it up somewhere. Where's the victory in that?'

'So maybe a sliding bookcase, or a hidden panel?' Juliet suggested.

'Quite possibly,' Dorothy said.

'I've only had a cursory look in the main rooms so far, and haven't come up with much, but I do want a closer look at that mirror in the hallway. The main and most important thing is that we don't alert Leonard to what we are doing. If he finds out it will all be over, because he will move the painting and then it probably will be put in a box or stuffed down the back of a sofa, never to see the light of day again,' I said.

'Okay, leave it with me and I'll have a think about it. I'll have a plan,' Juliet said.

I was aware that neither Dorothy nor I had actually asked Juliet to come up with a plan, but I hadn't had any success so far. Could it really hurt to have another pair of eyes looking, another brain thinking? Juliet was young and might well have ideas that Dorothy and I wouldn't.

Juliet looked excited again, but after a pointed look from me she began to scowl. I shook my head, uneasy about this unwanted alliance, but knowing we had no choice.

'Best we go and join the group,' Dorothy said, looking at her watch.

The patio was decorated with colourful paper lanterns in red, white and blue, all lit and gently moving in the evening breeze. There were ice buckets stuffed with bottles of beer and wine dotted around the edges of the table and in the middle was a huge basket of bread and bowls of salad prepared in Harry's professional style. The tablecloth was a giant American flag.

'God, save me,' Dorothy said. 'Does he have to have a theme for everything?'

Leonard was standing at a barbecue, wearing jeans with turn-ups and a checked red and white shirt. He had a Stetson on his head and looked ridiculous. He had a walking stick in one hand – an easy reminder of his riding accident – and in the other a giant pair of barbecue tongs, the sort that always made me laugh. Someone had bought Douglas a pair as a present for Christmas one year. The packaging had been robust with a picture of a bearded, muscled man on the front – very much not the look of Douglas who was more clean-cut and lean. The same year, the same friend had gifted me some dainty clippers for gardening. The reality was that I always used a bigger pair that could more easily cut the bushes and Douglas used a smaller pair of kitchen tongs for the barbecue because he found the others too big and difficult to wield. Leonard seemed to be struggling with his and was pushing large chunks of expensive-looking meat around the grill. Despite myself, my mouth began to water.

Country and western music was coming at us on the breeze from Leonard's hidden speakers. He was good at hiding things, I thought.

Caroline walked out from the house then. She looked pretty in a blue summer dress with white daisies printed on the fabric. Her hair was pushed up into a messy bun that looked, to me, a quick and simple thing to do, but had probably taken ages and she pulled down the sunglasses that she had balanced on top of her head onto her face. She went over, stood next to Leonard and slipped her arm around his waist. It was a sweet and affectionate thing to do and it made me more convinced that Caroline couldn't possibly know what Dorothy had accused her uncle of.

'At least no one can charge you with the crime of stereotyping, Uncle Leonard,' she said, laughing, and he rested his chin for a moment on the top of her head and closed his eyes. The moment passed and he went back to moving the meat around, then the rest of the party appeared from inside the house. They made a beeline for the table and began to pour drinks and pick up handfuls of crips and nuts. Everyone was full of their day in the saddle, discussing who was the best rider and how well Juliet had handled Lawn-mower. Lavinia appeared from the middle of the group and moved in my direction bringing an air of expensive scent with her.

'How's Dot doing?' she asked. 'She seems a little edgy. Is she okay?'

Dorothy had gone to sit in the shade and I was about to get her a glass of wine.

'Fine, she's fine,' I said. 'I don't think she's edgy.'

'And she's not showing any signs of confusion?'

'No, none at all,' I said, feeling uncomfortable.

I looked over at Dorothy and it suddenly occurred to me that I'd put myself in a vulnerable position. I didn't know Dorothy well at all. Perhaps she was actually showing the early signs of dementia and this whole thing with Leonard was in her mind. Should I just tell Lavinia and Miles and hand the whole thing over to them? I could be home by tomorrow lunchtime.

'She's had a difficult year after Philip, so maybe I'm looking for problems that aren't there. Just ignore me – you're doing a great job, Gina. Thank you.'

I didn't really know how to respond so I just smiled as Lavinia walked away. I noticed that Miles was sitting with his mother, so I took my time getting her a drink.

'I can't wait to get hunting.'

Juliet had suddenly appeared at my side, making me jump. She had a half-eaten burger in her hands and a blob of ketchup on her chin.

'You need to just...' I motioned towards her face and handed her a napkin.

'Leonard might be a master criminal, but he makes a mean barbecue,' Juliet said, wiping the mess from her chin.

'Keep your voice down please!' I hissed. 'Look, can we just have this evening without talking about it. We can get on with it tomorrow.'

'You're the boss,' Juliet said and turned and walked back to her parents.

I got Dorothy a glass of wine and myself a fizzy water, then I made my way over and sat in the seat Miles had just vacated. He was handsome, Dorothy's son. Movie-star handsome with very styled hair and a strong jaw. Unapproachably handsome, which was why I had yet to share more than a couple of words with him. He wore smart trousers and a shirt all the time, even for horse riding this morning, and hadn't dressed down for Leonard's barbecue in shorts like most of the others. I wondered what he would think about this painting hunt and why I hadn't told him and his sister. I swallowed a lump of concern about how this week might end and handed Dorothy her drink.

The evening was successful in the end. Juliet went back to acting as her usual sulky self and didn't at all give the game away apart from the occasional conspiratorial look in my direction, which just made me want to gnash my teeth. The food was as perfect as ever and I realised that I had a new soft spot for key lime pie, something I had never eaten before. It didn't go on too late as the thought of the day of quad biking loomed large in all of our minds. I really wasn't sure I could drive a quad bike and whether I should even try at my age. The thought of it made me queasy and the idea of nearly-ninety-year-old Dorothy on the back made me feel even worse. Surely Leonard didn't really expect us both to participate.

Leonard was on top form during the evening, despite his knee, and even his faux American accent didn't seem to bother anybody, well, anybody other than Dorothy and to be honest it was irking me a bit too.

I got into bed at just after ten-thirty, opened the book I'd bought with me and rested my head back on my pillows. I'd decided to dip back into some Agatha Christie recently and thought that as I was staying in an old country house it would be fun to read about a murder mystery in one. But, as I opened it to where I'd left my bookmark and continued to read *And Then There Were None*, I realised that what was happening in the house I was staying in wasn't an invented story from the golden age of crime fiction, but a real-life case of theft and deceit, of death and devastation. I closed the book, not really having the stomach for it, and replaced it on my bedside cabinet, then I got back out of bed and wedged the back of a chair under the door handle. Once in bed again I turned out the light and tried to get to sleep.

Outside, the peacock screeched into the night.

15

DOROTHY

The following morning, Dorothy woke early and lay in her bed thinking about what it was she was asking of Gina and now Juliet. A complete stranger and her own granddaughter. If Sophie and Luke found out before they found the painting then she was sure she was going to be in a lot of trouble.

She tried to put it to the back of her mind and concentrate on the day ahead first. She was going to be spending some time on the back of Gina's quad bike, so it would really be a test of how much she trusted the woman and also whether she could even get on it in the first place.

They met outside the front of the house and Harry picked them all up in a minibus. Leonard had gone ahead on his motorbike, apparently with his dodgy knee padded and supported.

Dorothy made another comment about it feeling like they were on a school trip and got a bark of laughter and agreement from Juliet and Miles, but a stern look from Paul.

'I have to say, I was expecting a little more from Leonard,' she said unable to help herself.

'What? More ice sculptures and less day out for the local scouting group you mean?' Miles said.

'I think that Len is putting on a wonderful week for us all,' Paul said. 'You could be a little more grateful. Who else would do what Len does?'

'You're absolutely right – no one else is capable of what Leonard does,' Dorothy said pointedly.

Paul looked momentarily mollified until his brain caught up with Dorothy's words and then he was left narrow-eyed and contemplative.

Gina turned in her seat and smiled at Dorothy over the head-rest, but Dorothy noticed she was looking a little apprehensive. Juliet had her head in her phone and her earbuds in as usual, but she was smiling at something she was watching. Dorothy felt disconcerted about Juliet filming people and hoped it was a short-lived exercise in her boredom this week. Lavinia, Dorothy noticed, was looking apprehensively out of the window; Miles was reading the newspaper; Sophie seemed genuinely excited about the prospect of driving around the countryside on four bumpy wheels; and Luke had his arm draped across the headrest, almost around her shoulders, but not quite. Rufus looked thunderous. Sandra and Paul sat side by side, barely touching, and looked a thousand miles apart. In contrast, at the back with their limbs as entwined as was possible and acceptable were the happy couple, and Dorothy smiled warmly at them. No matter what else happened this week, missing painting or no missing painting, these two lovely people would be married.

The lane to the farm building where the quad bikes were was potholed and the last mile was incredibly disorientating.

'I shall be glad to get out of this wretched contraption,' Dorothy said.

'Only to get onto another,' Gina told her.

'You will take it steady, won't you? I am eighty-nine, you know.'

'I'm seventy-one. I'll be taking it very steady,' Gina said. 'Do we really need to do this? I've honestly never driven a quad bike before. I'm not even sure how.' Gina had lowered her voice and her mouth was set in a grim, tight line.

'Seventy-one – that's no age at all,' Dorothy said. 'I'd certainly have been up for the challenge when I was that age, especially if I found myself suddenly single like yourself. The world is yours for the taking and you should take it, while you still can. Say yes to opportunities, say no to housework.'

'You do housework do you, Mum?' Sophie asked her with a grin.

'I've been known to wield a duster, yes,' Dorothy replied.

Her voice was animated, which in the confined space of the vehicle meant that everyone was suddenly privy to Gina's change in circumstances. Dorothy gave Gina an apologetic smile and decided she'd keep her thoughts to herself from now on.

The rattling and bumping in the minibus suddenly came to a stop and Dorothy could see that they were at a large building with a corrugated roof and huge sliding doors. A great place to store a lot of stolen items, she thought, but actually the doors were open and she could see that what it mostly stored was farm machinery and gardening equipment.

Leonard was standing outside the front and having a conversation with a young man in jeans and a black leather jacket. The man was looking down at Leonard's hand, which sat casually on his arm, and Dorothy didn't have time to tell whether the gesture was welcome or not, because Leonard removed it as soon as the minibus appeared.

The ground at the front of the building was a quad bike car park and there was another man, lying on the ground, who was fiddling around with the underneath of one. Two vans with large trailers were parked up and Dorothy suddenly felt a frisson of excitement or possibly alarm; it was hard to distinguish between the two. The day was glorious and the thought of biking around the countryside was suddenly very appealing.

An hour of instruction and squabbling later and they were finally off. They all had bike-style helmets on and had had to prove competency by driving around the yard before the two men would allow them out – Dorothy had stood back and watched that fiasco, thoroughly entertained. Gina had been very hesitant and Dorothy heard her say more than once that she'd be just as happy not doing it, but she'd had nothing but encouragement from the rest of the group and now stood with her arms across her chest looking as if she'd rather be anywhere else than here. Leonard had assured the quad bike owners that he would be in charge and fully responsible for the welfare of the group, which made Dorothy raise her eyebrows so far they disappeared into her hairline.

Leonard gave up his own large bike to Gina and Dorothy, which Gina later said was very considerate, but Dorothy suggested it was an act of unparalleled violence, because it meant he'd obviously sabotaged it and they were both likely to die. Her thoughts, it seemed, could not be kept to herself after all. The others had squabbled over the remaining vehicles, which all looked pretty good, but still much deliberation was needed. Juliet wanted the one with handlebars that matched her top; Caroline and Toby wanted ones that matched each other; Lavinia and Miles argued over whether she was actually coming, because *it really wasn't her thing*; both Sandra and Paul declared they were happy with anything before both rushing for the same bike; and Rufus sat down on the one nearest him, his face still looking like a gathering storm.

'Perfect,' Leonard said, and then went back into the shed for a shiny new one that elicited a groan from a few of the party. He started it up and then there were no words worth saying because they'd never have been heard anyway. Leonard manoeuvred out of the yard and, with a wave of his hand above his head, he encouraged them all to follow him.

Because Gina and Dorothy had been given the large bike it meant that Dorothy could sit comfortably behind Gina, although she had to be helped on to it by three people.

'I'm sure this isn't what a companion would usually be asked to do,' Gina said as she started her engine.

'Noted,' Dorothy said simply, but in her mind she was already thinking about Gina's fee for the week and how she'd definitely need to increase the figure. She was asking an awful lot of her.

When they set off, though, Gina proved a very competent driver and Dorothy settled into her seat and actually began to enjoy herself. Gina's shoulders lowered a little as they went and she seemed to relax a bit too.

Leonard's estate was huge: 3,000 acres in total, of parkland, woodland, lakes, farming fields and cottages, and he wanted them to see it all. He'd set them up with walkie-talkies so he could give them a running commentary about where they were and what they could see and, despite herself, Dorothy was enjoying every minute of it. Gina had the walkie-talkie attached to the handlebars of the quad and as Leonard didn't require a response to his commentary they could listen without Gina having to touch it.

As they headed out along the banks of a river and across to what Leonard called the Great Wood, Dorothy thought about Philip and what he would have made of all this. He would have been impressed – it would be hard to find someone who wasn't – but the way his relationship with Leonard had soured, Dorothy knew Philip wouldn't have wanted to accept an invitation to visit. He wouldn't have wanted to have given Leonard the opportunity to show off his superior collection. Perhaps Leonard wouldn't have wanted Philip to see other things he might have stolen. She let that thought roll around her mind for a moment. Of course! It couldn't just be Philip's painting. Leonard was someone who took what he wanted. There must be more to find and that thought made her smile.

She settled into the ride and watched the landscape roll past. The Great Wood had beautiful dappled sunlight sparkling down through the canopy of the trees. The distinct and resinous scent of pine was crisp and it combined with the damp earth and the musty smell of the woody debris. Gina had dropped back a bit and let the others get a little further ahead so the noise of their machines didn't distract too much from their peaceful setting.

'I'd like to stop and walk about,' she called out to Dorothy. 'These quad bikes are spoiling the atmosphere.'

'I agree,' Dorothy called back to her, 'but I am having a lot of fun too.'

'Keep up, stragglers, at the back. We're going down across the park and past the tower before we head into the village for lunch. You don't want to get lost.'

Leonard's voice came through the radio at them and Dorothy held on a little tighter as Gina picked up her pace again.

'Yes we bloody do want to get lost,' Dorothy said. 'Can he hear me through that thing?'

'No, don't worry. It's only when I press the button on the side.'

'Shame,' Dorothy said and Gina laughed.

'Do you know, Dorothy, I think you're amazing,' Gina called out as she took a corner at quite a speed and Dorothy whooped with delight from the back.

They caught up with the others at the tower and Leonard had no history for it, which made Dorothy a little cross. Another example of the man not realising what he had, not appreciating what was right in front of his face. This made her think about the thief not taking the best pieces from her home. An amateur burglar, or someone with specific instructions about what to take.

'There would be a wonderful view from the top of the tower,' said Gina quietly to Dorothy. 'I assumed that it would originally have been built as a viewing platform for a previous wealthy inhabitant of the estate. Perhaps to watch racing or similar.'

'No idea what it was used for originally, but I had it tarted up and it's now a holiday let. So remember that if you fancy a few days away from it all. I give good family and friends rates.' Leonard chuckled into the radio and then shut it off and carried on.

'Do you think the painting could be hanging in there?' Gina asked.

'No,' Dorothy said firmly. 'It will be where he can see it all the time. I really do believe it will be hidden in plain sight. It's in his nature to win, to covet and to then have at any cost. He won't have it tucked away like a guilty secret. He would almost want someone to stumble across it. That would be a game he'd like to play – you can be sure.'

'Woe betide the man who stands in his way,' Gina quoted from when Leonard caught her snooping in the library. 'I absolutely agree with you, Dorothy. The painting is definitely in that house.'

Leonard continued to tell them about the careful management of his land by park rangers and also the partnership with his tenant farming community. Dorothy noted that he might not care about the history of the place, but he was careful with what and who bought him money.

They came down off the higher ground and stopped in the small village at lunchtime. Leonard directed them down a long track and into the back end of the pub car park.

'They're expecting us at The Swan and you're all to have whatever you'd like for lunch because it's on me. I won't tolerate drink driving, though, even if it isn't on the public road, so go soft on the drinks – literally.'

Dorothy climbed off the quad with help from Gina and stretched out her back. Then she noticed that Harry's car was parked up. She was pretty sure she recognised the old, battered vehicle.

'What's he doing here?' she asked Gina who shrugged.

'Maybe he's here to see if anyone has had enough. Maybe he always trails Leonard around like a bodyguard. Perhaps he thinks that us two old ladies would give up at this point and need a lift back.'

'Well, he's completely off the mark. I'm loving it,' Dorothy said, and then followed Gina inside and they headed for the bar to get a coffee. The pub was old-fashioned and cosy. The bar was a solid hunk of mahogany and looked well worn and as if it had been the propping place of many a lonely drinker for a number of years. The seats were upholstered with a tapestry-style fabric and the wall lights, set to low, all had little velvet shades. Horse brasses and paintings of hunting scenes peppered the walls and the leaded windows told of an historic setting.

There didn't seem to be any sign of Harry, and Dorothy now wondered if she'd mistaken the car.

They found a quiet corner to tuck themselves into and, once they had sat down, Juliet joined them carrying a bottle of Coke and a packet of peanuts. She pulled over a chair from another table and folded herself into the small space between the two women. Once she'd sat down she ripped the packet open with her teeth and proceeded to pour the contents into her mouth.

'Really, Juliet, manners,' Dorothy scolded her.

'Sorry,' Juliet said with her mouthful. 'Did you want some?'

'No, thank you.'

'Have you thought any more about what we were discussing

yesterday?' Gina asked her after checking who was in earshot. It seemed that the rest of the group had settled in a small room off of the main bar. Dorothy could see Leonard's recognisable tweed trousers through the gap in the door and his signature move, jiggling his leg up and down; impatient, excited or just keen to always be moving on to the next thing, she couldn't tell which. She felt that if she could keep her eyes on those tweeds, they were safe for a moment.

'I really think that Grandpa's painting won't be the only thing Leonard has stolen,' Juliet said in a whisper. 'I'd be well surprised if he doesn't have a secret hiding place with lots of stuff hidden. I was reading about this bloke who had a false wall in his home and he was growing weed in the space behind it. The police found it because they had a helicopter overhead with an infrared camera that could see the heat lamps. Clever.'

'So, you think Leonard has a secret wall or something?' Dorothy asked her.

'Not necessarily a wall, but we should be thinking about the big spaces as well as the small. That way if we find some stolen stuff, but not the painting, we have enough for the police to do a proper search.'

Dorothy and Gina looked at each other for a moment.

'That's actually very sensible, Juliet,' Gina said. 'Well done. Perhaps I should start in the attic and see what I can find up there. Leonard will have things planned with all the guests arriving tomorrow, so I might be able to slip away when he's busy.'

'We,' Juliet said, 'we are a we now, don't forget. I'm not just going to come up with the ideas and have the glory snatched away.'

'There is no glory in this situation,' Dorothy said. 'This is a serious business.'

'What are you three plotting like the witches of Eastwick?'

Dorothy realised that she'd taken her eyes off of Leonard and his tweed legs, because they were suddenly standing right next to her.

'We were talking about doing something fun for Toby and Caroline. Maybe tying something to the back of the car, like cans. I've seen that done in movies. Lame movies to be honest, but it could be a laugh. Just married sort of thing. What do you think?'

Dorothy made sure not to look at Gina and kept her face neutral. She glanced between Leonard and Juliet, and was relieved to see that Leonard seemed animated by the idea.

'Actually that sounds like a fun idea, Juliet. Let me see what I've got that could work. I do think we should do a little better than some old tin cans, though. The others are ordering some food, so if you can do the same then we'll eat and go. Have whatever you want,' he said, waving a hand above his head as he returned to the rest of the group.

'I suggest,' said Dorothy in a low whisper, 'that we don't say another word until we can guarantee we're alone.'

Juliet and Gina both silently nodded their agreement.

* * *

They left the pub car park an hour later and Leonard told them he was going to take them back a different way so they could further admire his manor from a higher viewpoint.

It was all uphill to start with and because Dorothy and Gina hadn't dilly-dallied around after lunch like the others, they were ahead and Gina accelerated out of the car park behind Leonard with the others following some way behind. Dorothy felt more relaxed now, but that might have been more to do with the glass of sherry she'd had with her risotto rather than the fact she was more used to being on the quad bike. Leonard was setting quite a pace and Gina was doing her best to keep up with him. Dorothy thought it looked as if Gina was really enjoying herself and it was good to see her relaxed and happy. Then she had that stab of guilt again for what she expected from her. She pushed it back down and decided that Gina was an adult and wouldn't do something she really didn't want to do. What that said about the very enthusiastic Juliet she didn't like to think about.

Leonard had pushed further ahead and Gina seemed to have dropped back a bit. She was enjoying the view, perhaps, and not keen to rattle Dorothy around too much.

'I wonder what Paul really thinks of the inheritance,' Gina suddenly asked. 'How is it for him, touring the land that belongs to his brother and not to him? I sort of admire his support of Leonard. He doesn't seem at all resentful of the situation.'

Dorothy glanced behind her, but the others hadn't been so quick and were still a way back.

'I have heard, through Miles, that Leonard has left the entire estate to his brother in his will,' she said.

'Oh, perhaps it was Paul who fiddled with Leonard's saddle then,' Gina said, laughing.

'Possibly,' said Dorothy.

'I was only joking,' Gina said, accelerating again to catch Leonard up, but it set off something in Dorothy's mind.

'If he is trying to bump his brother off,' Dorothy said. 'We need to make sure he doesn't before we find that painting.'

They had nearly reached the summit of the hill and were closing in on Leonard.

'Leonard's got some liquid coming from the back of his quad bike,' Gina said. 'Leonard!'

Gina shouted out to him, but he was just that bit too far ahead. She pressed the button on the walkie-talkie, but there wasn't any of the beeping Dorothy had heard earlier. Surely the battery hadn't run down already. Gina handed it back to her.

'Can you get this working?' she said, and then she sped up to try and drive alongside him and get his attention. It was too late, though, because instead of stopping at the top, Dorothy watched as Leonard pressed frantically at the brakes and then disappeared over the edge.

16

GINA

I came to a stop at the top and climbed off the bike. My heart was in my mouth. I pulled off my helmet and left it on the seat.

'What happened?' Dorothy asked me.

'I don't know, but he was having trouble with the quad bike. I don't think he meant to drive off the edge. Did you get radio working?'

'No.'

'Did you try?'

Dorothy didn't answer that and then the others appeared behind us, everyone leaping from their vehicles to see what was happening. I walked to the edge and looked over, terrified of what I might see. Leonard's bike was upside down further down the hillside, but Leonard himself was lying in a heap a few feet away from me. The slope wasn't too steep and he either fell or threw himself from the bike as it went over.

Rufus and Paul were quicker than me and were already scrambling down the grass to get to him.

'Is he dead?' Juliet called out.

'No, I'm not bloody dead,' was Leonard's muffled response. I could see that Rufus and Paul were checking him over but hadn't taken his helmet off yet.

'He must have landed in the soft grass,' Lavinia said as she came to stand next to me and I hoped I was the only one who heard Dorothy say, '*Pity.*'

'This is becoming a bit of a habit, old chap,' Paul said to his brother as he helped him to stand and Leonard pulled his helmet off.

'I'm not imagining it, am I? After the saddle incident too, I'm sure someone has it in for me!' He looked pointedly at Paul and then turned his attention to Rufus, who shrugged.

I watched Rufus for a second longer and thought there was the merest hint of a smirk on his face.

'I think you're probably just accident-prone, that's all,' Paul said.

Leonard narrowed his eyes and then looked up to the rest of the group standing at the top of the incline.

'My brakes didn't work. That does not make me accident-prone,' Leonard said.

'Why on earth would anyone have it in for you, Leonard?' Dorothy asked. 'You've been a perfect host and gentleman this week and we're all having a wonderful time.'

I wanted to reach out my hand to stop the older woman talking, but she was too far away and it would have looked odd. I gave her a pointed look, but Dorothy's eyes were fixed the other way.

'Hear, hear,' said Lavinia. 'I think you've been incredibly unlucky, but you're not badly hurt, are you?'

'My head's been rattled around in my helmet, my arm feels sore and I doubt it's done much to improve my knee, but I'm not dead, no.'

'Let me have a look,' Caroline said, cautiously making her way down the grassy slope.

I watched as Caroline gave him a fair assessment and, deciding

that he was no more than a bit bruised and shaken, she helped him
to his feet. Rufus and Luke were righting the quad bike with some
help from Toby, and Juliet wandered down to get in the way.

'I think we're going to have to get the bike company to come and
retrieve this,' Toby said. 'It looks like there's some damage to it. You
can jump on the back of mine, Leonard.'

Luke got the number from Leonard and phoned the company,
explained the situation, and they said they'd come with the van and
trailer to fetch it. Then the men helped Leonard up the hill and
onto the back of Toby's quad. I helped Lavinia get Dorothy back on
and we set off at a sedate pace. We took a more direct route back
and missed seeing more of Leonard's land. He didn't bother with
further commentary and we were a sombre party arriving back at
the farm to drop off the remaining quad bikes an hour later.

* * *

We all filed into the house under a bit of a cloud after the turn in
events of the afternoon. Leonard was still complaining about his
head and how something untoward was definitely going on.

Harry appeared again, offering tablets and comfort to Leonard,
seemingly always around when he was needed. It was Harry who
helped Leonard upstairs to his bedroom so he could have a rest. I
wondered what Leonard paid him to be at his beck and call.

'Do you think there could be some truth in what Leonard said
about sabotage?' I said to Dorothy as we took ourselves off to the
library and found a corner to tuck ourselves into.

'I doubt it. I can't imagine anyone here wants him dead more
than I do,' Dorothy said. 'I can tell you I certainly didn't sabotage
his horse or his quad bike. Then again, with the ever-watchful
Harry, I doubt anyone would be successful.'

An image of Harry watching me as I went to bed last night

appeared in my head again, but just as I tried to concentrate on his expression, the image disappeared and I couldn't quite grasp his intentions. I had a horrible feeling that Leonard had told him to keep an eye on me and that we should be watching his movements as much as Leonard's while we searched.

I pushed myself up and out of the chair I'd only briefly sat in and stretched my arms. They felt stiff after an afternoon of clutching the handlebars of the quad bike. I walked over to the window and looked out. The peacock was strutting again around the lawn, his tail following him like the train on a wedding dress and the heron was back in the lake standing like a statue in the grasses that grew at the edge of the water. The surface shimmered in a white-gold glow from the sunlight and I could just make out the figures of Sandra and Rufus walking in the shadows under the trees. They seemed to be having a heated conversation, judging by Sandra's gesticulating arms and Rufus's grim expression. And then I wondered if I could really make that observation from such a distance. Being in this house with these people was beginning to make me feel suspicious of everyone and everything around me.

'Who, though? Who do you think would want harm to come to him?' I asked, not sure I truly believed that he was the target of someone's hate, well, someone other than Dorothy Reed.

'Anyone who's spent more than a few minutes in his company would be my guess. Now, I'm going for a lie-down before we have to suffer another evening with him,' Dorothy said.

This made me smile, because despite the circumstances Dorothy had clearly been enjoying herself the previous evening.

'I'll walk with you,' I said.

'There's no need; I'm more than capable.'

'I know you are, but I am supposed to be your companion. I think it's best if we keep to that as much as possible. I can't be seen to be wandering about this house all alone all the time.'

'That's a fair point, but you'll have Juliet shadowing your every move from now on.'

'What do you think Sophie would say if she knew what Juliet intended to do? Surely she wouldn't be happy with us,' I said.

'She wouldn't be thrilled, no, but she adored her father and if there is a chance to get Leonard for his part in the whole awful situation, then I have no doubt she'd understand.'

I wasn't convinced, but there was little I could do now anyway. It felt as if it was all rather out of my hands. I took Dorothy's arm and we were about to leave when I stopped, looking down to the other end of the room where I noticed a door that sat between two bookcases.

'Where does that door go?' I asked, but Dorothy just shrugged.

'Let's find out then,' I said.

Once out of the library, we found ourselves in a room that I hadn't seen before. It was oval in shape and was dominated by a huge painting that hung in the middle, directly opposite a large window. The light flooded in and because the painting had a thick layer of lacquer covering it, the image depicted on it wasn't immediately clear because of the glare.

'Well, that's interesting,' Dorothy said, and it made me stop in my tracks beside her.

'A *Vanitas* painting,' I breathed. 'A vanity still life.'

'What is it? What do you see?' Dorothy asked me. 'It's an eclectic mix, that's for sure.'

'Yes, a medley of items layered up and overlapping. You have a clock,' I said, pointing as I spoke, 'a watch, a just-extinguished candle and an hourglass. These are artefacts representing worldly wealth, combined with reminders of time and death in a mid-seventeenth-century, Dutch still-life tradition.'

'I prefer my art clean-cut and easily understandable. If a piece takes too long to interpret I tend to lose interest, although it hasn't always been that way. I think my patience and attention span is waning a bit as I get older. It's the same with books. I balk at anything over four hundred and fifty pages. I'd likely be dead before I'd got to the end.'

'I think after what you've been through, you're incredibly patient,' I said, my eyes not leaving the painting.

'So what's caught you about this piece particularly?' Dorothy asked.

'The trinkets and musical instruments, vases and shells you'd expect. Likewise, the bowl of fruit overflowing on the table with the red velvet curtain swathed across one corner, but that's Leonard's Martinware vase, there...' I pointed '...hiding behind that lute – and look, there's a glimpse of his motorbike too. This is either a modern painting, very well executed, or an original that Leonard has commissioned someone to add his own items to. God! That doesn't bear thinking about.'

As I stared and took stock, Juliet appeared from a staircase in the corner that I had also failed to see.

'How's Leonard's head?' I asked her. 'Have you heard anything?'

'He's having a lie-down, but he's still moaning so I think he'll be okay,' Juliet said.

'Shame,' Dorothy said and Juliet giggled.

I needed to have words with Dorothy. She kept reminding me to keep my head down and not give myself away, but she wasn't exactly following her own advice.

'That's horrible,' Juliet said, turning to the painting.

'An acquired taste, perhaps,' I said.

'Not one I'll be acquiring, that's for sure. Actually, it reminds me of those hidden object games I used to play on my laptop.'

'I'm not familiar,' I said.

'Games where you have, like, a list of things to find and they're cleverly hidden in among a load of other crap.'

'Juliet,' Dorothy chided.

'Stuff, then, hidden in among stuff,' she said, rolling her eyes. 'Either way, it's horrible.'

'Yes,' I said thoughtfully. 'That's exactly what this is and I feel there's some significance.'

'Something you can share now or do you need to dwell?' Dorothy asked me.

'Oh, dwell for now,' I said.

'I'm going for that lie-down, then. Thanks for driving me around today, Gina,' she said. 'I haven't enjoyed myself so much in ages.'

'You're welcome,' I said as Juliet linked her arm through her grandmother's and they began to walk away.

I glanced back just as the sunlight hit the painting again and the light bounced off an image of a mirror. I took a step closer and saw reflected in it a painting of a little coral-coloured, fan-shaped vase. Taking out my phone I snapped a quick picture and then hurried after the other two.

By the time I was on the main stairs up to my room with the fan vase back in my hand, I'd lost some of my previous excitement. Expecting a key or similar and finding nothing at all, I continued with Dorothy to her room and watched Juliet disappear to her own.

Now I really wanted to go hunting, but I had no idea how well or mobile Leonard was, or how long he'd be lying down for, so in a snap decision when Dorothy had closed her door, I decided to go and find out what everyone else was up to.

Harry was my first port of call in the kitchen where he was preparing the meal for that evening. Keep your enemies close and all that. Lavinia told me there was to be a rehearsal at the church this evening and then they had invited the vicar back for dinner.

Harry seemed to have a lot on the go and was chopping, stirring, sifting and shoving things into the ovens all at the same time. I thought the poor man could do with some help, but I wasn't about to offer. Instead I asked him if he'd mind me making myself a coffee.

'Not at all,' he said, genially. 'But won't you let me do it for you?'

'No, thank you anyway,' I said. 'I don't like to be a bother and you have a lot going on. I'm very happy to do it myself.'

He placed a white porcelain mug down on the counter next to the coffee machine, told me what to press, then went back to marinating some chicken.

'That smells lovely,' I said, really feeling that having Harry on my side was the best idea, or at the very least to give him no cause to suspect me of what I was actually doing: going through his master's personal possessions.

'Moroccan chicken, which I'm going to put in a pie. How are you feeling now? I was a little worried about you the other night. I was told to top everyone up, but I may have been a bit too heavy-handed,' he said, looking a little contrite. 'I did make sure you got back to your room, though. You probably don't remember...' He trailed off.

'I do, actually,' I said. 'Thank you.'

Was that all it had been? A heavy-handed waiter who didn't intentionally slip me extra alcohol and saw me back to my room to make sure I got there safely? Maybe I *was* becoming paranoid, and maybe I should change my reading material to something a little more uplifting.

'How is Leonard, by the way? He did take quite a tumble.'

'I think he's okay. Certainly nothing that will stop him in his current endeavours.'

There was a sour note to Harry's tone that sounded remarkably close to disapproval.

'Current endeavours?' I pushed.

'The wedding, just the wedding.'

'Of course,' I said, but there was a moment where we shared a

knowing look. Before I could summon the courage to say something more, Sandra came bustling into the kitchen.

'Oh, you have the same thought as me,' she said, eyeing my
coffee. 'And I'll take one up for poor Leonard.'

'I'll leave you to it then,' I said and made my escape back
upstairs, wondering why Sandra was taking a coffee to *poor* Leonard
when she clearly didn't like him.

* * *

Miles and Lavinia were discussing the seating arrangement for the
wedding breakfast with Caroline when I poked my head around the
door of the music room. Toby was back in front of the piano where
the gentle strains of Mozart could be heard.

'But Uncle Leonard wants to be on the top table,' Caroline was
telling them. 'He insisted that he won't be demoted to a guest in his
own home.'

'Hardly a place for the uncle of the bride,' Miles said.

'Quite,' Lavinia agreed.

'Does it really matter where everyone sits?' Toby asked, over his
music. 'We'll all be pissed and stuffed and waiting for the speeches
anyway.'

'I hope you won't be drunk, darling,' Lavinia said. 'You have to
make a speech before Rufus does.'

'I'm still not quite sure why you chose Rufus to be your best
man,' Miles said.

'I think it works well as he's Caroline's brother. A way for us to
bond as a family,' Toby said. 'I do hope he cheers up a bit, though.
He seems really down this week.'

'I'd quite like to say a few words,' Caroline said and Miles
unsuccessfully stifled a groan.

'It might be wise to limit it to the groom, father of the bride and the best man, sweetheart,' Lavinia said.

'But Uncle Leonard is making a speech.'

'As well as your father?' Miles asked. 'God, anyone else?'

'All right, Dad, no need to get your knickers in a twist. It's supposed to be a happy event, so I expect a few people might like to say some nice words. Don't worry, though, I don't expect you to be among them.'

Just as I was beginning to feel uncomfortable listening in and about to make my presence known, Miles noticed me hovering in the doorway anyway.

'Gina, are you okay there?'

He said this very much like someone talking to a member of staff, which was entirely reasonable. The trouble was, the relaxed manner that Dorothy and I had fallen into had made me forget.

'Just wondered what time the church rehearsal is?' I asked. 'I'll make sure Dorothy is ready.'

'We have to be there for six and it should be about an hour, then Leonard has arranged for our meal to be at seven-thirty. He has something special organised,' Lavinia said.

'Every meal has been very special,' I said. And it had been. The finest food had been consumed every day. Even the picnics and casual lunches had been beautifully cooked and presented. The barbecue was something else. 'What does Harry have planned for the wedding meal itself? I can't see how he can top what he's already cooked this week.'

'That is going to be a surprise,' Caroline said. 'But I think everyone will love it. He's got a catering team coming in to help him, though. Even Harry would struggle to feed eighty people.'

It was the first time I had heard how many wedding guests there would be in total. I began to wonder if with the place heaving with people I could slip away unnoticed and really put together all that I had learned in the hunt for this painting. Surely there would be an opportunity when everyone was eating in the orangery. It had occurred to me that I really shouldn't be needed at the wedding meal, maybe it would be enough to slip into the back of the church to watch the service. I was neither family nor a friend, after all.

17

DOROTHY

Dorothy and Gina made their way to the church, which was just to the right of the house and sitting on the edge of Leonard's estate. Through the gate and up the path they found themselves in the cemetery, which was in a state of semi-neglect, but that only seemed to make the place appear very peaceful. The ancient stones had begun to lean over the years and protruded from tall grasses and wildflowers, which were sheltered by huge oaks, sycamores and yews.

Dorothy watched as Gina ran her hand over the mapped flint that made up the walls within the stone-carved structure and then the ringing sound of a phone cut into the silence. Dorothy knew it wasn't hers, because she'd left it in her room.

'Douglas, again,' Gina said.

'Take your phone call,' Dorothy said. 'We are a bit early and it does seem as if your husband needs to speak to you.'

Gina hesitated for a moment and then put her phone to her ear as she walked a few steps away.

'Douglas, yes, hello.'

Dorothy tried to listen, but Gina was a little too far away.

Instead she went and sat down on the wooden bench under the trees and closed her eyes. She felt incredibly tired all of a sudden and brushed a tear away from the corner of her eye. It was the churchyard. It made her think about Philip. Well, it made her think about his not being here any more and that thought overwhelmed her. He'd been such a vibrant man, full of life, keen to experience all that was on offer to him. It made her so sad and also so angry that his life had been taken away in the way that it had. Yes, they were old, but her Philip had so much more to do, to give. Dorothy didn't think she'd ever despised anyone in her whole life, but now, this seething hatred of Leonard was taking her over and it had to end. She felt more than ever how imperative it was to find the painting.

Gina had finished her call and made her way towards Dorothy.

'We've had an offer on the house,' Gina said, looking a bit bewildered.

'Is that a good thing?' Dorothy asked.

'It's a quick thing. The couple are living in rented accommodation and want to move things along fairly speedily, apparently.'

Dorothy watched Gina for a moment as she sat down beside her. She could see she was overwhelmed, a feeling all too familiar to Dorothy herself. Hadn't she been wondering what she could do for Gina? Wasn't the answer staring her right in the face?

'I'd like to offer you the use of the boathouse for as long as you need it,' Dorothy said and Gina looked at her in surprise. 'You know the area, you grew up there, you worked around the corner in Richmond. I think it could work well and it will certainly give you a chance to think about where you'd eventually want to move to with no pressure.'

'That's very kind, Dorothy, but can I ask you about the advertisement for this job?' Gina asked.

'Of course,' Dorothy said, surprised.

'It's just that it said there might be a permanent position for the right candidate.'

'Did it, indeed,' Dorothy said, narrowing her eyes.

'Is that what you're asking me?'

'To be honest, Lavinia wrote that advert. I don't feel I need a carer, but my family do. Perhaps this could work to both of our advantages. You could come and stay independently in the boathouse and my family will think I've employed a permanent companion.'

'I don't know what to say,' Gina said and Dorothy noticed how vulnerable and lost she looked.

'Say nothing for now, just have a think about it. Like I said, no pressure.'

'Is this an offer conditional on me finding the painting?' Gina said with a wry smile and Dorothy laughed, happy to see her more animated.

'I'm not saying I don't want you to continue in your mission, but no, of course the two things are not related.'

Gina nodded, but Dorothy wasn't sure if she was convinced and that might be something to do with the fact that Dorothy wasn't really sure if her own motivations were sound. She glanced at her watch and got up.

'Let's get in there,' she said. 'I'm keen to find out who Leonard has as his vicar.'

They entered the church through the porch and a medieval oak door. It was beautifully cool inside, which was welcome after the heat of the late-afternoon sun, but it wasn't at all dark or sombre. There were three stained-glass windows, which cast pretty colours across the pews, but the rest were clear, allowing much more light into the interior, and the whole place was bright. They were the first to arrive and Gina took the time to pick up a leaflet and read out loud a little about the building while they wandered down to the font.

'The church was rebuilt in the Victorian era. There wasn't much left of the medieval structure other than the doors, the font – which is a fifteenth-century masterpiece of carving – and also there's a memorial coffin. The floor tiles are Victorian and we're supposed to look up at the ceiling, apparently. Its timbers are made from oak harvested from the Walstone estate. From Leonard's land.'

'Good afternoon, ladies,' came a voice from behind them and both Dorothy and Gina looked down from the ceiling to see the vicar. He was casually dressed in chinos and a short-sleeved shirt, but had his white collar tucked underneath. 'Or perhaps evening is more appropriate,' he said, looking at his watch.

'Hello,' Gina said. 'We're a bit early, I'm afraid.'

'No problem at all. I'm Peter, are you the mother of the bride?'

'No.' Gina laughed. 'I'm Mrs Reed's companion. Dorothy is the grandmother of the groom.'

'Ah,' he said stepping forward to shake Dorothy's hand. 'A proud day to come for you and your family. Toby and Caroline seem to be very well suited and I'm hopeful they will achieve all that they set out to, on the long path of their marriage.'

The words *till death us do part* flicked through Dorothy's mind and she felt, again, her loss.

'Do you have much to do with Leonard?' Dorothy asked, getting straight back to the point.

Peter looked a little bemused for a moment and it was obvious he was considering his response.

'Leonard seems very busy with all his art endeavours, and managing his estate, so I rarely see him any more to be honest.'

The word *endeavours* really made it sound as if Leonard was doing something very grand and important rather than indulging himself in criminal activity.

'Not a churchgoer then,' Dorothy pushed.

'In my opinion, Leonard doesn't allow himself time to reflect on the virtues of thought and prayer. I would say he has an agenda that excludes any god-like figure of any denomination.'

'Indeed, an agenda that also excludes him from any morals,' Dorothy said.

Before the vicar could respond the door opened and noise filled the quiet space with the arrival of the others, but Peter's words left Dorothy with something to think about. If she could get Gina to find the time to have a private word with him, they might learn more.

Caroline's friend, Katie, and her husband, Dan, had arrived, so the bride now had her chief bridesmaid and there was much laughter and conversation. They did quieten down when they saw the vicar, though. Leonard was sporting a crutch and had an unpleasant expression on his face, but he hobbled down the aisle, pausing to nod a brief hello to Peter, before seating himself in the first position in the pew on the left, usually reserved for the mother and father of the bride. Paul and Sandra exchanged a glance before moving in the same direction.

There was then ten minutes of chatter about positions and who should walk and stand where, before everyone slipped into their roles and the bride and her father, along with the bridesmaid, disappeared back outside, making it clear they were ready to start.

Dorothy chose a pew a little away from the front, keen not to get involved in the social order of the seating and Gina sat down next to her.

'I didn't say thank you before,' she whispered. 'About your offer, I mean. I will think about it, and thank you.'

Dorothy stretched her hand across and patted Gina's knee. Now the seed had been sown in her own mind, she was quite keen to have this woman come and stay with her.

Caroline walked in through the door, then, her arm threaded with Paul's. There wasn't any music and, of course no one was dressed-up, but Dorothy could hear Gina sniff beside her. She understood – it was the setting and with Gina's marriage seemingly at an end, it was unsurprising she'd feel tearful. She could hear her taking long breaths and she pulled a tissue out of her handbag and handed it to her.

Juliet took her position next to her parents and pretended to look bored, but it was an act that didn't come up to much scrutiny. Ever since she had revealed her recording of their conversation, Juliet had looked wired. Dorothy looked at Sophie rigid in her seat, her husband a little too far away, and she worried that theirs was another marriage that had run its course.

Caroline and Toby genuinely looked giddy with happiness as they took their places at the front to go through their vows and then Dorothy lost herself in the rehearsal service, hopeful that this young couple would be as lucky and as happy as she and Philip had once been.

* * *

'It feels like we really are married now,' Caroline was saying as they made their way back towards the house. 'I'm not nearly as nervous now we've had the practice.'

'You did so well, and it looked like you were really enjoying yourself. I'm so excited for you, Caro. Although, you do know that you have to sign the register for it to be official. The church is the fun bit, but not legal,' Katie said.

'So happy to hear the words *fun* and *church* used in the same sentence,' Peter called from where he was walking with Lavinia and Miles.

Caroline and Katie laughed at his words. 'Church gets a bad rep,' Katie said, 'but I always think that if you're not interested in the sermon, then look around you, because you definitely have the most beautiful buildings.'

'We do indeed,' he said, laughing too.

Katie seemed like a nice young woman. Already married to Dan, she was officially the chief bridesmaid, but as there were no others, she was the only bridesmaid. Juliet had been asked, but had refused to be dressed up like a *muppet*, in her words. Dorothy felt the girl might regret her decision when the ceremony was in full swing, but it would be too late by then.

Toby had hold of Caroline's hand, but her other arm was linked through Leonard's. Whether for his physical support or his perpetual need to be the centre of attention, it was hard to tell, but Dorothy watched the face of Paul behind his brother. He looked a little like a schoolchild not picked for the team. All this time she had thought that Paul should be commended for his stoic attitude towards his brother, but what if it was all an act? For a moment, she wondered if it really was Paul who had sabotaged the saddle and the bike. If Leonard died, Paul would be in for a great improvement in his situation. She rather wondered at his methods, though. They were rudimentary, almost immature in their execution. Even if he was successful, he'd never get away with it.

Dorothy pulled Gina's arm back and they slowed the pace until they were a little away from the others. She could just hear Leonard telling them all, that this time on Saturday they would be walking around to the orangery, but the rest of what he was saying was lost on the breeze that had picked up as they walked the length of the gravel driveway.

'Do you really think Paul could be trying to kill Leonard?' Dorothy asked quietly.

'I did say I was joking earlier. I don't really think someone is trying to kill him. I mean, think about it, Dorothy. How likely is that?' Gina whispered.

'As likely as someone breaking into my home, I would say,' she said wryly. 'If someone is trying to bump him off, I just want whoever it is to stop. I need Leonard alive for now, to face justice. There will be no relief for me if the painting is found and I don't get to look him in the eye as he's dragged away kicking and screaming by the law.'

'Dorothy, I think it would be in your interest to lower your expectations somewhat. I don't think there will be any kicking or screaming, whatever is found.'

'We'll see, we'll see.'

* * *

The dining room was a picture when they arrived a few minutes later. The curtains were pulled right back, allowing the room a lot of light that it hadn't had the last time they'd dined in there. Even though the decor was obviously unchanged, without that gloomy feel the whole place seemed more enchanting somehow. A clever use of lighting to create a completely different mood. Of course there was the addition of a lot of food. The table was heaving under the weight of what looked like a medieval banquet. Pies and platters of meat, cakes, bowls laden with fruit, puddings and jellies. It was impressive and it was also obscene. This food could feed so many more people than the present number of guests. It made Dorothy feel a bit angry, but she bit her tongue and smiled along with everyone else.

Leonard had disappeared off to get changed, he'd said, and

Dorothy wondered what ridiculous outfit he'd be wearing tonight. She imagined him in a full Henry VIII costume complete with fake belly, but when he did arrive a few moments later, she was surprised to see he had taken on more the look of a court jester. Dorothy realised how much less intimidating he looked when dressed up and smiled a broad smile just for herself.

He encouraged them all to dig into the feast and no one needed telling twice as the group descended onto the table to fill their plates.

Harry had outdone himself again and despite Dorothy's feelings about the amount of food that he'd produced, she couldn't help but admire his skill. Leonard wasn't eating, though; he had his phone to his ear and had slipped out of the room.

She wandered around the table to sit next to Juliet who had her phone out again too.

'I hope you're not recording,' she said sternly to her grand-daughter, who quickly switched it off. 'It has to stop.'

'Mind if I join you?' Gina asked them.

'Of course not,' Dorothy said. 'I was just telling Juliet that recording people's conversations had to stop. She's still doing it, you know.'

'For your Instagram channel?' Gina asked her.

Dorothy glanced over her shoulder to see where Sophie and Luke were. They were actually tucking into some wine with Caroline and Toby, Katie and Dan and Peter too. Their raucous laughter drowned out everyone else's chatter.

'I just made that up. I don't even have Instagram.'

'I guessed. I was joking,' Gina said. 'Why are you still recording?'

'Because I think there's more going on than Leonard and the painting. Here, listen to this,' Juliet said, tapping on her phone.

'Maybe not here or now,' Gina said. 'If you have something you really want us to hear, then later might be better.'

Juliet grudgingly put her phone away.

'Gina, if you get the chance, could you talk to Peter? I have this odd feeling that he perhaps knows something,' Dorothy whispered, and Gina nodded in agreement.

There was the sudden sound of a glass being struck and they all looked up to see that Leonard was back in the room and was standing at the end of the table about to make another of his announcements.

'A little word from me if you could all indulge me for a moment.'

'Me, me, me,' Dorothy said, under her breath, and Gina laid her hand on her arm. Dorothy hoped it was more a reminder than a warning.

'I have finally had word from the group who I hired the quad bikes from,' he continued. 'They got the bike back to base and had a good look at the problem. They pride themselves on their impeccable safety record and have never had an incident like this in all the years they've been in business.'

'Get on with it, man,' Dorothy breathed again and Gina took the reminder up a level by gently squeezing.

'In short, they found a hole in the brake pipe,' Leonard said.

There was a loaded pause as Leonard's stare bored into Rufus.

Paul filled the silence. 'Well, that's on them then, isn't it? Not having their machines in order – you could sue them.'

'Paul, you don't understand. They weren't negligent; it was sabotage.'

'Oh, not that again, what on earth makes you think that? Far more likely a faulty pipe than someone's malicious intent. They probably hadn't serviced it properly,' Paul said, getting aggravated with his brother.

'The brakes were fine on our way to the pub. I was using them as we came down the track into the village for God's sake. Sorry, Vicar.'

Dorothy noticed that Peter was staring at Leonard and his look was hard and cool. Was there something there – more than offence taken of casual blasphemy? she wondered.

'I came to a stop in the back of the car park, using the brakes,' Leonard continued. 'Then, when we left, the first time I needed to use them was at the top of the hill and they failed because, while I was inside the pub having my lunch, someone cut a hole in the pipe.'

18

GINA

Tentatively everyone started picking at their food again, but with Leonard simmering at the head of the table and casting his accusatory eye around us all, it did rather put a dampener on things. It seemed that nobody thought it was likely anyone had done something to his quad bike. And then Peter, who'd been quiet and contemplative up until that point, added his own thoughts.

'Do you have enemies, Leonard?' he asked. 'I can't think it's likely your family and friends would wish ill of you, so who do you think might be responsible?'

'Well, I don't have a particular person in mind,' Leonard said, glancing up at each face in turn around the table, including an unpleasant lingering look at me.

I swallowed hard and put my slice of pie back on my plate as a sudden wave of nausea took me.

'Perhaps a disgruntled tenant farmer? A person in the village with an axe to grind? A husband whose wife you've dallied with?' Peter asked.

There was a ripple of laughter at the last suggestion and I wasn't sure if it was the image of Leonard with a woman, or the word *dallied*, which surely belonged in the last century. Leonard had turned a shade of puce and the laughter died down.

'Perhaps,' Peter continued, 'someone from your art world. You're quite the collector, maybe you have someone who's after a treasure you've acquired.'

Peter said the word *acquired* as if it was a nasty taste in his mouth. Leonard levelled him a look, his face a more even shade now he seemed to have regained his composure.

A silence followed that was palpable and the scraping of cutlery on plates ceased. It was like watching a game of tennis, all looking from Leonard and then back to Peter. Now, though, all eyes were on the master of the house.

'All I know,' he said quietly, 'is that when I went into the pub for lunch my brakes were fine and when I came out the pipe had been punctured.'

'So nobody here could have been responsible then,' Peter said. 'Because everyone was inside the pub, weren't they?'

'I couldn't possibly say if anyone popped outside, could I.'

'Yes, but think about what you're actually saying. One of your nearest and dearest has a grudge against you? You're a nice bloke, Leonard, aren't you? What possible reason could someone have among your party to be involved in an unpleasant situation like that?'

More silence and then Leonard obviously seemed to realise he'd been cornered.

'You're right, Peter,' he said with a silly little laugh. 'I'm being ridiculous. It's the bash to my head. No one has it in for me – how could they possibly? Let's have no more talk about it now. Caroline and Toby are only two nights away from their wedding. Let us only have talk of good things.'

He stood then and raised his glass of red wine, encouraging everyone to do the same. Slowly and reluctantly we did, although

Dorothy hesitated longer than anyone else and I only had a glass of water to hand. After, when we'd settle back to eating, Leonard picked up a remote control from beside his plate.

'Music,' he announced. 'In all the excitement, I forgot the music.'

Pressing a button, the room was suddenly filled with medieval music. The sound of lutes and harpsichords surrounded us and I was surprised that Leonard hadn't ordered a group of troubadours to entertain us in person.

The rest of the meal was subdued, the conversation stilted and forced. By ten-thirty Peter was making noises about leaving and I had a sudden urge to talk to him. As the rest of the group started to depart the table to carry on drinking on the patio, I sidled over to him.

'When you go, may I walk with you, please? I have some questions about the monument in your church and would love to hear more about the history.'

If Peter was surprised he didn't show it.

'I'd be delighted,' he said.

Leonard had already left the room and wasn't, I assumed, in earshot, but those who were would be able to report a plausible excuse for my whereabouts if needed. Although, I could just as easily have gone to bed.

'I do need to see Dorothy up, if you wouldn't mind waiting.'

'You need do no such thing,' Dorothy said, her voice indignant. 'I have limbs enough for the stairs and to get myself to bed.'

'I'm going up now, Dot,' Lavinia said. 'You've been so diligent this week, Gina, you certainly deserve a walk down to the church.'

All settled, Peter and I set off from a side servants' door in a silent understanding that a big goodbye from the front would alert Leonard to our departure and neither of us were keen for that, it seemed.

The evening wasn't much cooler than it had been during the day and I was reminded of Lavinia mentioning about a possible storm come Saturday. If it was going to break I hoped it would happen before then. It would be awful for Caroline and Toby to have a week of hot, dry weather only to realise a downpour on their actual wedding day.

'What an evening,' I started. 'I wonder if Leonard had concussion after all his talk about sabotage.'

I decided to jump straight in and hoped that Peter wouldn't be too disappointed that church history wouldn't be featuring in our conversation.

'I didn't really think you wanted to talk about the church,' he said with a chuckle.

'I used to be an art historian many years ago, to be honest, and I would actually love to know more about your church, but I have a more pressing issue and wanted to entrust you with some of my thoughts.'

With time running out, I decided to trust and be honest with him. The week was nearly over and we were no closer to finding the painting. I hadn't even been looking today. It wasn't going to just fall in my lap and I needed to up my game.

'Ah, how interesting. So, what brings a former art historian to become a companion to an elderly woman?'

'A rather long story, a change in direction, you might say. May I get straight to the point?'

'By all means.'

'Do you think that Leonard is a criminal?'

'Ah, I see, *straight* to the point. And yes, I do. Why do you ask? As Dorothy's companion, I can't see why it would matter all that much. You'll be gone by the end of the week.'

I weighed up whether Dorothy's secret was only hers to tell and decided that as time was pressing I should just go for it. I also wondered whether I was being blinkered by the dog collar and who was to say how trustworthy Peter actually was.

'Dorothy believes that a painting belonging to her husband was stolen by Leonard and she's employed me to try to find it. Her husband died after a bungled burglary. They were supposed to be out and the thief broke in, took the painting and was leaving when Philip chased him, fell, and later died.'

'Goodness, I was not expecting you to say that. And she thinks Leonard broke in? Because I have to say, he usually gets others to do his dirty work.'

We'd reached the end of the driveway and were round onto the path leading to the church gate.

'No, she believes it was someone employed by him. Is that something you'd know anything about?' I asked him.

Peter steered me to the left and towards the lane that ran down to the rectory before he answered.

'I'll tell you what I know and what I believe to be true. Leonard is a man who likes people around him that owe him in some way. Harry, for example. I can't tell you what Harry did in a past life, because he wasn't specific, but Leonard knows about it and keeps him close. I know this because Harry told me. He's worried that Leonard will spill the beans, so to speak, and he's probably right to be worried, although I have told him to come clean. That way he can cut ties with Leonard and live an honest life, possibly behind bars for a short while, but honest all the same. I think he's wavering, but it's his choice. I believe Harry is currently helping Leonard to conceal stolen goods in the house. He's not so much a collector of art, but a thief of it.

'Harry hasn't confirmed this, but I've seen comings and goings. There's a good viewpoint of the back of the house from my spare bedroom window in the rectory and yes, I do realise how that makes me look. I just feel I ought to know what's going on under my nose. To be honest, I'm not sure how to act, yet.'

I didn't say anything as we walked up the path to his front door. I was taking it all in, though.

'I'm not all that surprised by what you've told me. It confirms what I thought. So, Harry isn't to be trusted then.'

'No, Harry *is* to be trusted and I suggest you go and speak to him. He's looking for an out from his situation in that house and if he can get Leonard to loosen his grip, he'll be onto the right path.'

'Surely he just needs to tell Leonard that he's leaving and see where the dice fall.'

'You're right, but that's for him to decide. If you talk to him, though, he might feel a sense of safety in numbers.'

'Or he might tell Leonard what I'm doing in his house and I could well feel the wrath of the man. You're asking me to put my faith in a criminal after all.'

We'd stopped at Peter's door and I declined his invitation for a cup of coffee.

'I should be walking *you* back now,' he said.

'No need, I'm more than capable,' I said.

'I can see that,' Peter replied. 'Gina, Harry will probably know where Leonard keeps his stolen artwork. He probably helps him to hide it. He might well know where the painting is. Maybe you could just ask him that. And if he's forthcoming, maybe you could encourage him to take the right path.'

'Maybe I could just phone the police and tell them Leonard has a house full of stolen goods,' I mused.

'I wouldn't do that. I don't think it's all in the house. Leonard has many places on his estate to tuck things away. The police will need more than hearsay and if Leonard finds out, he could well move the lot.'

'That's pretty much what Dorothy said. So, I'm looking in the house and may well be wasting my time.'

'Possibly; possibly not. I'm sorry I can't help you more than that, but I would urge you to talk to Harry.'

'You've been very helpful, Peter,' I said. 'Thank you for your honesty. I'll say goodnight.'

'Goodnight, Gina, I'll see you at the wedding on Saturday, no doubt.'

'I was rather hoping to duck out of it and go searching, but now I'm wondering if it might be a waste of time.'

I left the rectory and walked slowly back to the house, my head full of what I had to do next. Talk to Harry, the man who half terrified me, but who also cooked amazing food.

I could hear laughter coming from the music room and what sounded like Toby playing the piano again, but I walked straight past and up the stairs to my bedroom with no wish to interact with any of them. I thought briefly of telling Dorothy what I had learned from Peter, but she seemed tired earlier and was probably already asleep; I didn't want to wake her. I also contemplated going downstairs to see if Harry was around, but decided that the morning would be soon enough for that conversation and I'd have the night to think about how on earth I was going to broach the subject with him.

I pushed open my door, quite keen to sink under the covers, but to my surprise, Juliet was sitting on my bed.

'Where have you been?' she hissed. 'We're wasting time while you're busy chatting up the vicar.'

'I wasn't chatting him up, I was finding out information, if you must know.'

'Well, either way, Leonard is a bit drunk and he's in the music room and because of his knee and his head, he's not in a position to come chasing us up the stairs, so we need to hunt in his sitting room and the attic.'

'Now?' I asked. 'I was just going to bed.'

'Did you listen to anything I just said? We might not get another easy opportunity.'

Juliet was already up and to the door. She pushed past me and stood out on the landing with her arms folded.

'Come on!'

I hesitated because hadn't Peter told me that the stolen items might not even be in the house? They could be anywhere on his land. I really needed to speak to Harry before more fruitless searching. But I didn't want to tell Juliet what I'd learned from Peter. She already knew too much and she was just a young girl after all.

'Look, Juliet, this could all go horribly wrong,' I said. 'There would be serious consequences to being found snooping. It's one thing me doing it, but a whole other thing for you. I don't want to let your grandmother down, but I'm not happy about any of this,' I said and watched as she tilted her head onto one side and drew her lips into a thin line.

'I'm always snooping. I'm well known for it, so it would come as no surprise to anyone. If you're really not comfortable then go back to your room and I'll search on my own,' she said with a look of resignation.

'You are not looking on your own,' I said.

'They're all downstairs, a bit drunk and not remotely bothered about what we're doing.'

I supposed it couldn't be worse than being found in Leonard's bedroom and that didn't happen, luckily. I couldn't have her looking on her own; I'd have to go with her.

'All right then,' I said with huge reluctance. 'Let's go.'

I slid my phone into the back pocket of my trousers and we made our way along the landing, across the staircase gallery and up into the tight staircase that led up to the rooms above. I paused with my hand on the banister and took a breath.

'Let's be quick and quiet. No talking unless there is great need,' I said and Juliet nodded in response before sprinting up the staircase. I followed at a more sedate pace.

The attic space was not what I expected it to be. It wasn't a dark and dusty place, but rather a perfectly ordered area. Round skylights in the roof meant that in daytime it would be bathed in light, but for now, as I looked up, I could only see stars in the cloudless, ink-coloured sky. It was also quite a big space, but there wasn't much in it. It was surprisingly sparse.

There were shelves in the eaves with books that were ordered alphabetically as you'd expect in a library or a bookshop. I was surprised to see as I bent down to scan the spines that they were mostly commercial fiction paperbacks and had titles I'd seen published in the last few years. They weren't first editions, classics, collectors' copies or expensive hardbacks. There were also crates and boxes stacked neatly in the middle of the space where there was more headroom and I lifted the lid on one to see what was inside. It was full of vintage china teacups and saucers, the kind you'd use for afternoon tea. Nothing matched. It was a mix of designs as eclectic as the rest of Leonard's things. Juliet raised her eyebrows in surprise and opened another box. This time it contained vases, all chintzy and similar to the cups. Another had styled candleholders with the same designs, and another had trinket dishes.

'Does he just steal from old ladies?' Juliet whispered and I gave her a look. 'Yeah, but where's all the silver, the gold and diamonds? Why is he stealing stuff from car-boot sales?'

In one corner there were maybe twenty rugs rolled up and

stacked one on top of another. I pulled an edge back on one and was surprised to see it was a decent Persian, although a little threadbare.

'Gina!' Juliet hissed, and I turned to see her in the far corner, under one of the windows with the full moon casting a perfect circle of muted light onto her head like a halo.

It looked like she'd found a stack of paintings leaning against the wall. She was already pulling them back and letting them lean against her legs by the time it took me to get there. We worked through all of them, but they were mostly portraits. There were no coastal scenes and I could feel my natural tendency to calm slip a little.

'Absolute bloody waste of time,' I said, pushing the paintings back and crouching down on my haunches. I rested my elbows on my knees and my head in my hands. 'It's like Del-Boy's flat in here.'

'I don't know what that means,' Juliet said.

'Like it's all fallen off the back of a lorry.'

'Well, we're not giving up now! Sitting room,' Juliet whispered impatiently, tugging on my arm and then helping me to my feet. I stood up, grateful for the assistance.

I took one last look around the room in case we'd missed something, but it remained a huge disappointment. We left the attic as we'd found it and walked quietly down the stairs, round to the main staircase and on to Leonard's wing of the house. His bedroom door was open and he wasn't in it, neither the sitting room, and I had to assume he was still downstairs. I looked at my watch and could see it was nearly eleven. I doubted they'd all be down there for much longer, but I could just about still hear the faint strains of the piano and some distant laughter.

'Do you want to wait outside and call if someone comes?' I asked Juliet.

'What would be the point of that? By the time someone was up here, it would be too late, and what would I say about me being here anyway? Let's just both get in there and look.'

Juliet was determined even though I was dithering, but really at this point there was nothing else we could do other than forget the whole idea.

'Come on then,' I said and we stepped into Leonard's sitting room.

19

GINA

The room took you back in time to the seventeenth century. It was dark with oak panelling on the lower part of the walls and rich, red velvet covering the upper part. There was a gilded leather wall hanging with images of fruit and birds, plants and dragonflies. I stepped closer for a better look, but found myself sidetracked by the sight of a large tapestry. The leather work on the wall hanging was made to look ancient, but actually seemed to have been done recently. The tapestry, however, appeared very much like a seventeenth-century original. It was a scene depicting Greek figures and I felt sure I'd seen it or certainly something like it before. I began to wonder how deep Leonard was into the criminal underworld of art theft. This piece looked as if it should be in a private collection of someone far more deserving than him. I pulled out my phone and took a photograph then noticed the humidity detector on the wall beside it. At least he was looking after it.

Juliet was going through drawers and cupboards, but came back to stand beside me, empty-handed.

'It's not here,' she said.

We both looked around the room in silence until I began to

walk towards the windows. I pulled back the curtain to peer behind it, then stepped back and began to feel along the wooden panelling, away from the window and towards the corner of the room.

'Can you see?' I said. 'Can you see that the windows aren't even?'

Juliet looked to where I was pointing, to where there was a good foot or two more wall to the left of the second window.

'So? What does that mean? The room is wonky, so what?'

'You're the one who mentioned secret panels. Help me look.'

Juliet joined me in the corner of the room and began feeling around the panelling for anything unexpected.

'And why is the oak covering the whole wall here, when it's only on the lower part around the rest?'

'Gina!' Juliet said. 'Feel here.'

Juliet took my hand and made me run my fingers over a hole in the wood. I pushed in my forefinger, pulled and the wall of oak began moving towards us. We both stepped back to see what we'd uncovered.

'Wow! I think we've found his stash,' Juliet said.

We were looking into a secret room behind the oak panel and it was full of what I had expected to see in the loft. Vases, sculptures, both modern and antique, silverware and furniture. Nothing was displayed as such; it was purely a storage area. Some things were bubble-wrapped; others had sheets draped over them. What I could see, though, was quality. Like the tapestry in the sitting room these were all items of worth. I went to pick up a ceramic jug and stopped myself.

'Don't touch anything,' I said to Juliet. 'We don't need our finger-prints contaminating what could well be a crime scene.'

I took out my phone and snapped a couple of pictures, then I scrolled through my photo library until I found the one of the hidden objects painting, or rather the Vanitas. There in the corner of the secret room was something I'd recognised from the painting: a sliver jug. In the painting itself it had a snake coiled around it, but I was pleased to see that the actual jug here did not. I zoomed in on the photo and saw a ceremonial sword, which was also in this secret room. Did Leonard have his prize possessions painted on canvas and displayed in plain sight when the actual items were hidden? I took careful photos of everything without touching anything. As I did, I noticed that there were paintings stacked against an antique mahogany ottoman and both Juliet and I made a beeline for them.

I used my sleeve pulled down over my hand as a glove, which I wasn't sure was all that effective, before I riffled through them. It wasn't there. Plenty of wonderful pieces were in front of us but not the damn watercolour.

'It's not here,' I said, frustrated.

'What's not here?' said a voice behind us, and both Juliet and I spun around to see Harry standing in the doorway. 'Don't worry, he's still downstairs and won't be coming up until I go down to get him. What are you both doing?'

'Perhaps it's time we had a chat, Harry,' I said, and was surprised to hear how confident I sounded, because my legs had turned to mush.

'Possibly so, but not here and not now. You need to close that up and get out of here. I need to get Leonard to bed and if he finds you up here it won't be pretty.'

'What do you think he'd do?' I asked. 'Hurt us?'

'No,' he said, quickly. 'He wouldn't do that, and besides, I wouldn't let him. He'd get you out of his house and move all of this before you could get the police here, so don't even bother. You need to be smarter than that.'

His phone buzzed in his pocket and he pulled it out to read the message.

'That's him now. I need to go down and you'll both be gone by the time I get back up here with him. Is that clear?'

'But I need to talk to you,' I said again.

'Okay, but later. I've still got a whole lot of food to prepare for the hordes coming tomorrow. Give me half an hour and come and see me in the kitchen.'

He didn't wait for a response, but just left us standing in the middle of Leonard's secret room.

'Is there any point in me telling you to go to bed?' I said to Juliet.

'I mean, you can try, but I'll ignore you.'

I took some last few photos and we pulled the door closed carefully behind us.

'Fine, come on then.'

Out on the landing, I took Juliet's hand and pulled her quickly away from Leonard's private domain. Once we were back in a safer part of the house and then down towards the servants' staircase, I stopped, suddenly remembering that earlier Juliet had some information she wanted to share.

'Who did you record?' I asked her. 'On your phone, you said you recorded something important.'

'Oh yeah, that. It's just a sound recording, though, unless you want to look at leaves,' she said with an embarrassed smile.

I suddenly wanted to give this girl a hug, because actually she was pretty bloody brilliant. I didn't, though; I just grinned at her instead.

She took out her phone and handed me one of her earbuds and we sank back into an alcove to listen.

The sound was quite faint and Juliet had to turn up the volume and play the clip again. Once she pressed play, the sound was of Rufus's voice talking urgently in my ear.

'It's exactly as I told you, I found a compromising video of the two of them together.'

There was a moment of interference, sounding very much like Juliet rustling in the bush before Rufus's voice again.

'*But don't you see, we have him now. No more blackmailing unless we are the ones doing it.*'

'*I don't care who Leonard is shagging, no one else will either. It doesn't change a bloody thing.*'

This sounded like Sandra.

'*You haven't seen it.*'

'*I don't want to see it. Is someone there?*' Sandra's voice descended to a whisper that I had to strain to hear and then all that could be heard was the sound of Juliet's rapid breathing for a moment before Rufus spoke again.

'*Mum, we can use this before it gets any worse.*'

'*Worse! How the hell could it be any worse?*'

I stared at Juliet long after she'd stopped the recording.

Within half an hour Juliet and I were drinking mugs of hot chocolate that Harry had made and were ready for him to enlighten us on the situation with Leonard. According to Peter, Harry was a criminal and I'd certainly been wary of him since arriving in this house, but for now I had decided to trust him. After all, things upstairs, just a short time ago, could easily have gone a very different way.

He had his back to us as he began to prep salmon en croûte for eighty people. I found I could only watch for so long and then I rolled up my sleeves, washed my hands and began rolling out the pastry. Harry smiled at me gratefully, while Juliet raided the biscuit tin.

'So, what were you both doing in Mr Price's private space?' Harry asked.

I continued to roll and thought about a measured response.

'We were looking for a painting that he stole from Granny,' Juliet said before I could.

'Juliet!' I said.

'Well, we were in his secret stash of stolen stuff, weren't we. No point pretending!'

'We don't actually know he stole any of it. He could be using that room as a security measure,' I said, and Juliet levelled me a look that told me exactly what she thought of that as an idea.

'It's okay,' Harry said. 'I know that Leonard works away from the rules of the law when he acquires some of his art.'

'You know he took Dorothy's painting?' I asked.

'I heard about it, but it was before I came here. I don't know the details and certainly not enough to get him convicted.'

'And do you know where it is?'

'No I don't, sorry.'

'Someone mentioned that Leonard likes to employ people that he feels he can manipulate. Is that something you're aware of?' I asked him, wincing a little at my words.

'If you mean, am I under Leonard's control because he has information about me and my past then, yeah. I did something I'm not proud of and when I found it impossible to get employment, Leonard stepped in. In a way he has helped me. He's given me a good job doing something I love and paid me well, but it's come at the price of me helping him while keeping my mouth shut. He's hardly lifted me out of the world of crime. In fact, he's kept me right in the thick of it.'

'And now?' I asked. 'Why have you decided to talk about it now?'

I rolled and cut the pastry, copying what Harry had done and then passed the sheets over to him where he folded his prepared salmon inside.

'Because I don't want to be here any more. I don't like Leonard and his dealings have got out of hand. He's a kleptomaniac of the worst kind. He rarely sells pieces on any more. It's all about the having of them. It's not about money; it's about ownership. The stakes are getting higher and I don't want any more involvement. I'm handing in my notice after the wedding.'

I wondered at the idea Harry would be handing in his notice as if he was on some sort of official contract.

'How are you involved exactly?' I asked. 'Do you steal the artwork?'

'No, I'm just the delivery guy,' he said. 'Worse, I'm more like a getaway driver sometimes.'

'Harry, can you tell me where the rest of these stolen things are? I assume it's not only that crap in the attic and what we found in the secret space of the sitting room. I really need to find this painting of Dorothy's.'

'The attic, yes, some of that is stolen, small scale from people he knows in antiques. Pinched from house clearances and the like, not all crap if you have time for a closer look. Some he's actually bought, to be fair, or taken in payment for his silence. Some is bigger stuff, the tapestry and a few ceramics around the house. That secret stash is all stolen.'

'That tapestry,' I said thoughtfully. 'I really thought I'd seen it before somewhere. I may have been mistaken.'

'You're an expert?'

'I used to work in the arts, a very long time ago.'

'Ah, I didn't think you were just a companion. You seemed to have an edge to you.'

I was about to ask him what he meant by that, but he'd continued talking.

'He told me the tapestry was taken from a collection that was being moved from an exhibition back to its place in a stately home.

It was many years ago, so many it seems that he feels he can display it freely. Stolen work, hanging in plain sight.'

'Maybe I read about it; that's why I remember it,' I said. 'You know, Dorothy said exactly that about hanging in plain sight. She thinks he's so egotistical, he'll have her painting somewhere clever.'

'I doubt it will be somewhere clever, but it will be somewhere he can see it whenever he wants to. His bedroom perhaps? What is the painting of, anyway? How big is it?'

'It's a watercolour of a coastal scene, with a beach and headland in the background and a lighthouse. About so big,' I said holding out my hands to give him a rough idea of its size, although I only had Dorothy's word on how big it actually was. 'I have looked in his bedroom, but couldn't see it there.'

'There are many other places on his land that he stores things. He has barns and sheds, the temple. He has that holiday home where I know for a fact he has a couple of very prominent pieces locked in the tower.'

Juliet had been very quiet up until this point and Harry suddenly turned to her.

'What are you doing? Are you recording this conversation?'

He made a lunge towards her phone, but she pulled it back and stepped away.

'It's just for my own personal use,' she shrieked.

'Juliet, give me that phone,' I said, holding out my hand and Juliet handed it over with a thunderous look. 'I'll make sure this is deleted, Harry. She's just a bored kid at a family wedding.'

Juliet opened her mouth to say something, but I stopped her with one penetrating look. Then after a couple of swipes across the screen, I turned the phone around so Harry could see it was gone, then I handed the device back to Juliet, who looked at it in exasperation.

'Nothing matters much now, anyway,' he said, his voice as resigned as his position.

'Harry, I have to ask, what was in my drink the other night?'

'Sorry about that. Leonard slipped extra alcohol in your drinks. I think he was going to try to get you talking. He doesn't trust you for some reason. Well, now I can see why. He shouldn't have done it, though. I know I was as bad for handing them out.'

'Did he get me talking? I really don't remember.'

'No, because I slipped extra in his and he wasn't really fit for conversations. It was why I made sure you got to your room. I was worried after I saw how much he was pouring.'

'And he thinks someone is trying to bump him off,' I said. 'With his record, it could be anyone.'

'I think it's Paul,' Juliet said. 'He looks around this house with a sort of longing. I wouldn't like it if I'd lost out on such a big inheritance.'

Harry didn't say anything and I wondered if he knew who it was.

'Thank you, Harry,' I said, 'for your honesty. Not many people would be so decent. Apart from anything else, you're here feeding the guests, rather than doing a disappearing act. Commendable.'

'Thanks, Gina, but once the catering team come on Saturday I won't be hanging around for long. But if I find the painting, I'll let you know.'

I nodded and put the rolling pin back on the worktop. I washed my hands again and dried them on a towel.

'I'm going to leave my phone number,' I said. 'In case you find anything or think of anything that might be useful to Dorothy.'

In a gesture of complete faith, he handed his phone to me, unlocked, and I put my number in under the name *The Companion*. He laughed when I gave it back to him.

'That makes you sound sinister,' he said.

We left the kitchen and walked back up the stairs, but once we were out of Harry's earshot, Juliet rounded on me.

'I can't believe you deleted it. That was such a stupid thing to do. It was evidence!'

'I had to make sure Harry knew it was off your phone. I'd like to think he could be trustworthy, which I know sounds like an odd thing to say about a criminal, but we can't really trust him. And, anyway, I only deleted it after I'd sent it to myself,' I said.

Juliet's eyes widened and then a huge smile broke out on her face.

'Nice one,' she said.

Despite my reservations about what I was doing for Dorothy and how Juliet was mixed up in it now as well, I still managed to feel a little proud of myself for my quick thinking. I also felt like we were close now. Surely it couldn't be long before the painting appeared.

20

DOROTHY

Dorothy had slept badly. She'd been restless all night with a terrible headache and when Gina knocked on her door at seven-thirty she'd really not had the energy to get up.

'I think this is all too much for you, Dorothy,' Gina had said. 'I think it's time to hand it over to Miles and Sophie and let them do whatever they feel is right. It's too stressful for you.'

'No,' Dorothy had croaked from her bed. 'We're so close now – I can feel it.'

So Gina had agreed to leave her for a few more hours and then they'd make a decision about what was best to do. She left Dorothy with her tea tray and her newspaper open at the crossword.

It was now lunchtime and Gina had returned with more tea and a glass of water. Dorothy had managed to get some sleep, her headache had subsided and she was determined to show Gina that she was fighting fit. The trouble was, she wasn't exactly on top form, but she intended to rally.

The rest of the guests were arriving, bringing a whole other level of excitement, and Gina was at the window describing the scene outside the front of the house.

'Two coaches have pulled off the main road onto Leonard's driveway and there's a sea of colourful summer dresses. Caroline and Toby are there greeting them along with Miles and Lavinia, Paul and Sandra. Of course Leonard isn't there,' Gina said. 'He'll want to make his entrance later. There's no way he would stand on his own driveway waiting for guests to arrive. He has his minions for that. He'll probably appear in a puff of smoke, at the garden party.'

Dorothy laughed. 'You definitely know that man now, Gina,' she said.

'So, why are the guests here a day early? What's the plan?' Gina asked.

'Caroline didn't want a tacky disco, as she put it, after the wedding breakfast. She wanted to disappear off with her new husband on their honeymoon before everyone got incredibly drunk and disorderly. Apparently, Lavinia had reminded her that some guests had come an awfully long way and were staying overnight. And what were they supposed to do with their evening when the meal would most likely be over by five-thirty? She said the rest of us would have already had a week's worth of fun and would probably be glad of an early finish, but the guests might feel short-changed.'

'That does make some sense,' Gina said.

'Well, Caroline arranged with Leonard that the guests would be invited a day early for an afternoon and evening of fun. That way they could be as drunk as they liked and it wouldn't spoil her day. She's also booked most of the rooms in a large hotel in Norwich for the two nights and arranged for the guests to take over the bar once they get back on the Saturday. Leonard suggested a garden party for today and he's organised the coaches for the two days. Between them they have thought of everything.'

'Are you going to be well enough for a garden party?' Gina asked her.

'I'll be fine if I can sit quietly in the shade.'

Gina turned back to the window to watch what was going on down below, but Dorothy pretended to be busy with her crossword as she hadn't quite got the energy yet to get out of bed and join her.

'This whole week is quite surreal,' Gina said, turning back to Dorothy. 'Do you know what I mean?'

'I do, when time begins to have no meaning. It feels like we've been here for weeks already, not days.'

'When I was fifteen I was hit by a car when I was crossing the road. It was entirely my own fault as I'd been reading a book at the time and not concentrating, something my mother later ripped shreds off me about, but that was after she had smothered me in love at the hospital. My leg had been seriously injured in the impact and I needed several pins to bring the bones back together. It wasn't a great start to us returning to the UK. I was in hospital for three weeks in the end and time had stopped making any sense. You know what it's like, all that bleeping and buzzing, a constant noise, day and night, and alongside the pain, deep sleep had been impossible. That was a surreal experience too.'

Dorothy thought back to those surreal and painful days in hospital with Philip and her new reality caught up with her again, as it often did. It still felt surreal, not having her husband with her.

'I'm sorry to hear that your week here is similar to three weeks in hospital in crippling pain,' Dorothy said, and Gina laughed.

'I didn't really mean it like that,' she said, but Dorothy understood.

'So tell me exactly what happened after you got back from talking to Peter,' Dorothy probed, as Gina sat in one of her chairs.

Gina relayed her conversation with the vicar, not that any of it came as much of a surprise to Dorothy. He'd just confirmed what she'd known for a while. But no matter what he said about art being scattered across his estate, Dorothy remained convinced that her painting would be in this house.

'Well, Juliet and I then went to the attic room – she insisted she'd go alone if I didn't go with her. There was an odd collection of stuff up there. Then we went to his sitting room and I found a tapestry that I'm sure the police would be interested in. Most importantly we found a secret doorway in the oak panelling and inside was his Aladdin's cave. That Vanitas painting in the oval room is almost a record of his stolen items. He hides them in that secret room and gets someone to paint them in plain sight. You are so right about this. I'm afraid not your painting, though.'

Dorothy had been sitting forward in anticipation, but now slumped back against her pillows. Although, she knew that if Gina had found it, she would have already told her.

'Why is it so bloody hard to find that painting? All the stolen items in the world won't help me. He might go to prison for his theft, but not for the one he should be inside for.'

She reached for her tea and Gina stepped forward to help her when she saw that Dorothy's hand was shaking. Once Dorothy had taken a sip, Gina placed the cup back onto the table and continued.

'Then Harry found us.'

'Oh God! What happened?' Dorothy was leaning forward in anticipation once more.

'It's okay. He was ready to talk about his involvement with Leonard. Here, Juliet recorded it.'

Gina handed Dorothy her phone and pressed play on the voice recording. They both listened in silence as the conversation unfolded for the second time.

'So, we could just go to the police with this, I think,' Gina said. 'What do you suggest? It could all be over with a proper search warrant.'

Dorothy shook her head. 'Leonard is a slippery snake and will find a way to wriggle out of this, leaving me with nothing and possibly with family who wouldn't talk to me. Like I said before, I want to find the painting first. Let's see if Harry does. Now he knows about it, he might realise he has seen it before and does know where it is.'

'But he said there was stuff in the stables, the roof of the temple and goodness knows where else. We can't look in all those places and I don't think Harry has any intention of hanging around after the wedding. It's not like he's going to work out his notice.'

'No,' Dorothy agreed, 'I very much doubt he'll do that. Let's just see though. Let's get through the wedding and then see.'

Although Dorothy could very well see that Gina wasn't convinced.

'So what, then? Go and chat to the guests, enjoy the wedding and let whatever is going to happen, happen?' Gina asked.

'I think that now Harry knows what we've been doing, that might be the best idea. He might still just tell Leonard what we've been up to. He doesn't owe us anything, after all.'

'You might be right, Dorothy,' Gina said. 'But you know I do have some confidence in him – possibly misguided. Oh, and Juliet recorded a brief conversation between Rufus and his mum.'

'Anything interesting?'

'Well, it was odd. Rufus telling Sandra that he'd found a compromising video of Leonard and someone, unnamed.'

'Oh dear,' Dorothy shuddered at the thought.

'Yes, and something about them having him now, and black-mail, and how could it be any worse. Not sure it really helps with what we're trying to do, to be honest, but Juliet will play it for you if you want to hear it.'

'Okay, and in the meantime we have a garden party to get ready for,' Dorothy said.

'Yes, but only if you're well enough to go?'

'I shall make every effort to join in. That way, I won't miss out on any opportunity to make Leonard squirm. I know an awful lot more about him now.'

Dorothy thought Gina looked lovely in a pair of pale-blue linen trousers and a cream blouse, but she noticed Gina never wore short sleeves and thought she must be hot. Dorothy herself had chosen a light summer dress in lavender, which Gina helped her into when her arms didn't seem to want to work properly.

'I love that your dress has such deep pockets,' Gina said. 'Not enough women's clothes have pockets.'

'That's all to do with us having to have good silhouettes. I used to subscribe to that rubbish, but not any more. Pockets are useful; silhouettes are not.'

They made their way slowly down the stairs and outside into the parterre garden where Leonard had arranged to have several separate gazebos constructed with tables and chairs underneath. Every table had a vase of lemon-coloured roses and jugs full of ice and sparkling elderflower. Music filled the air from another gazebo where Dorothy could see a string quartet playing. The guests looked relaxed and delighted to be there while Caroline and Toby flitted between the groups, making sure everyone was having a good time. Dorothy watched as Gina took a couple of glasses and filled them.

'I really want to hate him with everything I have heard about him,' Gina said, 'but I do have to commend him on another fabulous set-up. He's a wonderful host.'

'I think you're to be congratulated on your kind nature, Gina. It's an excellent trait to see mostly good in people. But, please don't confuse wonderful host with narcissistic show-off with head up own arse,' Dorothy said, causing Gina to splutter out some of the juice she still had in her mouth. 'I, however, wish him a grizzly death where he is dragged through the snow by rabid wolves and torn limb from limb. Ah! Yvonne, how lovely to see you.'

Dorothy turned from Gina to greet her old friend who was wearing a large pink hat and a matching dress with plunging neckline in, what Dorothy knew to be, her wonderfully extravagant signature style. They leaned into each other to kiss cheeks and then choose seats in the shade.

'Gina, my oldest friend – Yvonne. Yvonne, my newest friend – Gina.'

Gina extended her hand and Yvonne shook it vigorously.

'Pleasure,' Yvonne said. 'Although I can't possibly be your *oldest* friend, Dorothy. I'm only eighty-nine, the same as you,' she said with a deep laugh. 'I have a proposition for you, dear.'

'Oh? I'm all ears,' Dorothy said and then noticed that Gina was giving her a pointed look and turning her head in the direction of the rose garden. Dorothy looked to see Peter walking under the arch covered in white blooms.

'Dorothy, would you like me to stay with you, or shall I go and mingle?' Gina said, extending the syllables of the word *mingle*.

'Oh, please do go and mingle. I have a lot of catching up to do with Yvonne. And, Gina,' she said. 'If you happen to go back indoors, would you be so kind as to fetch me that little packet of tissues I've left on my bedside table. No rush, mind, just in a while, if you're going.'

Dorothy touched Gina's arm and smiled as Gina placed her glass back on the table.

'Of course, no problem at all,' she said and then after a nod at Yvonne, Dorothy watched her as she made her way across the lawn, past the sculpted topiary, down the steps towards the sunken rose garden in pursuit of Peter.

21

GINA

'Peter!' I called out as I picked up my pace. I looked back over my shoulder to see that Dorothy and Yvonne were chatting animatedly, Leonard was in deep conversation with a couple holding a baby and that Juliet had found a young lad to speak to. As everyone seemed occupied I wondered if I should really be indoors on the hunt, with that pretext of fetching Dorothy's tissues, but for some reason I felt drawn to talk to Peter again.

He was already inside the confines of the rose garden by the time I caught up with him and he had his head stooped, his hand cupping an orange rose, his nose inside the petals. The garden was set up in an oval shape, reminding me of the room in the house with the stolen items and for a moment I wondered if Dorothy's painting could be out here, but just a quick glance told me there were no hiding places. There were four borders, though full of rose bushes. I thought it would have been spectacular in June, but now during the last few days of August, there were only a few blooms left. Some of the remaining buds may never open and a good north-easterly wind would see the last of the flowers off. I could see a bench at one end near a water feature that was set into the wall. A bronze lion's head dribbled water onto stones below. Down here the music and chatter was faint and I imagined that bench would be a perfect place to sit and contemplate life, or to read a book, or just to look at the roses with a glass of wine. I had a sudden urge to do all three.

'Hello, Peter,' I said and then realised I'd made him jump as he dropped the rose. 'Wonderful garden party.'

'Yes, it is. Leonard has outdone himself again. Hello, Gina.'

Peter walked to the bench and sat down. He leaned his head back against the wall and closed his eyes for a moment.

'It's so peaceful here, you wouldn't imagine that this house could harbour such a wealth of secrets.'

While his eyes were closed, I took a moment to look at him. He had dark shadows under his eyes, and what could have been loosely called designer stubble yesterday had gone beyond that and his fingernails were bitten down to nothing.

'I spoke to Harry. I think he's on the brink of doing the right thing. Well, he's on the brink of leaving.'

'That might well be the best thing for Harry to do. Leonard would never send him on his way with a reference anyway, so maybe disappearing and starting over is as much as can be expected. I wish him all the luck.'

'Are you okay, Peter?' I asked sitting down next to him. The metal bench was cool on my back through my blouse and with the garden being sunken and shaded from the sun, it was welcome.

'I'm tired,' he said. 'I'm very tired.'

'Just got tomorrow to get through and then can you take a break, a holiday perhaps? Is there a Mrs Vicar?'

Peter laughed then, a dry hollow sound that came out through closed lips.

'A holiday and a Mrs Vicar. How wonderful those two things sound, but sadly I have neither time nor inclination.'

I wondered which he didn't have time for and which he didn't have inclination for, but I brushed it aside as none of my business. I was about to tell him about Leonard's secret room and how I felt we were only a coastal scene away from justice, when Leonard himself appeared in front of us, walking down the steps into the garden.

'Well, this looks cosy,' he said.

He had a glass of champagne in his hand and appeared a little drunk as he slurred his words and swayed on the bottom step.

'A companion who never seems to be by the side of her ward and a vicar who likes—'

'Leonard, are you okay, old chap?' Peter said standing up and moving forward to the steps. He caught hold of Leonard's arm and steered him towards the bench. 'Sit down before you fall down. I think the sun has got to you.'

Leonard did as he was told, but poured the remaining liquid down his throat before dropping the glass to the ground where it broke in two.

'Gina, do you think you could get something to put the glass in, my dear? I don't want any of the children here to hurt themselves,' Peter said.

'Of course,' I said, quickly walking back towards the steps. When I reached the top I glanced back and could see that Leonard had his head in his hands and Peter was standing over him, actually towering over him. He was saying something that I couldn't hear, but the tone was urgent and angry. Peter no longer looked tired; he was animated.

By the time I came back with some newspaper I'd found in a kitchen cupboard and a dustpan and brush, Leonard and Peter had gone. I cleared up the glass then sat back down on the bench. I had so many thoughts swirling around my head, but couldn't get a grip on any one of them. What was Rufus involved in and who was blackmailing whom? Who was with Leonard in his compromising video? My mind automatically went straight to sex, but really it could be images of theft. Perhaps there were compromising CCTV images of Leonard and Harry, stealing.

I decided that it was time to go and get those tissues that Dorothy requested.

A team of catering staff had arrived to get the food out for the garden party. Harry had already done a lot of the work, but it was too much for one person to do completely. Now there were about fifteen staff hurrying back and forth from the kitchen and out to an area set up for serving. It was basically a long trestle table covered in white linen and under the shade of another gazebo. There were bain-maries to keep the vegetables warm and portable ovens for the salmon en croûte.

For now, people were still walking around the gardens, drinking and chatting. They weren't quite ready for lunch as waiting staff with sliver trays of canapés were still circulating. Dorothy was where I had left her, still in her seat, but now talking to a couple. Yvonne and her pink hat had disappeared. I raised a hand to Dorothy and she waved back and then offered me a thumbs up. Leonard could just be seen quaffing more champagne, surrounded by guests all seemingly enraptured by whatever he was saying. He wasn't swaying now, but only because he had his back against a hedge. Peter was nowhere to be seen.

I walked quickly around to the main entrance, through the front door and straight up the ornate staircase. I was into Dorothy's room in moments and with the packet of tissues in my pocket, I was across the landing and up towards Leonard's personal staircase. I felt a sense of liberation at last. Leonard was too drunk to get here anytime soon and everyone else was enjoying themselves in the garden. Besides, I wasn't sure how much I cared now. Let someone challenge me on what I was doing. I was only one secret oak panel away from my own challenge. Let the house of cards fall where they may.

I stopped in Leonard's bedroom doorway and stared at his perfectly made bed. Unwanted images of him in so-called compromising positions came unbidden into my head, but I laughed them off. One thing Leonard was, was a grown man and his sex life – as long as it was consensual – was absolutely nothing to do with me.

I took my time to scan the room. The last time I had been in here, I was flustered and felt under pressure to look and then leave as quickly as possible. Now, though, I just looked. My eyes moved across his bed and that beautiful crewel-work embroidery, over his wardrobe, his chest of drawers, the paintings on the walls, those huge drapes and back to the Chinese cabinet.

Walking over to it, I pulled the handles the same as I had last time and the same as before, it was locked. Then I began to really rummage. I opened his bedside drawers, slid my hand under his pillow, crouched down and looked under the bed. I checked his bathroom cabinet, lifted vases to rattle them, picked through trinket dishes with coins and rings. I stopped and stood still again. I let my eyes roam once more and then they fell upon one of the paintings with an unsympathetic frame around it. The picture was a modern print of a coastal path. Nothing like the one I was looking for, but the frame was odd. It was an overly large, ornate, gilt frame, which didn't at all go with the picture. But more than that, the bottom of the frame looked slightly deeper than the top. I walked over to the window and looked outside. Leonard had a perfect view of most of the parterre garden from here and I could see him still talking to the group.

Back in front of the picture, I ran my fingers along the frame. The left-hand side felt different to the right and as I fiddled with that edge something popped under my touch and a slice of the frame fell into my hand. Behind it was a tiny key, stuck into the recess. A tiny key that likely opened an antique door on an old piece of furniture.

Without much thought, I pulled it away and walked back to the Chinese cabinet, stood for a second at the side of Leonard's bed, looking at the door, my heart now pumping faster. I leaned over his covers, pushed the key into the lock and turned. I held my breath as I pulled open the two doors and peered inside. What was inside made me jump. A stuffed bird stared back at me with one beady eye; the other was missing. It was the worst case of taxidermy I'd ever seen. There was nothing else, no painting, and I allowed myself a full minute for the utter disappointment to flow through me as I stared at that ugly, bloody bird and the terrible job someone had done on it. Then I closed and locked the doors, returned the key, slid the piece of frame back into place and left Leonard's bedroom.

I walked back down the landing so lost in my despondency that I almost didn't hear the noise coming from Leonard's office. I hesitated outside the door, listening to the definite sound of drawers opening and closing, and of rummaging. I knew the sound very well after my own exploits for the last ten minutes. I knew Leonard was still in the garden – I'd just seen him – so I decided to open the door and catch whoever was in there. It went against everything I knew to be right and sane, but let's be honest, that ship had sailed at the beginning of the week when I first started invading Leonard's privacy.

The handle was cold under my grip, but as quietly as I could, I turned it, pushed the door open and found Peter with his hands in Leonard's drawers.

'Peter!' I said, completely surprised to see him there.

'Gina, thank goodness it's you. This is not what it looks like,' he said. 'Actually, who am I trying to kid, it's exactly what it looks like. Leonard has something of mine and I'm trying to find it.'

'Not you as well – he seems to have something of everybody's. Is it some artwork?'

'Um, no, it's a memory stick with some important stuff on it and...'

He trailed off, looking uncomfortable and I made the connection in my mind: compromising video. I'd been imagining an old video tape, but of course no one had those any more. A recording could easily be on a memory stick.

'Peter, I think I may know what you're looking for and I think I may know who has it. Let's go downstairs where it's safer to be and have a chat.'

Peter looked mortified sitting in the window seat of the library while I told him I thought Sandra or Rufus might have his memory stick and how I came to know about it.

'I'm so embarrassed,' he said. 'I didn't know that Leonard was recording us.'

I swallowed down my surprise. I wouldn't in a million years have put Peter and Leonard together. And there was me asking about a Mrs Vicar.

'You shouldn't feel at all embarrassed. Leonard is breaking the law here, recording you without your consent. Another one to add to his list of misdemeanours.'

'Leonard was so charming when we first met. I was quite swept away with him and my new position here. The setting is so romantic, much more so than the city I was working in before, and I honestly thought we had something serious going. Quite quickly, Leonard made it clear he didn't do commitment, only casual, and I realised I was deluding myself. So, I carried on with my work, built up the community around the church and kept out of Leonard's way. When Harry started, though, I saw a lot more comings and goings and, already suspicious about the amount of artwork that Leonard seemed to be collecting, I approached Harry to see what he knew. That was when he told me his whole sorry story.

'I just kept an eye for a bit, but then seeing how unhappy Harry seemed to be, I spoke to Leonard and suggested he let him go, that Harry had as much on him as he did on Harry. Leonard just laughed, said he knew enough people who could make it all disappear before any police involvement. I thought he just meant the artwork, but now I'm not so sure. When I said I would take it further, he told me he'd recorded us together. I was mortified and he said that I should keep quiet or at any time during any service he could easily show my parishioners who I really was. I know how vain that makes me, but imagine, Gina, halfway through a christening and Leonard has secretly rigged up my projector. My time here and anywhere else would be over. I'm a weak man it turns out, because I should have done more.'

'He's despicable,' I said. 'I'll get the memory stick back for you. I promise.'

I said this confidently, but in truth I wasn't sure how and also, could we be certain there weren't more copies? Did I just walk up to Rufus and demand he hand it over? 'I'll do my very best,' I said.

* * *

Outside in the garden the guests were beginning to take their seats for lunch and I lifted a glass of champagne from a passing tray and downed it before smiling at the waiter and returning the empty glass to him. I joined Dorothy with a sad shake of my head as I handed her the packet of tissues and she patted my hand in solidarity, but all I wanted to do was go home. I couldn't see how I was going to find the painting. I might be able to get the stick for Peter, but that really wasn't enough. Leonard had thwarted me as he had so many other people.

Someone put a plate of salmon en croûte down in front of me and I ate it in silence while everyone around me talked and laughed and the quartet played their soothing music. I didn't feel soothed, though; I felt an odd combination of irritation and despair. I also had an unsettling urge to phone Douglas and beg him to come and get me. I took another glass of champagne and decided to move through the rest of the day in a haze.

22

GINA

Saturday morning arrived sooner than I would have liked. I lay in bed contemplating the ache in my head and the glasses of champagne I'd consumed at the garden party. In the end I had enjoyed myself and made sure Dorothy had done the same. She seemed to have perked up a bit as the day went on. There was no further talk of the painting, I didn't mention the crippling disappointment I'd experienced after the Chinese cabinet incident, but I did have a bird, one beady eye and a bad job of taxidermy rolling around my head. I also had the added problem of how I would get Peter's stick back. Today, though, there would be a wedding and tomorrow I would be going home to a house that would not be mine for much longer. I felt both relieved and rather twitchy about that.

Dorothy's kind suggestion of me staying in her boathouse was actually rather appealing if I was honest, but I needed to square it all in my head. Was I just running away from the problem of where to live long term, or did it offer me some breathing space to decide?

There was a knock at my door and without waiting for me to say a word, Juliet walked right in.

'Morning,' she said brightly. 'We don't have long now and we should be looking. I wondered about the temple, after what Harry said, although I get that plain sight might be more Leonard's style. Either way, we're running out of time. Did you tell Granny about Rufus?'

'Morning, Juliet, do you not usually wait for someone to invite you in before you do actually come in?'

'I'm not a vampire! I knew you'd be awake – you don't really lie in. So, where are we going to look? It's seven-fifteen and Granny's still asleep.'

'Good,' I said, taking stock of what I was wearing – pyjamas – before pushing back my covers and swinging my legs around until I was sitting on the bed. It was only as I stood up that I realised my arms were uncovered and saw Juliet's eyes move straight to my scars. I pulled my robe around me and she looked away. 'I don't want your grandmother bothered; she seems very tired. I think this whole week has been too much for her and I can't even imagine what your uncle Miles, let alone your own mother would think about what we've been doing.'

'They'd be made up.'

'I'm not so sure, but it's a bit late now anyway. It's not in Leonard's bedroom; I looked yesterday, again. Maybe it is in the temple, maybe it's in a barn somewhere on his land. Personally, I think we have enough, with the photos and the voice recording, to go to the police and let them sort it. I'll wait until Harry has left; I feel I owe him that.'

'Even if he murdered someone?'

'I don't think it's anything like that,' I said, quietly. 'I think it's probably theft and on the scale that Leonard is dealing, it would come with a heavy sentence, but to be honest that's not why I'm here.'

'You're here to find a painting. Come on, Gina! Think how happy Granny would be if we found it.'

'She'd be made up,' I said with a smile. 'Okay, give me ten minutes to wake myself up and we can go and look in the temple if it makes you happy. Will you be a love and get me a coffee?'

We didn't see Harry in the kitchen when we went down to pinch some breakfast. The place was swarming with the catering staff, though, and we only managed to grab a couple of bananas and cereal bars from the pantry. I made another coffee to take with me.

We passed through the main entrance hall as Sophie was walking down the stairs. She was wearing her pyjamas and it reminded me that it was still early.

'Juliet, have you seen your father? He came down for coffee ages ago and seems to have disappeared. Why are you up so early?'

'I said I'd show Gina the temple and thought it best I keep out of the way. I haven't seen Dad.'

'Out of the way in case you get talked into being a bridesmaid?' Sophie asked with a gentle smile on her lips.

'I'd rather wash my face with an angry hedgehog,' was Juliet's response and I bit down on my lip to stop myself from laughing.

Sophie sighed and shook her head.

'Is it okay with you if we pop out for a walk?' I asked. 'Dorothy is still asleep, but I won't be long.'

I couldn't help remembering Sophie's voice on Juliet's recording and how she didn't think I was needed, which was why what she said next surprised me.

'Of course, Gina. You've been wonderful. Mum has loved having you around. I do think she needs her rest, though. This has been a very exciting week.'

I nodded while a horrible guilty feeling flushed through me and Juliet rolled her eyes.

'Exciting? Do let me know when that starts,' she said dramatically.

Sophie disappeared off in pursuit of her husband and some coffee and Juliet and I left through the front door to avoid the beginnings of the wedding production going on in the back of the house. We took a slow walk around the side of the house, past the beautiful herbaceous border, the gravel path that led to the rose garden and along the line of yew hedging that was so perfectly cut into rectangles that you'd be forgiven for thinking it was fake.

The storm Lavinia had spoken of at the beginning of the week showed no sign of appearing. The sun was already a blazing ball hanging against a powder blue background and it reminded me of the colour of Dorothy's boat.

We walked along the grass where the rhododendrons grew, because that was where the shade was. Even at this early hour the heat from the sun was penetrating. The temple, where we'd picnicked the other day, was also in shade and I glanced back towards the house before I ascended the steps. Could that be Leonard's face looking out of his window? In truth, I couldn't really see a face from this distance, but I was sure that two figures at the temple might be noticed.

'So let's have a look and see if there's any secret hiding places here,' Juliet said with a sparkle in her eyes. I prayed that it would be in a perfectly easy hiding space that we'd find in seconds and I could hand it to Miles who would be delighted or *made up*, as Juliet suggested, and Leonard would put his hands up and say *fair cop*.

It became apparent in those few prayed-for seconds that we would not find the painting in the temple. There were no hiding places, the stone was impenetrable and all we found in half an hour of further searching, was a woodlouse, a sweet wrapper that someone had dropped and a tiny weed growing in a crack. Harry had been wrong; there was nowhere here to stash a painting.

'Right, well, I'm done,' I said, irritated. 'Shall we head back?'

'I feel like you're giving up,' Juliet said.

'With good reason.'

I sat down on the top step and peeled the banana that I had in my pocket.

'This wasn't the role I was expecting when I arrived on Monday, you know,' I said between mouthfuls.

'Defeatist talk,' Juliet said, her hands on her hips.

'I thought I'd just be looking after an older lady. Perhaps making sure she took her medication, help her into her slippers.'

'Granny taught me how to do a cartwheel when I was five; that's eight years ago. She was eighty-one. She'll never need help with her slippers.'

I finished the banana and wrapped the peel in a piece of tissue I had in my other pocket.

'My grandpa was the best,' Juliet continued. 'When he died, it ripped a huge hole in the family. You know, like a space that can't be filled and will forever be this flapping void that we all feel, all the time. I was told, at the time, that he had a fall, like old people do, that he fell on his steps and it was just one of those things. But now, of course, I know that's not the case. Someone is responsible and I'd feel I could help to fill that flapping void if I did what I could to find who. That means finding the painting.'

Juliet took her hands off her hips and sat down next to me and I put my arm around her shoulders.

'I've seen some sheds out past the greenhouses. We could go and look in those,' I said knowing I was humouring her and wasting time, but felt I ought to do it all the same.

'Anything to get me out of being a bridesmaid.'

'Surely it's too late now anyway?'

'Oh no, Mum has a dress for just in case I change my mind.'

I stood and held my hand out to Juliet who took it. I dragged her to her feet and the two of us left the temple and cut back through the trees, out of sight of the house towards the kitchen gardens.

Back in my room I rummaged for something to wear and pulled out a navy dress that had a high collar and a simple belt at the waist. No one was going to be remotely bothered what I looked like and I needed to be comfortable. I opted for a pair of ballet pumps that were light and quiet. Although, I had no plan now for further searching and, to be honest, I was playing a bit of a countdown until this would all be over. Dorothy would be disappointed, but what was I to do. I picked up my phone from the dressing table to put it in my bag and noticed another message I'd missed.

> Georgina, I've spoken to Alice who said you're working! News to me and might have been nice to know. Not sure why you didn't say when we spoke. We need to make a decision on this offer. It's not as much as I'd hoped, but it would mean we can both get settled in our new situation. Please phone me back ASAP. D

There was so much to process and I really didn't have the head-space for it, so I packed all those thoughts inside that place in my mind where I'd go back later to retrieve. Some would be easy to access and action, and others might just stayed buried forever.

I looked at myself in the mirror, pulling the collar away from my neck as it was already making me feel too hot. The atmosphere was really becoming oppressive. A high neck coupled with long sleeves would not work on a day like today. Then, I took the dress off and dumped it on the bed, slid a different dress from its hanger in the wardrobe and slipped into that instead. It was a fairly simple pink and tan jersey dress, but nipped in at the waist in a flattering way with a braided belt. It did have a bit of a low neckline though, so I rummaged in the cloth bag where I kept some jewellery and pulled out my mother's silver and tourmaline necklace, hoping it would disguise a few creases on my skin. I realised as I fastened it around my neck that I rarely wore it. It was quite a statement piece and I'd not had many opportunities for a while. I'd like to think that there was some significance to me wearing it today. I could consider it a lucky charm and this would be the day I'd stumble on the painting, but I didn't feel that lucky.

I held the stone in my hand for a moment and remembered my mother: her gorgeous auburn hair, her smile and the way she looked like a statue of Persephone when she was deep in thought. I remembered her hands too and how they were never lined and old because she'd never become lined and old. The ring that belonged to her own mother, she used to wear on the third finger of her right hand. It was gold with tiny garnets set into a flower design and now sits on the third finger of my right hand.

'Where would you look for the painting, Mum?' I asked the room and the room didn't respond. It never did.

I stepped up to the mirror again and had a good look at myself, wondering how I compared to Douglas's Little Miss Maidenhead. I decided that for my age I didn't look too bad, then tugging the neckline of my dress up a bit, I slung my bag onto my shoulder and left the room.

23

DOROTHY

Dorothy was standing in front of the full-length mirror to check her appearance when Gina knocked at the door. She hoped the word *mutton* wasn't going to be forefront on everyone's lips when they saw her impractical slingbacks with killer points at the toe. The look was toned down with a silk floral dress that had cream and lilac peonies splashed across the fabric.

'You look fantastic,' Gina said. 'Those shoes! Some might kill for them.'

'These are shoes to kill *with*,' Dorothy said, brandishing one of the points. 'Might come in handy later. Although, maybe they're too much. I might end up killing myself trying to walk up to the church.'

'You look the perfect picture of grandmother to the groom. How are you feeling?'

'A little better, thank you. You look wonderful. You should wear dresses more often. Who knew you had such a trim waist. Although, with the cut of that dress I feel eyes will be centred a little higher.'

'Oh God, is it too much? I can change.'

'Goodness, no! You are perfect as you are, although, aren't you too hot with those long sleeves? Don't you have anything strappy?'

'I don't really do strappy to be honest.'

'Lots of women are worried unnecessarily about their arms as they get older, but I say be comfortable and sod what others think.'

Dorothy watched as Gina hesitated and then slowly pulled up the sleeve covering her right arm to reveal terrible scarring across her skin. It looked as if she'd been burned and badly. It took every bit of her strength not to gasp.

'Goodness, Gina, I don't know what to say.'

'I was burned in a house fire,' she said, simply. 'It was started deliberately. I was there with my mother, but only I made it out alive. I don't like the staring that comes with a scar like this. I find it's easier to just keep it covered up.'

'An arson attack! That's terrible and your poor mother too. How horrible for you. I'm so sorry you had to go through that and of course I understand why you cover it, but maybe among friends or family you don't feel that way?'

'I feel that way all the time with anybody I'm with to be honest. But I've been feeling like I need to reinvent myself recently. Not sure how to go about doing that.'

'How about learning to love the person you already are,' Dorothy said with a sympathetic smile.

'You're probably right – it's too late to try and be someone else now anyway.'

'Firstly, I say it's never too late to try something new, but in this instance I would ask you, what do you think is wrong with you, and who else do you propose to be?'

'Excellent questions for another time, perhaps,' Gina said walking over to the window while pulling her sleeve firmly back down. 'I'm afraid Juliet and I were not fruitful in our search this morning and we are seriously running out of easy places to look.'

'Where is Juliet now?' Dorothy asked.

'Gone to have an argument with her mother about what she can wear to the wedding.'

'Ah, perhaps it's for the best that she didn't get talked into that bridesmaid dress. I still have faith, you know.'

'In the bridesmaid dress?'

'In the painting.'

'The coaches are here,' Gina said, looking down onto the driveway. 'Lots more colourful dresses, but with hats this time. I feel sorry for men at weddings; they do get the short straw. Tight collars, long-sleeved shirts and jackets, strangulating ties. Women get to wear floaty silk, and hats to keep the sun from their faces.'

'There is a caveat to that,' Dorothy said. 'Shapewear underwear. There is nothing more sweat-inducing than that. Floaty on the outside maybe, trussed up underneath.'

She took a good look at the back of Gina as she watched the goings-on below. Her shoulders were a little hunched over all the time. She was always trying to make herself *less* somehow. And now, of course, Dorothy understood why that was. It made her feel even worse than she already did about what she'd asked Gina to do. Hadn't she wondered how biddable Gina was when she first met her? This woman needed love and care, not to be manipulated. But it was too late to change things now. Dorothy swallowed hard and considered that Gina might get as much of a boost from finding the painting as Dorothy would herself. And then she wondered if, as time was running out, she was still setting herself up for a huge disappointment.

'I'm sorry we weren't successful this morning. We searched the temple, the greenhouses and even some sheds,' Gina said as if she could see into Dorothy's mind and read her thoughts.

'I admire your resolve and I'm very grateful to you, Gina, but I have to refer back to my original point about it hanging in plain sight. He won't have it tucked away like a dusty nothing he pinched. He was incredibly competitive with Philip. I remain convinced that he will have it somewhere where he can see it as a daily reminder that he won. I'm honestly surprised it's not hanging over his bed.'

'I understand what you mean and now I've spent a few days with the man I can completely see that he would do that, but I have honestly looked and looked and can't think where else would be in plain sight. Harry is his right-hand man and has access to most of Leonard's personal spaces, but even *he* hasn't seen it. I'm at a loss. But we do have evidence of considerable theft and we can go to the police with that. I know it won't give you quite the comfort you're seeking, but maybe it might have to be enough.'

'We still have today and maybe even tomorrow morning before we all have to leave. Let's not lose all hope quite yet.'

'Shall we go then? I expect everyone is waiting in the entrance hall. I wonder what get-up Leonard will be sporting today?'

'I dread to think.'

Gina handed Dorothy her handbag from the bed and then took her arm.

'Let's leave that here,' Dorothy said, handing the bag back. 'I might very well need you to fetch that for me later.'

Peter had reserved the first two pews for the immediate family and Gina showed Dorothy to the front next to Miles and Lavinia, and Sophie and Luke. Juliet sat sullenly on the end wearing some lovely caramel-coloured trousers and a pretty blue silk top. She had pulled the side of her hair up into a silver clip. Dorothy smiled at her and she offered up a resigned shrug in response.

'I'll be more comfortable sitting at the back,' Gina said as Dorothy tried to get her to sit with them.

Dorothy didn't push it and hoped that Gina intended to slip out while the service was going on. She pulled Gina closer for a moment and made sure that her son and daughter-in-law were in conversation with Sophie.

'I forgot to ask you about Peter,' she whispered. 'Did you glean any information from him?'

Dorothy noted that Gina hesitated for just long enough for her to think that she had found out something, but she obviously decided to keep it to herself.

'No, just chit-chat,' Gina said, but Dorothy didn't believe her.

Peter was hovering with a Bible in his hands, walking back and forth, smiling at the guests, but when his eyes found Gina the smile faded and Dorothy saw him give her a brief nod. What that was supposed to signify, she wasn't sure, but he certainly looked a bit twitchy.

Gina left her then and found her way to the back of the church. Dorothy sat down next to Juliet and patted her knee.

'Am I allowed to say you look lovely?' she said, and Juliet gave her a half-smile.

'How about you just think it, Granny, and I won't talk about your shoes.'

'No Leonard yet,' Dorothy said to Sophie.

'I expect he's planning an entrance to upstage the bride,' Sophie replied.

'Oh, I see I'm not alone in my thoughts about that man then.'

'You may have been at the beginning of the week, but I've nearly had enough of him now,' said Sophie and Luke sniggered beside her.

Dorothy turned in her pew and her eyes travelled over the sea of hats and perfectly coiffured hair back to Gina, who seemed quite content sitting with a couple Dorothy had been introduced to at the garden party yesterday, but she couldn't remember their names.

The church looked lovely with the addition of the floral arrangements near the altar. The florist had done an amazing job in lemon-coloured roses and white lilies and even the ends of the pews had pretty little displays, the scent of them filling the cool air. The organist was playing Bach's 'Wachet Auf' and there was a quiet, but excited chatter among the guests.

The door opened then and Leonard finally walked in. All heads turned to watch him walk down the aisle as if he were the blushing bride. Dorothy was disappointed to see that he was dressed in traditional tails with his black hair slicked back and flicking up on his collar. He had a lemon rose in his buttonhole and Dorothy's honest and unwanted thought was that he looked quite handsome. She turned her attention to Peter and he was staring straight at Leonard with an expression that seemed to be a little savage. She wondered what his problem was, but then didn't everyone eventually have a problem with Leonard? Once Leonard reached the front he turned to survey the room and his eyes alighted on Dorothy. He smiled broadly at her, almost smugly, and she returned it with one of her own. *Please let today be the day,* she thought. *We surely must find it today.*

The strains of Pachelbel's 'Cannon in D' began and the door swung open to reveal Caroline having her veil rearranged by Katie. Her dress was as beautiful as Dorothy knew it would be. Traditional but not frothy, strapless but not sleazy, detailed but not fussy. She was a vision in ivory silk. Katie's dress was a simple design of the same material, but in lemon, and it suited her perfectly.

They began their walk down the aisle with all eyes on them apart from Toby, who Dorothy noticed was steadfastly looking forward as Caroline had apparently told him to do. Paul looked every bit the proud father with Caroline on his arm. Dorothy felt quite choked and reached for her handbag for a tissue, but of course she didn't have it. Sophie held one out for her and as she took it, she was aware that Juliet had a hand to her own face and was pretending to scratch at her cheek while secretly wiping a tear away.

Dorothy noticed as Katie walked past her that she was wearing a silver chain around her neck with a bird pendant in pale yellow enamel and it was a perfect match for her dress. She was sad that Juliet hadn't wanted to join them, but she could understand that for some, being on show was not a happy place to be.

They took their positions, Peter began to speak and the next time Dorothy looked behind her, Gina was gone.

24

GINA

It was the pendant that caught my eye. Katie looked beautiful in her lemon dress with ruched sleeves and sweetheart neckline. It gave her the perfect amount of cleavage for her necklace and the bird to sit comfortably.

Oddly it made me think about that ghastly stuffed bird in Leonard's Chinese cabinet and why he might have it there, what terrible taste he had in some things. And then my brain really started whirring. That bird had made me jump and I'd shut the cabinet noting that there was no painting to be seen. I should have looked more carefully; perhaps the bird was there as a deterrent, something to stop you looking any further. My hand reached for my mother's pendant. Wasn't I hoping for some luck today? Was this it? Was this the thunderbolt moment I'd been waiting for?

I watched as Leonard suddenly gave Dorothy a huge smile, but couldn't see what her response was. He really was exactly as Dorothy described him – odious. The organ music stopped, Peter began the service and then I quietly got up and slipped out of the door, holding the handle tightly until it closed silently behind me. Then I began a brisk walk back to the house via the woodland path.

Even with everyone inside the church I still felt I needed to keep to the shadows. Once I was back at the house I went inside through the door from the garden. The reception was to be solely in the orangery and the guests would be leaving from the front, so there wasn't any activity on this side of the house at all. The kitchen would be where it was all happening. All that food had to be taken up and kept warm before being served. Harry and his team had their work cut out for them.

I slipped in through the patio doors and made my way round to the main entrance hall and up the stairs to Leonard's wing. This was becoming a habit. Then as quickly and quietly as I could, I opened his bedroom door and stepped inside.

The first thing I noted was that Leonard's bed wasn't made and his curtains weren't tied back in perfect pleats as they had always been before. The second thing I noted was that the Chinese cabinet was open, the bird was lying on its side and behind it, where before there had been a lacquered back panel, it was open and a deep chamber – which would have been a perfect hiding place for a small coastal watercolour – was empty.

I sat down on the edge of his bed and let the full weight of disappointment wash over me. It was over. He'd known what we were doing. How could he not with me and Juliet tramping around his house? We'd been as subtle as Dorothy's shoes. Leonard had moved the painting – in a hurry by the looks of it. That broad smile he'd given Dorothy in the church earlier had been smug. Now I really thought about it, it hadn't been friendly; it had been victorious. I had honestly thought I'd been sneaky and clever, quiet and unassuming. I'd been a complete fool.

* * *

I slipped in through the door during a rousing rendition of 'Lord of the Dance' and managed to get back in my pew without making a fuss. The wife of the couple I was sitting next to did look questioningly at me, but I just mumbled something about needing the loo and the woman had nodded sympathetically in that united way women did – middle-aged and older women knew the score when it came to the loo.

The service was finishing and according to the order of service we were singing the final hymn. And then Peter was thanking everyone and congratulating the couple and the highly spirited 'Toccata' from Widor's *Organ Symphony No.5* began, signalling that it was time to leave. And I felt like crying at the sound of that music. I dabbed at the tears with a tissue before they could ruin my make-up. It wasn't just the painting and how close I'd come to finding it, but it was Douglas. He had played this at Alice's wedding. With permission from the organist he had taken over for the end of the service and had played us all out of the church. I took a deep breath, determined not to make a fool of myself. I tried not to blame Douglas for the disappointment I felt right now, but actually I did. I wouldn't be here in this church trying not to cry at the music if he hadn't left me. I'd be at home in Thame, gardening through a Saturday afternoon and then planning to cook a Saturday night curry and watching the time closely to see the numbers reach the magic six o'clock so I could open some wine. Instead I was at a stranger's wedding after a fruitless week, not quite being a companion and not finding a bloody painting.

Outside I hung back as the photos were taken. I couldn't face Dorothy knowing that I'd been so close to finding the watercolour. If I'd not been spooked by that bird I might have had the sense to explore the cabinet further when I'd had the chance. For years that had been my job, my career: to examine, explore and to discover. I'd failed considerably.

I watched Leonard like a hawk, but he didn't show any sign of being bothered by me. He didn't look like a man who had wrenched a hidden painting from his room knowing I was hunting it. In the end I went and chatted to a woman from Scotland and the woman's brother who were friends of Lavinia and Miles. They talked about books they'd enjoyed recently and how beautiful the city of Madrid was, how generous Leonard was for letting Caroline use his home for her wedding and that they were looking forward to the party they had planned back at the hotel later. Most of what they talked about went over the top of my head as all I could really think about was getting the train back home. And really that gave me no comfort at all.

It took an hour for the photos at the church and then Caroline encouraged the photographer to move towards the orangery so that the guests could all get a drink.

Leonard's staff were serving champagne and glasses of Buck's Fizz from silver trays. Then canapés circulated too. Beautifully made and delicious, the miniature bites would help soak up the alcohol that was flowing fast and furious. I thought that Caroline had made the right decision to leave early while everyone would still be on a high.

I took a glass of orange juice from a passing tray just as Leonard began tapping on the side of his own. The chatter died down instantly and all eyes were on him. When I really looked at him, I noticed that he looked tired too. His face was drawn and he had dark shadows under his eyes, but he was making every effort to look upbeat. The effect was that he appeared maniacal somehow. He looked slightly deranged.

'Thank you all again for coming and I would like to offer my hearty congratulations to the beautiful bride and her handsome husband.'

Leonard paused so everyone could shout *hear, hear* and then he continued.

'An incredible amount of work has gone into today and I hope so much that you are all having a wonderful time...' Pause for more praise directed at Leonard. 'And now to the moment you've all been waiting for... I have created for you a seven-course tasting menu with the finest ingredients sourced from the best producers in the UK. This really is something to behold and I hope you enjoy.'

As the group moved towards the open doors of the orangery I walked over to where Dorothy was standing. She had hold of Sophie's arm on one side and Juliet's on the other. I was slacking in my role as companion now too, although no one had said anything to me.

'Shall we get you inside so you can sit down?' I said and Dorothy nodded gratefully.

'Thank you, Gina. Come on, Juliet, let's go and find your father,' Sophie said.

'Can I sit with Granny?'

'We are sitting with Granny, and Gina and Granny's friend Yvonne is going to join us with her husband, Bill.'

'I don't have to sit with you,' I said. Being in the church was one thing, but a guest for the meal was something else.

'Of course you're going to sit with us,' Sophie said. 'You are very welcome.'

'Thank you,' I said, rather wishing I could disappear back to the house.

Juliet shoved her hands into her pockets as she walked away, and Sophie followed her, tucking the back of her daughter's hem into her waistband. I felt for her; thirteen was a difficult age. I still remembered how I had felt then. All my thoughts seemed fixed. I was never going to wear make-up and couldn't understand why anyone would waste their precious time applying it. I'd never get married or have children, I'd be far too busy with my donkey sanctuary for that nonsense. I'd travel the entire world, whilst also managing to look after my donkeys. I'd be a vet and a pop star and live in a cottage by the sea. But, within six months I'd totally reinvent myself. I'd be a scientist and work in a lab; I might have children, but no more than two and I'd still never get married. I'd seen first-hand what marriage could be like for some women. And so it went on. My mother had been brilliant through those times. Always encouraging me to do whatever I wanted rather than squashing my dreams as being as ridiculous as they probably were. And up until the point that she left my father and we moved back to the UK, I hadn't fully grasped how incredibly difficult it had been for her.

I realised with a horrible sinking feeling that it wasn't just Dorothy who was going to be disappointed, Juliet was very much invested in this too. Perhaps I could just leave Dorothy to break the news to her after I had disappeared back to Thame. I certainly wouldn't be moving in with Dorothy now.

What would my mother have done? The thought landed in my head unexpectedly. She would have been upfront and honest about it. She was someone who faced things head-on. No matter the consequences.

I took Dorothy's arm and we began to walk towards the door. Caroline and Toby were waiting to greet their guests and Leonard was hovering behind them like an annoying fly that needed squashing.

'You'd think he'd cooked the whole menu himself the way he announced it. I for one will be so glad to be going home tomorrow. I can't bear to be near that insufferable man for any longer than necessary,' said Dorothy.

'You and me both,' I said.

'Congratulations, my darling grandson and his beautiful wife!'

We'd reached the front of the queue and Dorothy was

embracing Caroline and Toby. I was face to face with Leonard and I couldn't think of a single thing to say.

'Gina, how have you enjoyed your week here as Dorothy's carer?'

'Companion, and very well. You have a wonderful home with some beautiful pieces and it has been the perfect venue for this wedding. Caroline and Toby are so lucky to have had the opportunity to have their special day in this special setting.'

I ran out of platitudes then and anyway, Dorothy was giving me a look.

'Are you quite well, Leonard?' Dorothy asked. 'I have to say, you look a little peaky.'

'Quite well thank you, Dot. Very much looking forward to this meal. What do you think of a seven-course taster menu? Sounds pretty amazing, doesn't it.'

'Philip and I had a taster menu in a Michelin-starred restaurant once. It was rather lacking in substance and we stopped for chips on the way home. Shall we, Gina?'

I suppressed the giggle that was threatening to erupt out of my mouth and guided Dorothy past the incandescent Leonard.

We were the first to arrive at the table and I pulled out the chair for Dorothy. Everyone else in the room was standing behind their chairs waiting for the bride and groom to take their own seats, but judging by the queue to greet them it might be a while.

'Just sit for a bit,' I suggested. 'If you want to, you can stand back up when they come in. No one's going to mind.'

Dorothy sat down gratefully and helped herself to a glass of water from the table. It was decorated just as Caroline described with a beautiful low-hung chandelier above us and displays of trailing pale-yellow and white flowers in the centre of the table. There were gifts of little boxed chocolates for each guest to take away, but a lack of table confetti, which pleased me. I'd often been to weddings where the table was littered and you were forever picking it from your sleeves.

I hesitated over whether to bring Dorothy up to speed with what I had found out about Leonard and Peter, and then decided that it was best not to. It really wasn't anyone else's business and he'd already had his privacy violated by Leonard; he certainly didn't need me spreading nasty gossip too. I opened my mouth to let her know that Leonard had moved the painting and that it was unlikely we'd find it now, but then I closed it again. I'd leave that disappointment until after the meal. I should let her enjoy it. There was time enough to deliver that blow later.

We were joined then by the rest of our table. Yvonne sat down next to Dorothy with Bill on the other side of her. Juliet sat next to me, and Sophie and Luke sat opposite. I noticed that Sophie found Luke's hand as he reached for the menu on the table in front of him and they shared a sweet smile. Juliet might be very much relieved and I was sure Dorothy would be too.

Then the first course arrived and someone poured me a glass of wine. I picked up the menu from the table in front of me. *Amuse-Bouche and Breads* it read for the first course.

'Go easy on the bread if we've got seven of these to get through,' said Dorothy.

'What, not stopping for chips on the way home?' I said.

'I made that up, of course. I just wanted to wipe that smug smile from his irritating face.'

'It worked – he looked thunderous.'

'One must get one's digs in whilst one can.'

In fact, it was hard not to devour the whole lot of miniature homemade breads, piquant butter and tiny cup of intense mushroom soup. So I did and then reached again for the menu to see what was next.

There was relaxed conversation around the table during the

next two courses of *Pea and Mint Tart* followed by *Hand-Dived Scallop Ceviche*. I tried to include Juliet in the chatter about our week in Leonard's manor, but she wasn't offering much apart from pointed looks. I would have to tell her, but I wasn't looking forward to it.

'I've been invited to go away in October,' Dorothy said.

'Where?' Sophie asked her.

'My friend was supposed to be joining me for a cruise around the Med, but her hip replacement has been brought forward and she's desperate to get it done,' Yvonne said. 'So I asked if Dot would like to come with me instead.'

'And she knows I won't go,' Bill said.

'Yes, you'd never get Bill on a floating hotel. You're keen, though aren't you, Dot?'

'I am,' she said. 'Let's get this week done and then we can talk about it properly.'

I noticed Sophie give Luke a dubious look, but then the conversation moved on to various joints being replaced. And Bill seemed like he had a lot to say on the matter. I glanced at Juliet and smiled as she gave me a look that said *kill me now.*

Then my phone pinged in my bag by my feet and as I bent to retrieve it and discreetly read the message on my lap I saw it was from Juliet who wanted to know what was happening and what we were going to do next. I quickly responded, saying we'd talk after. I also noticed I'd missed a message from Alice confirming our lunch next week. I didn't respond to that.

'Sorry,' I said to the group. 'My daughter messaging me. I'll talk to her later.'

'You have a family?' Sophie asked me. 'I'm sorry I've not asked you anything about yourself.'

'You've no need to. I'm here to look after Dorothy,' I said and we all turned to look at Dorothy who was looking a little paler than earlier. Another job I wasn't doing particularly well. 'I do have a daughter – Alice – and a son – Christopher, Chris. Alice has two little girls, so I'm a granny too, which is lovely.'

'And you're newly single, I think you mentioned on the minibus the other day?' Sophie said, but before I had the chance to respond and say it had been Dorothy who had divulged that tit-bit of information, the staff were bustling around and clearing the plates away and I could hear someone talking behind me. I looked round to see two waiting staff standing close together and whispering. I caught only a few of the words they were exchanging, but it was enough. Harry had disappeared.

25

GINA

'Would you excuse me for a moment,' I said.

I pushed my chair back and without looking at those seated at the table I got up and left as quickly as I could. I walked past the huge refrigerated van that had been used to bring the food and drink from the house. The staff had a table to plate up and a portable oven to keep those plates warm for all the courses. There was a posh toilet block that had been erected, but I walked past that too, hoping no one inside the orangery could see me, but then I didn't really care any more. I made my way back down the path to the house.

The kitchen was alive with energy. Flustered staff were cooking and preparing dishes ready to go in the van when it returned. Everything was lined up and they clearly had things under control despite the furore and also despite the fact that Harry was nowhere to be seen. I asked a couple of them if they'd seen him. Two shrugged that they didn't know who I was talking about and another said he'd disappeared.

I left them to it and made my way back up the stairs to Harry's room. I knocked on the door, but there was no answer, so I decided to chance it and go in. I half expected the door to be locked, but it wasn't and I hesitated with my hand on the handle, not entirely sure what I was going to find. Then I took a breath and pushed open the door.

Harry's bed was made perfectly, his curtains were neatly tied back and there was no sign that he'd ever been there. So, he'd done it, his version of handing in his notice. That was it then. He hadn't found the painting before Leonard; that tiny glimmer of hope was extinguished. We were all vacating the house tomorrow and nothing at all had been resolved.

I sat down on the end of his bed and rubbed my hands across my eyes, suddenly feeling every one of those missing hours of sleep from the last few nights. Then I remembered my carefully applied mascara and got up and looked in Harry's mirror. Disaster, I looked like I'd been crying or as if someone had thumped me in both eyes. I'd need to wash my face and reapply my make-up. Then again, did I really need to go back to the wedding? Was my presence all that important? Did we still need to keep up the facade of me being Dorothy's companion? The trouble was that it wasn't in my nature to abandon a situation. I'd need to see it through to the end no matter that the finish line had been crossed and we were definitely in last place. I returned to my own room to sort my face out.

Two things happened as I opened the door to my bedroom: my phone pinged with yet another message at the same time as I noticed there was a package on my bed. I ignored my phone for the moment and picked up the package. It was the size of a tea tray and I knew immediately it was a painting. I could feel the edges of the frame and when I pulled back the bubble wrap, used to cover it, I could see that it wasn't just *a* painting, it was *the* painting. My heart leaped at the sight of it. After a week of trying to find it, it was just there on my bed, easy as that. Now I could see it up close and in the flesh, so to speak, I realised I'd been a bit dismissive of it before. It was actually a lovely watercolour of a coastal scene: a headland and a beach with a stretch of rocks and a lighthouse. I turned it over and the artist had written *Bamburgh* on the back. If my geography was correct, I was pretty sure it was a coastal scene from the North East.

Had Leonard given up? Was he finally ready to admit his part in this whole sorry story? From what I had learned of him over the last few days, I knew this couldn't be true. Leonard didn't give up. It wasn't in his nature.

It was when my phone pinged a second and then a third time that I took it out of my bag and read the messages. The first one was from Dorothy asking if I was okay. I hesitated over my reply, full of wanting to tell her all about the painting, but it occurred to me that Leonard must not know right now that I had it and I couldn't fully trust Dorothy not to march up to the top table and expose him. He would obviously take it back given any opportunity. I had to get it out of this house and find a better hiding place. But where?

The other messages were from Harry. The first was a photo of the painting sitting at the back of the Chinese cabinet with the words 'for what it's worth' typed underneath and the other message said to phone him on this number. I dialled the number straight away.

'Harry?' I said when the call connected.

'Yes,' he said simply and I could hear from the background noise that he was driving.

'So you've gone then? I don't blame you.'

'I had to. I can't be there when the police come and you'll phone them now you have the painting. You have found it haven't you? It was behind the panel in that white cabinet. I've sent you a picture, although it doesn't really prove much. Could be useful, though.'

'Yes, thank you, Harry, you're a star.'

'I'm a criminal, Gina, and it's hard to stop that when you keep mixing with people like Len.'

'Please find some better people to mix with, then. Stay away from the Leonards of the world.'

'I was born into a family of Leonards. It was drugs mostly and how easy it is to get your kids to deal for you. Hard to ditch a learned lifestyle, but it's more than that. You try and stay away, do a good job, do something decent with your life, but somehow the Leonards always find you.'

'You are an amazing chef. My advice would be to go as far away as you can afford to and start again. Do you need some money? I don't have a lot, but could stretch to a one-way plane or train ticket somewhere.'

'Gina, you're a good person and probably had a good start in life.'

'You'd be surprised,' I said.

'I don't need your money, thanks. I may have lifted a couple of things Leonard won't miss too much.'

'I'm not going to judge. Just use it for good, please, and thanks again. I can't tell you how much this will mean to Dorothy.'

'My advice is to get that painting out of the house before he finds out it's gone. Hide it well until you need it.'

'Was someone trying to kill Leonard?' I asked him. 'There was a time we thought it might be Paul.'

Harry laughed.

'It was me,' he said, 'but it was only a half-hearted attempt, clearly. My heart wasn't really in it. I didn't fancy going down for murder. Oh, but there's something else. I didn't want to say the other night in the kitchen with the kid being there because it's her family, but the person who took Dorothy's painting is one of them. Leonard told me, but he didn't say who. You'd better prepare Dorothy for disappointment as well. I've got to go. Thanks, Gina.'

'Good luck,' I said and then he was gone.

I smiled. I finally had everything I needed to give to Dorothy so she could expose Leonard. Looking at my watch I realised I'd been gone for half an hour. They'd be halfway through the fourth course by now. I was no longer hungry as my stomach was full of butterflies, but I did need to get back before Leonard realised I wasn't there; if he hadn't already. Remembering that I had to stay calm and act as if nothing had changed, I typed back a message to Dorothy to say I'd come back to the house for some paracetamol for a headache and I'd be back within half an hour once the painkillers had taken effect. I spent five minutes washing my face and making it as presentable as possible, then began to look for a hiding place in my bedroom. No, I needed to do what Harry had suggested and get it out of the house. Where though? Who did I trust enough to hide a painting? And then I remembered the church.

* * *

The church was, of course, deserted. Peter was currently enjoying the meal with the rest of the guests. He had an open-door policy though and I was able to walk straight in. Peter felt like an ally now. He didn't like or trust Leonard the same as Dorothy and I was convinced he'd help given the opportunity. Also the church was probably not a place that Leonard would think to look, certainly not in the short term when it mattered. In the long term, I very much hoped the business would be out of my hands.

I quickly looked around for a good hiding place. I tried to wedge it down the back of the radiator, but it wouldn't fit. I lifted the lid of the font, but changed my mind in case there was a christening tomorrow and Peter wasn't the first to find it. I even considered the monument, but I'd never have the strength to push the lid on it and surely it was incredibly disrespectful even if there wasn't a body inside.

'Argh! Come on, Gina,' I urged myself. 'You don't have time for this.'

Then I remembered Dorothy's words *hidden in plain sight* and thought about hanging it on the wall. My eyes roamed until they fell upon the wooden plaque where the hymn numbers were listed. I pulled over a chair and stood up on the seat so I could reach the plaque. When I pulled it off the wall I could see it was made like a box with a space behind it. With great luck and the bubble wrap removed, the painting fitted just inside and I replaced it on the wall. I hoped that this would all be resolved one way or another before tomorrow's service when the hymn numbers might need to be changed. To be honest, the next step of this drama would begin to play out as soon as Leonard saw the painting was gone from his room, if Dorothy didn't get her victory accusation in first. Surely that would be tonight.

As I climbed down from the chair I could hear a low rumble of thunder in the distance as if I needed a reminder of how alarming this whole adventure was. Lavinia's storm was coming.

Pushing the chair back into its space I rushed from the church, shoved the bubble wrap into the dustbin out the back and I was off to the orangery, my heart racing.

Everyone had just finished their main course of Norfolk lamb as I sat back down and I had missed not only that but also the palate cleansing lemon and fennel. I reassured the others at the table I was fine now and it was just a minor headache. I also apologised for disappearing and gave Dorothy a smile, wishing I could say more. Leonard, at the top table, stared at me for longer than was comfortable through very narrowed eyes but I looked away, a genuine headache beginning. So, my disappearing act hadn't gone unnoticed. I poured myself a large glass of water and then took my phone out of my bag and put it into my pocket. I had proof of the painting being in Leonard's bedroom, or certainly a photo of it on my phone and it suddenly felt much more precious. If Leonard got hold of it and deleted it, what did I have? I suddenly worried that all I'd done by hiding it in the church was pass the blame onto Peter. But no, I'd got Harry's word on where it had been, if Harry's word would be believed. I pushed all of the scenarios out of my head because I was being just a little bit paranoid.

I had done all I could for now. I felt happy to wait for dessert and cheese and biscuits to arrive.

26

DOROTHY

Dorothy was beginning to flag now and had kicked her shoes off under the table. Gina looked wired, though and Dorothy wondered if she'd had too much to drink on top of the painkillers.

She had been mostly confident all week that Gina would find the painting and she'd been certainly hopeful, but time was almost up now and even *her* optimism was waning. She was also feeling a bit under the weather and could really do with resting somewhere quietly. She decided to keep her old lady card up her sleeve for a little longer.

She managed to get through the speeches – through all the words of love from Paul, the thanks and gratitude from Toby, the tales of drinking games and fun from a rather drunk Rufus and the sickening words of self-congratulations from Leonard. All she wanted to do was have a quiet time to herself, preferably horizontally.

And then Dorothy squeezed her feet back into her shoes and they walked round to the front of the house to see the bride and groom off. The car was a Rolls-Royce Silver Shadow and the couple looked so happy as they walked down the red carpet and under the floral arbour, pausing for more photos. It was much prettier than Lavinia had described it to her, the whole thing festooned in lemon roses and white lilies. It would certainly make for some lovely photographs for the album.

Toby had his arm around Caroline and she had her head on his shoulder. The photographer was snapping away and not for the first time Dorothy felt a stab of guilt at what she'd orchestrated. The fact that the couple had no idea what had been going on while they had been enjoying their wedding, in fact what had been going on while they had been enjoying their week, suddenly made her feel terrible. Using their wedding was never going to be her finest moment. Maybe she wouldn't feel quite so bad if they'd been successful.

Leonard had indeed tied some silver and yellow bells to the back of the car, which was a lovely touch, and Dorothy thought that he was the oddest of men. Someone capable of causing both extreme trauma and great joy.

Caroline whooped in delight at the bells and after enveloping everyone in the warmest of embraces, including Leonard, she ordered everyone to stand in a group so she could throw her bouquet. Gina, Dorothy noticed, stood as far to one side as it was possible to be. The beautifully handcrafted bouquet flew through the air and was caught by one delighted guest who looked straight to her unsuspecting boyfriend, but he smiled gamely. Then the new couple climbed inside the Rolls and the car set off down the driveway with everyone cheering and waving behind them.

Within minutes two coaches arrived to whisk the rest of the guests away and Dorothy marvelled at the foresight of this. Without the bride and groom, their guests were suddenly a bit of a nuisance to Leonard.

Once they had all departed Leonard turned to the remaining group.

'Well, that really was a golden wedding day. Let's have champagne in the garden now we have the place to ourselves again,' he
said and without waiting for a response, he walked inside the
house.

'Well, I think that all went marvellously,' Paul said and Sandra
agreed. 'Shame you had to get so drunk though, Rufus.'

Rufus shrugged. He seemed to have lost a bit of the sparkle he
had during the wedding earlier. Perhaps the booze was really
affecting him. It was quite hot standing out on the driveway.
Dorothy was certainly feeling it now.

'Why don't we go and find some shade?' Gina suggested.

'Great idea,' Lavinia, said looking up. 'Although, shade may
just have found us. Did you all hear that rumble of thunder
earlier?'

They all looked up then to see a mass of dark clouds gathering.

'I did say there was a storm forecast. Luckily it didn't arrive
during the wedding.'

'Can't believe our little boy is married,' Miles said.

'And to our little girl,' said Paul, laughing. 'Our families will be
entwined from here on.'

'Why anyone would want to be entwined with us is a mystery,'
Rufus said, grimly, and followed Leonard into the house. The group
fractured then, but agreed to meet shortly in the garden for the
promised champagne. Gina held Dorothy back as the others
walked away.

'Dorothy, what would be the icing on the cake for this wedding?'
she asked.

'A swift removal of these uncomfortable shoes would be a good
start and then, I suppose, a chilled glass of champagne wouldn't be
the worst thing.'

'You look exhausted,' Gina said to her. 'Come on then, let's get
that sorted.'

She took Dorothy's arm, led her inside the house and up the stairs to her bedroom.

Dorothy sat in her chair with her head back against the wall. She was worried that if she did lie down on the bed she might never get up again.

'Are you feeling okay?' Gina asked, but Dorothy didn't have the energy to answer and she closed her eyes. 'Dorothy?' Gina tried again while laying her hand gently on the older woman's arm.

'I'm just tired, Gina,' she said. 'I think the wine I had at lunch and then the sun has got to me a bit.'

'Are you well enough to hear some news?' Gina asked tentatively.

Dorothy opened her eyes then, her brain firing up again at Gina's words.

'Yes, if it's good news,' she said, sitting forward.

Gina crouched down and took both of Dorothy's hands in hers.

'We have it; we have the painting,' she said, the brightest of smiles on her face. 'Harry has left, but he found it before he went. It was a parting gift.'

'Where was it?' Dorothy asked quietly.

'It was just as you said it would be, hidden in plain sight in the Chinese cabinet in his bedroom. When I went looking it wasn't there, but I could see where it would have been and thought Leonard had moved it, but it was Harry. He knew where the key was. Turns out he was pretty decent after all.'

'Where is it now? Have you hidden it?'

'Yes, I've hidden it in the church. I doubt Peter would find it, but after talking to him last night, I do believe we can trust him.'

'So, it's over,' Dorothy said, tears springing into her eyes as she fully comprehended what Gina was telling her. 'Justice for my Philip at last.'

'It is partly over, but you need to decide what to do now. I suggest you hand it all over to Miles and let him deal with the police and Leonard. I think you've done your bit.'

'I think *you've* done more than my bit actually,' Dorothy said, catching Gina's hands tightly in her own. 'I will be forever grateful to you.'

* * *

It was a delighted Dorothy who accompanied Gina down into the garden. The others were a glass ahead of them and Dorothy readily accepted one from Leonard with a very large smile on her face.

'You look invigorated, Dot, my dear,' Leonard said, surprised at her countenance. He looked a bit uncomfortable with the change. As much as Dorothy would have loved to have told him right then, about the painting, she held back. Gina was right and she needed to hand it all over to Miles now. He would know how best to act. She decided she'd allow herself a little bit of a victory speech, though and she raised her glass.

'I just wanted to say that it has been a wonderful day. Two young people are now married and on their way in life. I think Caroline and Toby are well suited and I wish them all the happiness.'

She took a sip of her drink and everyone followed her cue.

'And I want to thank my companion, Gina, who has been a great comfort to me this week. I shall be forever grateful for the care and consideration that she has afforded me.'

They all quietly sipped again.

'And to you, Leonard for opening up your house and showing us all what fabulous treasures you have collected. For finally giving me the opportunity to find *one* real gem among them.'

Everyone sipped again, but neither Leonard nor Dorothy did. The two of them had their eyes locked together, and Leonard actually looked like he was squirming under Dorothy's steely gaze. And Dorothy watched as his expression changed and there was a moment of clarity. He suddenly placed his glass down on the table and turned for the house.

'Please excuse me for a moment. I need to go and speak to Harry,' he said, and quickly walked away.

'I haven't seen Harry all afternoon,' Paul said.

'He's gone,' said Juliet. 'I saw him leaving as we walked round to the orangery. I went back to the house to charge my phone and he was sneaking out the kitchen door with a huge bag.'

'Bit off, leaving Leonard in the lurch,' Paul said, and Sandra gave him a long-practised withering look.

'I really don't know why you have such a soft spot for Leonard,' she said. 'He constantly takes whatever he wants and now he's taken away our future.'

'It was hardly ours in the first place,' Paul said sitting down heavily in a garden chair. Picking up the bottle of champagne he sloshed some into his glass. 'I really don't know why you have it in for him all the time. He's been the perfect host all this week and given our Caroline a wonderful wedding. I think you could be a little more grateful.'

'And, like Rufus, I think you could be a little less drunk,' Sandra hissed and then turned her back in a gesture reminiscent of Juliet.

Dorothy and Gina shared a look and then Gina moved a bit closer to her.

'Do you think I should go and tell Peter where I've hidden the painting?' Gina asked her quietly.

'Yes, go and do that, then we have him onside when we call the police. Take Juliet with you and let her know. Battle lines are about to be drawn and I'm going to have a long-overdue conversation with my son and daughter.'

27

GINA

Juliet and I walked quickly down to the rectory while I filled her in on what had happened.

'So, it's all over and no one had a fight or anything good then?'

'No one has had a fight yet, Juliet. There's still time.'

'What now then? Granny gets her painting back, Leonard goes to prison and everyone else lives happily ever after?'

'I don't know about that. I have to say, though, Harry said the thief of the painting is one of the family group. I just wanted you to prepare yourself.'

'I bet it's Rufus. He seems mad and sad all the time.'

'Well, I don't know about that, but it would be a big shame if it was him. And I don't know what Leonard could have on him.'

'He cheated in his uni exams or something like that – I know that.'

'What? How do you know that?'

'I heard him talking to his mum. I didn't catch all of it, but she was saying something about how he'd shamed the whole family and that there were far-reaching consequences or something. Leonard's name was mentioned, but the sound quality wasn't great on the recording. I kept it, though. And to be honest, I thought it was pretty cool.'

'Cheating on your exams is absolutely not cool!' I said, horrified.

'No, I know that, but getting away with it is,' Juliet said.

We had reached the rectory at this point and I leaned forward and knocked on the door. It was a few minutes until Peter opened it and I had begun to wonder if he was in the church. His hair was a little dishevelled where he'd clearly been asleep.

'Gina, Juliet, you've caught me having a nap. It might have been those lovely refreshments at the reception,' he said running his fingers through his hair and laughing. 'Everything okay?'

'We've found the painting and I've hidden it behind the wooden plaque with the hymn numbers in the church. Dorothy is currently telling her son and daughter and Harry has gone and he's left us with the news that the original thief of the painting is one of the group,' I garbled.

'And I think it's Rufus,' said Juliet.

'Goodness, it's all going on then. How long have I been asleep exactly?' He glanced at his watch, but I knew it was a rhetorical question.

'We wondered if you could come and mediate for us?' I asked him. 'Not sure how Leonard will react and when might be the best time to phone the police. But then, that really isn't an issue for me to worry about; that really is for the family to sort out, I suppose.'

'You've been such a good friend to Dorothy this week. I'm sure she is ever so grateful.'

'Granny will be delighted,' Juliet said. 'I bet she'll leave that painting to you in her will.'

Juliet laughed, but I suddenly felt uncomfortable. Leonard was unpredictable and had now been cornered in his own home.

'I think we should get back, but what should we do about the painting?'

'We can't confront him without it,' Juliet said.

'You won't be confronting anyone, young lady,' I said.

'God, you sound just like my mum.'

'Where are we with what's going on? What does Leonard know?' Peter asked.

'So far, Dorothy has just hinted that she's found the painting, but only a slight mention and Leonard went dashing off into the house saying he was looking for Harry. But of course he won't find him because we know he's gone.'

'So it's likely he'll be looking for Harry, find him and his things gone, and then may go and check on the painting. He may well think that Harry has taken it. He might even think that Harry has taken it to protect himself. Is that too much of a stretch, do you think?'

'Yes,' Juliet and I both said at the same time.

'Let's leave the painting where it is for now – it's a great hiding place, Gina. Leonard won't look there. Let's get back to the house and see how things stand.'

We left the rectory and walked back towards Walstone Hall. The gathering clouds were becoming darker and angrier-looking and I didn't think we'd be in the garden for long.

Everyone was exactly as we had left them, but now they were animated and arguing. Leonard was nowhere to be seen.

'You've been doing *what* this week?!'

Miles had his voice raised and Dorothy was standing with her hands on her hips.

'I didn't want to tell you because we've been through this before and firstly I didn't want to get your hopes up if we couldn't find it and also because, if you're honest, you didn't really think Leonard had taken it,' Dorothy said. 'You thought I was being a silly, grieving old woman and I do understand that.'

'Of course I didn't think he'd taken it! Do you think I'd be merrily using his house as a wedding venue if I thought for one minute that he had been responsible for the death of my father! Oh, Mum,' Miles said, stepping forward and folding Dorothy into his arms. 'I'm sorry we didn't listen to you. I'm going to bloody kill him.'

'Uncle Len has always taken whatever he wanted,' Rufus joined in then, but he seemed to struggle to get out his words with the amount of alcohol he'd consumed. I glanced at Sandra and she looked stricken. Then, she sat down next to Paul, poured herself a glass of champagne and drank the lot down in one go.

'Dorothy,' Sandra said as she poured herself another. 'I think it's time to—'

'Celebrate,' Dorothy said. 'Yes, we *should* be celebrating. Leonard is a nasty and manipulative man and I am so glad we have him at last.'

I had my eyes on Sandra as the woman drank down the contents of a second glass. She was going to be catching up with her son at that rate. I watched as Rufus put his hand on her arm and gave her a nervous glance. I felt that things were going to take an unpleasant turn, if they could even be more unpleasant. Was Rufus the thief? Did Sandra know and was she about to reveal his secret? But no, I suddenly realised the truth.

'So, where is this painting then?' asked Sandra.

'Don't tell her,' I blurted out.

'Why ever not?' Dorothy asked.

'Because—'

'Please don't, Gina, please don't,' Sandra said in an anguished whisper.

'Because I think she's the thief.'

There was a moment of stunned silence with the whole group staring at me and then Sandra collapsed into a chair with her head in her hands and all eyes turned to her. I walked over to stand next to Dorothy who looked troubled and then I helped her into a chair too.

'Sandra, please tell me this is a sick joke,' Paul said in a low voice, his hand on his chest as if he might need to restart his own heart. 'You didn't break into Dorothy's house. You couldn't have – it's impossible.'

'I wish I could say it was a joke,' came Sandra's muffled voice from between her hands.

'But, Philip,' he said.

'That wasn't meant to happen. They weren't meant to be there,' she said and she was crying now. 'I'm so sorry, Dorothy. I hate myself.'

'Don't you dare,' Miles said. 'You don't get to cry and be upset about this. My father is dead because of you. How could you!' Miles's voice broke at the end of his words and he took deep ragged breaths to try and regain control. Lavinia, who looked traumatised herself, took his arm as much to comfort him as to comfort herself.

I had my own hand on Dorothy's shoulder and I could feel her shaking under my touch. I hadn't done what Harry had suggested and prepared her. I had been taken over by the excitement and hadn't remembered what I'd said to Dorothy before about repercussions.

'What did he have on you?' Dorothy asked, her voice quiet and controlled. 'How did Leonard get you to do it? Not money?'

'No, not money, I would never have done it for that,' Sandra said.

'What then? You'd better start being honest now,' Miles said, but there was only silence from Sandra.

'It was because of me,' Rufus said. 'Mum did it because of me.'

'Well, you'd better start talking then,' Sophie said, her expression furious.

I realised that Dorothy's family had all moved closer to her in some sort of protective stance and I moved back a little to accommodate them.

'I had my degree certificate forged,' he said. 'So basically I was taken on at the law firm under false pretences. Uncle Leonard knew someone who could help me and to start with he was just happy to have helped, but then he wanted me to do something in return. He told me he wanted Philip's painting and he wanted me to steal it. I told him I wouldn't do it, but then he became more and more demanding. I went to Mum because I was out of my depth, with work and then with this. I just wanted it all to go away. Mum went to see Uncle Len and said that she would do it if that would be the end of it all. And then, of course it all went wrong and it's all my fault.'

'Yes it bloody is!' Paul shouted. 'I don't know my own family. How could you both have done this?'

'It's Leonard's fault,' Peter suddenly said. 'And someone needs to go and find him before he disappears too. We can pick this all apart later, but it stops with him.'

'Peter's right,' Sophie said. 'Let's get him out here to give his account.'

'I don't want him anywhere near me,' Paul said. 'I might actually do him harm.'

They all moved towards the house then, apart from Sandra who'd been told not to move a muscle by her husband. Paul looked as if he was going to say something further, but then, as if he couldn't bear to be near his wife, he followed the others with a resigned sigh. She began to talk to Dorothy, but Dorothy cut her off before she could really get going.

'Sandra, I can't hear another apology, not now. I might be able to tomorrow, but not now please. It's all a bit raw.'

Sandra nodded and then buried her head back in her hands.

'Gina, I think you should go and help the others. You have a better knowledge of this house and all its hiding places now. I'll go to my room.'

I helped Dorothy up to her bedroom and then followed the sound of scurrying steps until I found the rest of the group. I showed them the secret room, but he wasn't in there, the attic or any of the rooms in his wing. The others had scoured the rest of the place and it was clear very quickly that Leonard was nowhere in Walstone Hall.

* * *

The first drops of rain began to fall as we all walked back out into the garden, so we gathered up glasses and bottles and took everything back inside.

'I'm going to take the golf buggy over to the tower in case he's decided to hole himself up in there until the morning,' Paul said.

'Good idea,' said Miles. 'I'll come with you. He might need persuading to come back, which will be easier with two.'

I thought about a scuffle between the three men and was glad Dorothy wouldn't be around to witness it.

'Is it okay if I go to my room?' Sandra asked.

'As long as you're there when I get back,' Paul said.

'Of course I will be,' she said, but Paul just gave her a long look.

After they'd gone, the rest of us decided to sit in the music room and I offered to make some coffee. It was as I walked back up the stairs with the tray that the first flare of lightning lit the sky and it illuminated the darkening hallway as it flashed through the window. It was shortly followed by a crack of thunder and then the rain really came down.

We sat in relative silence as we waited. The coffee was drunk, the biscuits ignored and it was an hour and a half before the men returned without Leonard. They were soaked through and I went to make more hot coffee as Lavinia found towels and dry clothes.

'He's not in the tower, nowhere we can see driving around his land. His bike, his car and the minibus are here, so wherever he's gone is on foot in this storm,' Miles said.

'It looks as if he rummaged for some clothes in his room,' Sophie said. 'A couple of drawers were pulled out, so I'm guessing he must have left pretty quickly after he realised the painting had been found. He's had a good head start and, to be honest, he could be anywhere by now.'

'Should we phone the police?' I asked tentatively.

I wasn't entirely sure how I would be received as the person colluding with Dorothy all week. Juliet luckily had kept her mouth shut about her small part in it so far.

'I think we should leave it until the morning, get some sleep and decide what's best to do. This is far more than just Leonard being a thief. There's much more to consider,' Miles said and Paul looked relieved.

I wanted to point out that the longer it was left the further Leonard would get, but decided that it was their business. We all dispersed then and I was very glad to slip inside the covers of my bed. I was exhausted, but sleep wouldn't come easily and I lay awake listening to the storm crashing outside for hours before I finally drifted off.

28

GINA

I woke at six-thirty to a tapping noise outside the bedroom window. I'd not slept well, with the storm raging all night and my dreams had been a mangled mix of art, fire and death. The thunder had finally rolled away in the early hours and now the sun was shining through the gap in the curtains. I pushed the covers back and then pulled the curtains open. The tapping was the last of the rain dripping from the roof and onto the windowsill.

I wasn't sure what they were going to do today. Nothing had really been decided. Sandra had been suitably contrite, but what would happen to her once the police arrived? Surely they would phone the police. Leonard had to be found and would need to answer for his part in all this, not to mention the stolen items in his home. But he'd be long gone. He had money and if he'd thought to take his passport he could be anywhere by now.

Most importantly I needed to check on Dorothy. She'd had a huge shock last night and I hoped she'd managed to get some sleep. I wrapped my dressing gown around myself and walked to Dorothy's bedroom.

I tapped lightly on the door, not wanting to wake her if she was asleep, but her voice came out clearly and very much awake.

'Come in.'

'Good morning,' I said, closing the door behind me. 'How are you feeling this morning?'

Dorothy was sitting up in bed with her pillows pushed up behind her back. She had a book in her hands, open at the first page. I guessed she didn't really have the headspace to concentrate on a story. Not when she had her own going on.

'I did sleep quite well, surprisingly. Now I feel both relieved and sad and that won't change. How could it possibly?'

I sat down on the end of the bed and folded my arms across my chest.

'How do you see things playing out today? How would you like things to be resolved?'

'I'd like Leonard to turn up and accept responsibility for everything and I'd like to go back to that time yesterday evening before I found out that Sandra was actually the person responsible for the death of my husband, even if it was an accident. I do see it was an accident; I always have. I was so fixated on Leonard that I took my eyes off the thief themselves. Sandra is clearly incredibly sorry and it's obvious she didn't want to do it, but she still did. She chose to do Leonard's bidding to save the reputation of her son. A mother's love should only go so far.'

'But you do have the painting and evidence that Leonard had it in his possession. That was what this was all about, so don't lose sight of that victory in all of this other mess,' I said.

'You're right, and I'm so grateful to you for that.'

'Well, it was Harry who found it in the end – don't forget.'

'Yes, but he wouldn't have even looked if you hadn't approached him and explained the situation. This is all because of you, Gina.'

I wasn't sure how I felt about upending a happy family on what should have been such a joyous occasion.

'Can I get you a cup of tea?' I asked her.

I wanted to be practical and helpful, but not give over my own opinion in what was going to be a very tricky situation to resolve.

'I would love one, thank you. Miles said we'd all meet and talk at breakfast when everyone had had a chance to think about what was best to do, but I doubt that will be for a while and I'd love a drink.'

Dorothy had given up the pretence of reading the book and as I got up and left the room she closed it and rested her head back against the pillows.

The house was silent. All the wedding paraphernalia had been cleared up and removed yesterday afternoon. Harry was gone and all the family were asleep, or certainly in their rooms. I took a moment to wander the downstairs rooms alone, to soak up the beauty of the house on what was going to be my last day in it. I'd checked the train times and had a taxi booked for early afternoon. Dorothy and her family had more to deal with, but I was going home.

In the kitchen I boiled the kettle and pulled some cups down from the cupboard. I found a pot and a tray, some sugar and a couple of biscuits that I put on a plate. Then I stood with my back against the counter and waited for the kettle to boil.

I thought again about Dorothy's offer of her boathouse. It was actually a very appealing offer and if I was going to rent a flat somewhere then could it be there? I'd talk to Alice and Chris and see what they thought about it. I needed to talk to Douglas and discuss this disappointing offer too. I sighed thinking about all I had ahead of me.

I thought it was the noise of a boiler groaning for a moment and looked around me to see where the boiler was, but couldn't find one anywhere. I opened the dishwasher to see if someone had been up and put it on, but it was empty. I walked towards the window in case the noise was coming from outside. Perhaps an animal had wandered into the kitchen garden to eat the vegetables. Not my problem, I thought as I glanced out of the window.

There was a body at the bottom of the steps. I could see a body in a crumpled heap with limbs in positions they had no business being in. I yanked open the kitchen door and rushed to where they lay. It was Leonard. His clothes were soaking wet. There was dried blood in his hair and on the concrete steps. His right leg looked broken, the angle it was in. He was a pitiful sight.

'Leonard,' I said, crouching down next to him. 'Can you hear me?'

He groaned again and I put my hand out to touch him, but then took it back. I had no idea what I was doing, but I'd seen enough medical TV programmes to know that trying to move a person after an accident like this wasn't a good idea. If he'd fallen down all these steps, which it looked as if he had, he might have damaged his spine. I didn't want to make his injuries worse.

'I'm going to get you some help,' I said, and brushing aside the thought that there was some kind of twisted justice in Leonard lying broken on the steps, I rushed back into the house to phone for an ambulance.

* * *

Leonard was carried out on a stretcher and into the waiting ambulance a couple of hours later with the whole party there to watch it happen. Paul climbed in beside him and then turned to Sandra.

'Someone needs to go with him, if only to make sure he doesn't try and do another runner. Will you be okay?' he asked his wife.

He said this with a note of concern, but I was sure the concern was about whether she would try and run.

'Yes,' she said. 'I have things I want to say to everyone. I'm not going anywhere.'

Dorothy seemed delighted when the paramedic closed the door. Not so much in Leonard's injuries, I assumed, but more that he was found and could face the justice he deserved.

'He'd fallen while trying to make his escape last night,' I said. 'It isn't nice to think of him there all night, injured and with the storm going on around him. He was soaked through.'

I glanced around at the gathered group as the ambulance drove away, but I didn't detect much sympathy.

'He's lucky to be going away in an ambulance for treatment. I'd like to break his bloody neck!' Miles said.

'This is the best way, though,' said Lavinia. 'A dead man can't be brought to justice.'

All eyes turned to Sandra.

'I know you'd probably all like me dead too and I do understand. I've thought about it myself over the last year. Can we all go in and I'll tell you what I'm planning on doing?'

We all filed back inside the house and decided to go down to the kitchen to make coffee and sit around the table there. In an unsaid understanding we all seemed to realise a glamorous backdrop for this conversation was not needed.

I made the coffee again and rounds of toast, which got picked at by a few. Then I hung back.

'Do you want me to go?' I asked. 'I shouldn't really be here.'

'You absolutely should,' said Dorothy, motioning for me to sit down beside her.

'So,' Sandra started. 'I know you all must really hate me, but please let me tell you what I'm planning to do and I hope that might go some way to gaining your forgiveness.'

Dorothy grunted, but then she sat back in her chair and crossed her arms over her chest.

'I'm going to call the police and tell them what I did. I'll tell them that Leonard pressurised me into it so that will link to him having the painting, but I'm not going to drop you in it, Rufus. I'll have to make something else up.'

'No!' Rufus said. 'No more lies. If you're going to tell the truth then let it be the whole truth, otherwise it undermines what you did. I will confess to my cheating. To be honest it will be a weight off my head. I know I'll lose my position at the firm, but I'll just have to live with that as it was my own fault and I had no business pretending to practise there anyway. We'll do it together, Mum.'

Rufus reached for his mother's hand across the table and held on tight to it.

'For what it's worth,' Dorothy said, 'I don't wish ill on you. All of my venom is for Leonard. I know you didn't mean for Philip to be hurt and I'm grateful that you used his phone to call for help while he could still speak. But, I am glad you're going to confess to what you did, Sandra, because you could have said no. All this confessing now could have been done before that awful event. I think your punishment is how you've been suffering since that night and I hope whatever is dished out to you by the law is slight.'

'Thank you, Dorothy. I am truly sorry.'

They finished their coffee and Sandra got up from the table.

'I'm going to phone the police,' she said.

Out in the hallway I caught up with her as she reached for her mobile phone.

'Sandra, can I have a quick word before you make that call, please?'

'Sure,' she said with a weary voice.

'I believe you and Rufus have a memory stick containing a

movie of Leonard with Peter,' I said, and Sandra turned to me in surprise. 'Someone overheard you talking.'

'I do. Rufus gave it to me. Leonard had it and was telling him how he was keeping Peter on a short leash because of it. Rufus found it in his study the other day. He was looking for anything incriminating to use against him when the time came and he found the stick. I was going to give it to Peter. It was so awful of him to use something like that and I wanted to break the cycle.'

'That's good of you, but can you give it to me? You might not be in a position to give it back once the police arrive and I'd hate to see it fall into other hands.'

'Okay,' she said. 'I'll get it quickly now.'

'I'll come up with you. I need to pack,' I said and followed Sandra up the stairs. Even though I believed she would phone the police and not run off, I still felt some kind of responsibility to make sure it happened. Once she had handed over the memory stick, I hovered while she made the call. Then I went to pack up my things ready to go.

29

GINA

Dorothy clutched me to her in a warm hug. It had been a hell of a day, coming fast on the back of a hell of a week and also a hell of a year for Dorothy, but now, finally, she could do what she really needed to do and move on.

'I'm just so grateful to you, Gina,' she said. 'I don't think I'll ever be able to tell you how much.'

'There's really no need, Dorothy. It was my pleasure and privilege to be able to help you get the result you wanted.'

I said the words like I meant it and I did, but I actually felt quite wooden. My body felt heavy with all that had happened. Finding Leonard on the steps like that would stay with me, I realised. However bad a man he actually was, it didn't take away the shock I had felt at coming across his injured body. Had it been too much to ask of me? Yes, I thought that it probably was. But it was done, and now I could go home, such as home was now.

I noticed, with thankful eyes, that my taxi was making its way down the driveway towards me.

'The easiest way to show you is to put it in the most simplistic of terms,' Dorothy said, cutting into my thoughts and dragging me, reluctantly, back to the here and now.

'I'm not sure I understand,' I said.

'Your fee,' said Dorothy.

'Oh,' I replied, not wanting to get into a conversation about money, although the seven hundred and fifty pounds would be very welcome.

'I have your bank details and will make a transfer before the end of the day.'

'Well, thank you, I won't pretend that it isn't going to be very useful.'

'My dear, Gina, you have earned every single penny and more and I am indebted to you. Perhaps when you get home and sort out what needs to be done, you might still consider coming and staying in the boathouse for a while, or maybe we could work something out with your role as companion?'

'I wouldn't want to take a job where I wasn't really needed, but I will certainly consider the boathouse,' I said. 'Thank you.'

I made my goodbyes brief to the rest of the family, but I did linger a little with Juliet.

'It's been a real pleasure to meet you,' I told her.

'You made this week a whole lot more fun than I thought it was going to be. So, are you going to become a super sleuth and go around the country solving crimes?'

'God, no.' I laughed. 'I won't be solving anything more involved than a crossword puzzle for as long as I live. I hope to see you again at some point.'

Unexpectedly she stepped forward and slid her arms around me in a tight hug. I hugged her back and felt a little tearful. I could see my taxi making its way down the driveway, so I let her go.

'I'll be in touch soon,' I said to Dorothy, and then after a final wave to everyone, I opened the door of the taxi and while the driver wedged my suitcase into the boot, I sank gratefully onto the back seat.

'Could you make a brief stop at the church as you go past, please. I promise only to be a couple of minutes.'

'No problem,' he said. 'I've got time and you're paying after all.'

I walked up the pathway that cut through the cemetery and pushed open the oak door. I wasn't entirely sure that Peter would still be in here after the morning service, but it was closer than his house and worth a quick look. He was actually cleaning the floor, which surprised me. He had a mop and bucket of soapy water and was splashing it merrily around.

'Hello, Peter,' I said. 'You look busy.'

'What's happening at the house?' he asked. 'I've been so busy in here cleaning after the morning service, but really I should have come down to see if you needed any help.'

'You know Leonard tried to run last night, once he'd realised the painting had been found, but he had an accident and fell on the back steps. He's got a head injury and badly broken his leg, but an ambulance has taken him this morning and Paul has gone with him.'

'This morning? Why wasn't it called last night?'

'Unfortunately he wasn't found until this morning. We should have thought to check the back of the house but we didn't, did we. We all assumed he'd have gone out of the front or even through that side door.'

'Is he going to be okay?'

'I don't know, Peter. I hope so. He did look in a bad way, but he survived the stormy night with injuries so he's fighting – that's for sure. He's not a good person, but I don't wish that on him.'

'Have you come for the painting? Is Dorothy going to call the police?'

'The police are on their way, but I haven't come for the painting.

The family will come for that. I'm actually going home now. But I wanted to give you something that Sandra found.'

'Oh?'

'This,' I said, handing him the memory stick.

He took it from me and swallowed audibly, his face a picture of embarrassment.

'Thank you,' he said. 'I appreciate you doing this for me.'

'I don't like that Leonard has all these people at his beck and call. If he survives, I hope he faces up to what he's done, to all those lives he's ruined.'

'I'd like to think that were true, but I know he won't. He will feel he's been betrayed by people he considers should be thankful to him. He operates in a way that leaves him always in a place of virtue. When he goes to prison, and it seems there is enough for that to happen, he will still be surprised and disbelieving about the situation he finds himself in. He will never change and I hope he is inside for a long time. Thanks again,' he said and slipped the stick into his pocket.

Once it was out of his hand he seemed to relax and smiled at me. I decided it was time to get going. The taxi was waiting outside for me anyway.

'It was lovely to meet you and I wish you all the best,' I said.

'You too, Gina, you too.'

I closed the door of the taxi, the driver started the engine and then pulled out of the driveway and onto the main road toward Norwich.

'Had a nice time?' the driver asked me. 'Was it an eventful wedding?'

He wasn't the same driver who had brought me to the house and it proved to be true what the previous driver had said about it being a big house but a small village.

'It was the most eventful wedding I have ever been to,' I said, before pushing my sunglasses onto my face and resting my head gratefully back against the seat.

I pulled my suitcase up the path to the house and unlocked the front door. The first thing I noticed was the slightly musty scent of dead flowers and I could see that the vase of roses I'd left on the console table were way past fresh and heading firmly into dried flower territory. The pale-pink petals littered the surface and the water had a hint of green to it. So much for setting the scene for house-hunters.

I left my suitcase in the hallway and went straight to the kitchen to make a cup of tea, but of course the milk was almost off. It had only been a week, but it felt as if the house was turning against me. Instead I made a black coffee and took it out into the garden to see whether the storm had stretched this far and what damage might have been done to my plants, and then I set to work.

'Hello, Georgina.'

I spun my head round from where I crouched, pulling at some weeds, to see Douglas was standing on the lawn. He was wearing a white linen shirt, which showed off the tan that still lingered from his trip.

'I would prefer it if you knocked on the door or let me know you're coming. You don't live here any more,' I said, turning back to my task and annoyingly I wished I'd put a brush through my hair.

'I did send you a message. You don't answer them.'

'Oh, I'm not long back. I think my phone is still in my bag,' I said, pulling off my gloves and getting to my feet. 'I don't suppose you brought some milk with you?'

'No,' he said, bemused. 'Didn't think to.'

'Black coffee it is then,' I said, walking past him and into the house.

He followed me inside and after a long lingering look at his piano, he stood watching me make him a drink and instead of feeling uncomfortable I felt some strength in the fact that this was my domain, not his. Except that actually it wasn't, not for much longer anyway.

'So the offer isn't as high as I'd like, but, Georgina, I won't leave you stuck, you know. We'll make sure you get somewhere half decent to live.'

'Will *we*? Half decent, lucky me. Who's *we* anyway, Douglas?' I asked him and he did look a bit uncomfortable for a moment.

'I meant you and me, we.'

'Not Little Miss Maidenhead?'

He looked stunned at that, but he rallied.

'This isn't about anyone else you know,' he said, without actually denying the existence of anyone else. 'This is about reaching the grand age of seventy-three and wanting more. I'm sorry if that is hard to hear, but it's the truth. I won't leave you in the lurch – you have entitlements.'

'You won't leave me in the lurch! You left me with a letter explaining that you'd gone off to rediscover your youth and that the house was being sold from under me. I consider myself well and truly lurched. And I don't want entitlements; I can look after myself,' I said, slamming the mug of coffee down on the counter next to him and delighting in the fact that a couple of drops flew out of the top and landed on his sleeve. That stain would be tricky to get out.

'You can look after yourself? You haven't worked for forty-three years. How much does your companion job pay? Hmm.'

'I should never have left my job.'

'You weren't capable of doing it. After all that happened with your mother, you were a mess.'

'You were there; you knew what happened. If I was a mess, there was good reason,' I said, quietly, and he looked at the floor. 'And perhaps I would have been capable, with the right support.'

'I did nothing but support you. You were able to stay at home with all the comforts while I went to work.'

'You took advantage of me, Douglas. You took advantage of my state of mind. You turned me into a doormat over the years and then casually wiped your feet on your way out.'

He just stared at me, flabbergasted. I was a bit flabbergasted myself as the realisation hit home. He'd used me, not supported me. I felt almost euphoric as this thought landed.

'I've had a very busy week and I'd like you to leave,' I said with my arms folded firmly across my chest and, to be fair to him, he did.

* * *

Later, I ran myself a bath and soaked my tired body. It wasn't just the afternoon of gardening and the encounter with Douglas that had made my limbs and head ache, but a week of feeling tense all the time. I had felt uncomfortable, unsure, pressured and, at times, even threatened, but mostly I had come away with a huge sense of accomplishment. Dorothy had called me a problem solver and that had felt really good. Then I remembered Leonard's broken body at the bottom of the steps and shuddered.

The bath water was cooling and I got out and wrapped myself in my fluffy robe. I pushed that lingering image of Leonard from my head, and instead thought about Dorothy's bittersweet victory. The happiness she felt in being right in her assumption about the painting was imbued with sadness about the part Sandra and Rufus had played. There could never be true happiness when you looked at the bigger picture. Leonard was terribly injured and may not survive to serve his punishment, Sandra had to live with the awful choice she had made to save her son's reputation and future career, and Rufus was planning to leave that situation now anyway, making the choice his mother had made all the more pointless.

'Gina,' I told myself. 'If you are ever going to be a good companion you will need to learn to leave it behind when you leave the job.'

I found a lasagne in the freezer and opened some wine while I waited for it to finish turning in the microwave and, still in my robe, I went and stood in my show-house living room. Everything was immaculate, not a magazine was out of place on the coffee table, no photographs on the sideboard because I'd already packed them away, nothing at all to say who lived in this house. As the pings from the kitchen told me my dinner was ready I had an overwhelming sense that this house wasn't mine any more, because I'd already moved out.

30

GINA

Alice arrived the following Wednesday lunchtime and I had set up the table in the garden with a lovely spread for lunch. I'd bought cheeses and fruit, there was fresh bread and Alice's favourite hand-cut crisps. I had a bottle of Sancerre in the fridge too, but wasn't sure whether Alice had driven or got the train. Looking at the spread, I wondered if this would be the last meal I'd ever have in this garden. It had only been three days since I'd come back from Norfolk, but I'd made a decision about what I was going to do and was keen to get on with it.

I'd had a conversation with Dorothy yesterday on the phone. I'd originally called her to say she'd made a mistake with the bank transfer and had mistakenly added a nought on the end of the figure. But Dorothy made it very clear that there was no mistake and that I had earned every penny and more. When I had tried to protest, Dorothy shut that line of conversation down quickly by saying that if I wanted to give it away then I could; it was my money and I should use it in any way I felt was fitting. If I felt that offering it to a charity of my choice was what I wanted to do then it was up to me. In the end I had just thanked her and been grateful for that boost to my savings.

In fact, it was this that had made me look again in *The Lady* online magazine. Maybe I could try another position as companion. There were enough wanted ads looking for them. It wasn't only about the money that Dorothy had generously given me; it was how happy the woman was now. Despite the accompanying heartache, I had helped her into a position where she could move on.

She told me that Leonard was improving in hospital and the police were looking into the accusations. Sandra was, at the moment, helping them with their inquiries. Rufus had gone straight to his employers and had told them of his deception. Rightfully they had let him go, but apparently he was finally happy and free of what had been hanging over his head and, oddly, had decided that a career in the theatre might be more for him.

It was a week that I would never forget. A companion and painting hunter. I'd done a good job, but if I was to be companion again I'd be looking for a position that was far less taxing.

There was a woman looking for a someone to accompany her on holiday for a fortnight, but that was an all-expenses-paid job rather than just paid. There was a man whose wife had died and he needed help downsizing from his old family home to a smaller property and then to care for him until he found someone in the new community to take over his needs. There was man in Cornwall and a woman in London, and I kept looking, but hadn't found the courage to apply.

In the meantime I'd had a phone call from Lavinia who'd said that Dorothy was struggling a bit and feeling very tired after the week away. Would I consider Dorothy's offer of the boathouse and also keep an eye on her until she got back on her feet? In the middle of the night when I'd woken and couldn't get back to sleep, I'd decided to take it.

'Hi, Mum.'

Alice was at the side of the house where I'd propped the gate open and I looked up from the table of food to see my daughter with a bunch of flowers in one hand and a bottle of wine in the other. Good, I thought, she'd got the train. This would be far more relaxed.

'Garden looks lovely.'

I caught her and gave her a hug, which she returned.

'How are you, darling? How are the girls and Jim? I must come and see them soon. I miss them.'

I had been so wrapped up with things here, I realised it had been a good month since I'd seen Lou and Meg. After the ups and downs of the week I'd just had, I had a sudden wish to wrap both of my granddaughters in my arms. Of course Chris still had my car so I'd need to get the train to Alice's. But that was no matter.

'We're all fine. It's you I'm worried about. I mean, working as a companion at your age is a bit weird, don't you think.'

'It's a slight change in direction in my life, that's all,' I said and was horrified to feel my lip trembling. 'Shall we have some wine?'

I filled two glasses before Alice could decline.

I began cutting slices from the loaf of sourdough and Alice stood watching me while sipping her drink. I was desperately trying not to blurt out what I was thinking, what I was feeling. Douglas had left me; after forty-three years of marriage he'd disappeared off to the other side of the world on a whim. The only reason I'd been looking at jobs and flats I couldn't afford was because of him. It hadn't been my choice. I would have been quite happy staying here in this house until it became too much for me or I died, whichever came first. Instead I had been abandoned and put out to pasture.

And the truth now was that I had discovered something during my week away, and it was that I quite liked myself. I was actually pretty okay and had something more to offer. I wasn't quite dead yet. I picked up my wine glass and took a large gulp.

'How's work?' I asked after Alice sat down. We began to pile cheese onto bread, and roll up slices of the cured meats I'd bought at the local deli. I offered Alice the plate of grapes and dried fruit.

'Good,' she replied. 'I'm hearing rumblings of redundancies, but Hannah says it won't be me and actually I'm more likely to be promoted within the next six months, which will be about bloody time.'

Alice worked for a marketing company and had been sidelined for promotion many times when the girls were younger. They just wouldn't take her seriously, assuming that the kids came first, but now they were older – eight and eleven – it seemed that now was the time. And Alice had worked damn hard for it too. I took my hat off to my daughter. She juggled and ran herself ragged, put herself out and generally proved herself to be someone who could be relied upon.

'That's wonderful, Alice – you deserve it,' I said holding up my glass. 'Here's to being seen for all the work that you do and promoted accordingly.'

'Thanks, Mum. How was your weird week in Norfolk anyway?'

'Challenging, but rewarding,' I said, taking the wine and topping up our glasses. 'Put it this way: I shall be more careful when applying for my next position.'

'You're going to do it again?'

'Yes, I think I will. Also, I've found somewhere to live.'

'Right, I'm sorry for going on at you on the phone the other week. I'm cross with Dad for being an idiot and I shouldn't have taken it out on you. I know you've got to sell the house. So, where are you going?'

'The woman I've spent the week looking after has a boathouse at the end of her garden on the Thames at Hampton. She's offered it to me for a while, well, for as long as I want it.'

'A boathouse? It sounds poky. Is it?'

'It is quite small to be fair, but beautiful and has a lovely balcony looking over the water.'

I wasn't quite sure why I felt I needed Alice's approval, but I did. I wanted her to be happy for me. I'd already phoned Chris that morning to let him know what I was doing and he was thrilled for me. Alice was never going to be as easy.

'Everything has changed and I don't like it,' she said, a little petulantly.

'Everything has changed for me too,' I reminded her.

'I know,' she said.

Alice finished her mouthful and then took a sip of her wine.

'I don't even know what we're all going to do for Christmas,' she said.

'Alice, it's only August.'

'Yes, but we always came to you and we can hardly cram ourselves into your boathouse.'

'I don't see why not. Alice, this is quite hard for me, but I would like you to be happy for me. Can you do that?'

She looked at me across the table and smiled.

'If it's a boathouse, there's a boat I assume?'

'Of course – Dorothy has a blue narrowboat.'

'Do you think we could take the girls out in it?'

'I don't know,' I said. 'We could ask.'

She took my hand across the table and straightened my mother's flower ring on my finger, then stared at it for a long moment.

'I love you, Mum, and I am happy for you,' she said.

31

DOROTHY

Gina moved into the boathouse a week after they returned from Norfolk and Dorothy surprised herself with how happy this made her. She felt as if the two had made a close connection during that rollercoaster of a wedding week and to have her new friend by her side was wonderful. She didn't want to admit it to her family, but it turned out she did need some help.

Miles carried Gina's bags and cases up the stairs into the boathouse and then left to get started on the lunch they were all going to have in the garden.

'I really should have cleared more of my things away so you can make it your own space,' Dorothy said, picking up a vase from the walnut sideboard.

'I don't mind at all. I haven't brought any soft furnishings or trinkets with me so it will be nice to have some lovely things around me. Douglas suggested we keep the house furnished until the sale goes through in case anything goes wrong. It's never as easy to sell an empty house.'

'Sensible,' Dorothy said, although she didn't really like to compliment the idiot who had let Gina get away.

'We should leave you to unpack and settle in,' Lavinia said. 'Come on, Dot. Shall we go and lay the table?'

'Lunch on the lawn in half an hour,' Dorothy said and then left Gina to it.

* * *

Dorothy had decided to invite Erik round for lunch and was interested to see that he chose to sit next to Gina.

'It's Erik with a K,' Dorothy said after she introduced them.

'I'm not sure Gina needs to know that, unless she's planning on writing him a letter,' Miles said and everyone laughed.

'Is it a Scandinavian name?' Gina asked him.

'Danish,' he said. 'My mother was Danish, but my father is Welsh and I grew up in North Wales, so I'm a fair mix.'

'I love North Wales,' Gina said with a smile, 'such beautiful countryside.'

They tucked into the quiches and salads that Lavinia and Miles had made and Dorothy poured them all glasses of the cloudy lemonade she had decanted into a jug and stuffed with ice cubes and slices of lemon. It wasn't as warm as it had been in previous weeks, but pleasant enough to sit outside.

'Do you have a boat too?' Gina asked Erik. 'Is it obligatory when you live here?'

'I do. I have a narrowboat like Dorothy's,' he said.

'Do you take it out much, or is it just an expensive place to sit and have coffee?' Gina asked and Dorothy watched as her cheeks flamed.

Erik laughed; a deep bass sound that rumbled from him and when he stopped, Dorothy noted that he locked his piercing blue eyes onto Gina.

'It was just something Dorothy said when she showed me her boat,' Gina said, seemingly desperate to explain her odd question.

'Guilty,' Dorothy said simply.

'In truth, Gina, it is mostly an expensive place to sit and have a coffee and I'm lucky to have it, I know. I should take her out more. Perhaps you'd like to come sometime when you're settled in?'

All eyes turned to Gina then and she took a long sip of her lemonade before answering.

'That sounds lovely, Erik,' she said. 'I'd like that.'

Dorothy smiled to herself. It was a deeply satisfying feeling having these two people that she'd grown fond of, connecting like this. It was something she would be encouraging wholeheartedly.

When lunch was over and everything cleared away, Dorothy was pleased to see that Miles and Lavinia were leaving. Gina looked a little overwhelmed and probably just needed to settle quietly into her new space, alone.

'I promise it won't always be like this,' Lavinia said. 'We never just turn up unannounced. Dorothy doesn't like it.'

'Of course I don't like it. It's rude not to let someone know you're coming,' Dorothy said and it wasn't lost on her that her son and his wife shared a knowing smile.

'You all just do whatever you did before and I'll fit in,' Gina said.

'Well, we're both very happy that you're here,' Miles said. 'Mum is incredibly independent, but everyone needs a helping hand from time to time.'

Erik said goodbye not long after the other two had left and then opened the little gate next to the boathouse and disappeared into his own garden. Dorothy and Gina settled onto the loungers under the willow at the water's edge with a cup of tea each.

'It's really beautiful here, Dorothy,' Gina said, looking out over the water. 'You might never get rid of me.'

'Fine with me,' Dorothy chuckled and closed her eyes.

She must have nodded off, because when she woke her teacup was on the table, stone cold and Gina was chatting over the fence to Erik. Dorothy watched the two of them together and how Gina kept touching her hair and Erik stood straighter than usual with one strong arm on the top of the fence post. Dorothy smiled. They could be a couple of teenagers. Nothing changed with age when it came to blossoming attraction. It was always timeless.

Gina returned to Dorothy with a paperback in her hands.

'Have you joined Erik's book club?' Dorothy asked her.

'He's lent me the latest Karin Slaughter and wants to discuss it when I've read it. I'm already thinking it might be a bit scary for me.'

'Erik loves a book chat. I've not been too on board recently and can't seem to settle to a story, but maybe with you here that might change.'

'He suggested a bottle of wine and that a narrowboat book chat was in order. You'd be up for that wouldn't you, Dorothy?'

'That sounds fun,' Dorothy said, but she already knew she'd find an excuse to duck out of it. Gina and Erik didn't need her playing gooseberry. She decided not to say a word, though. She had a feeling that Gina might run a mile if pushed too hard and too fast. Nature had to take its course, nice and gently.

'Have you decided to go on the cruise with Yvonne?' Gina asked her as she sank back down onto the lounger.

'I have. I phoned her yesterday to confirm. Do you know, for the first time in ages I feel a sense of adventure again. I know I'm an old lady and some things are past me now, but there's some life in me yet and I feel open to some new experiences. Do you feel like that too, Gina?'

'Um, a bit,' she said.

'Because there was something I wanted to ask you. There is something I've wanted to do all my life and for some reason I've never got around to it. I don't want to ask Miles or Sophie to go with me because they'd fuss and besides, neither of them are keen on heights.'

Dorothy glanced across at Gina who looked alarmed.

'It's not as bad as it sounds. Perhaps you could look it up online for me?'

32

GINA

Tranquillity was the word that sprung to my mind as I took in the scene below me. The countryside was so beautiful from up here and apart from the occasional sound of the burner it was peaceful too. Half an hour into our flight I'd finally loosened my grip on the edge and decided that I was up here now and should just enjoy the experience. Dorothy was sitting across the basket from me sipping from a glass of champagne, her face was a picture of happiness.

'Is it how you imagined it would be, your first flight in a hot-air balloon?'

'It's wonderful,' Dorothy said. 'Even better than I expected.'

I had to admit I was thoroughly enjoying myself now, although I wasn't keen when Dorothy first suggested it. I loved watching balloons flying over our house in the summer months, but never imagined I'd have the guts to go up in one. After a serious talking-to from Dorothy and then myself, I had made the decision that I needed to challenge myself more. Certainly the week in Norfolk had proved that I had more gumption than I thought. It really is something when an eighty-nine-year-old woman has to talk you into doing something adventurous.

I leaned my elbows on the edge of the basket now and watched the villages go past far below me. It was a beautifully clear day and we'd set off from a field outside Canterbury just after dawn. When choosing her flight, Dorothy had said, what would be better than flying over the Garden of England. Looking down now, I could only agree with her.

Our pilot, Amanda, had taken us through a safety briefing, shown us around the balloon and basket, poured us champagne and offered us a plate of lovely canapés, then left us to watch in wonder at the world below us.

'We should do more things like this,' Dorothy said.

'More gentle, sedate things?' I asked.

'Well, more experiences all round. Perhaps bungee jumping or paragliding?' Dorothy said with a glint in her eye. Amanda chuckled beside me. She'd seen me gripping onto the edge of the basket as if my life depended on it as we first took off. She'd be surprised at me doing anything more fast-paced than walking, I would imagine.

'You can do whatever you like,' I said. 'I'll drive you and wait in the car for you to come back down to earth.'

Dorothy laughed and then sighed deeply in the most contented and relaxed way. She then raised her glass.

'Here's to you, Gina. Before you arrived at my house that day, I had nothing to look forward to and now everything is completely different. I feel as if the whole world is open and available to me, and you have given me that.'

I felt a little choked all of a sudden and swallowed down a lump in my throat.

'And do you know what else? I think you're on your way too,' she said.

* * *

Later, back in the boathouse, I opened the doors out onto the balcony and took a cup of coffee with me to the little table in the corner. I realised that from here, on the far edge, I could see into Erik's garden and to where he was stretched out on his lounger with a book and what looked like a glass of wine. I moved away, keen for him not to see me watching him and pulled a chair over to the other side, then I settled myself down and watched the boats sailing past on the river.

I needed to make sense of the life that I was living now and try to claim it as my own, but it didn't feel like that. It felt very much as if I had stepped into someone else's life, thrown on their clothes and climbed into their bed. I knew it would take time.

I had a sudden urge to record what I was doing and thought I might buy a journal and keep one like I used to do when I worked with my mother. Then I thought about Jullet and her voice recordings and wondered if that might be a better way to do it. After all, I used to do much the same at work. Tentatively I picked up my phone and opened the voice memo app. I had no idea what to say and considered turning it off again, but then changed my mind and pressed record.

'I am on the balcony of my new home. It's a boathouse on the Thames at Hampton and I can see Ash Island from where I sit. It's September now and those hot and endless summer days are gone. I long for crisp autumn mornings where the sunlight tones itself down to a pale amber.'

I pressed pause on my recording for a moment and thought about what I really wanted to say. I was talking, but what was I really saying? What was I doing? What was my role now?

I'd thought I was no longer needed. I'd been the centre of my children's existence, but they had grown up and even my granddaughters, Lou and Meg, didn't need me any more. They loved me, loved seeing me, but they didn't need me.

Douglas had once told me, many years ago and admittedly post-coital, that he'd die rather than lose me. But there he was living in his flat in Maidenhead, very much without me, and the last time I'd seen him he was still breathing.

But Dorothy had needed me and it sounded from the advertisements in *The Lady* that others might too. I drank what was left of my coffee and then pressed record again.

'My name is Gina Knight. I'm seventy-one years old and somewhat surprisingly find myself in the autumn of my life. I have always said that September is my favourite time of the year and here I am heading into the season of bonfires and cardigans, of fiery trees and homemade soup, of squirrels digging in the lawn and spiders moving into the bathroom.

'I am here and I need to find a way to embrace this glorious time while it is still available to me. I need to prove that September is, indeed, my favourite month.

'Recently I became a companion to an elderly woman and it turned out I was pretty good at it. It seems that I'm a problem solver—'

'Gina?'

I pressed stop on my recording as Dorothy's voice carried up to me from the garden. Jumping up from my seat I called out for her to come up and met her at the top of the steps.

'Can I gate-crash your boathouse for a bit?' she asked, and I noticed she had a plate of biscuits in her hand.

'Of course you can and it's your boathouse, you know.'

'Not at the minute it's not. Honestly, Gina, I'm here as a neighbour. Actually, I've just got off the phone with my friend and there's a bit of a problem. I thought I could talk it through with you if you're free.'

'I'll put the kettle on,' I said and invited her in.

I walked over to the sink and filled the kettle while Dorothy made herself comfortable on the sofa and put the plate of biscuits on the table. It was the first time she'd been in here as a guest since I moved in and I tried hard not to feel awkward about it. It would take time.

'Tea?' I asked her and she nodded. 'What's happening with your friend?'

'I've known Gerald and Meredith for years. He was an architect and has many prestigious projects to his name. Sadly, now he has dementia and all that is lost.'

'That is sad,' I said pouring milk into our mugs. 'It affects so many people now.'

'It certainly affects Meredith as she has to look after him. She adores him, though, always has and she's losing that lovely man of hers.'

I stopped stirring for a moment and wondered what it was like to adore your husband as Dorothy did Philip and Meredith does Gerald. I felt a pang of regret and then pulled the teabags from the mugs and dropped them into the food caddy in the cupboard under the sink.

'She has help, usually, because they've just moved in with their daughter and son-in-law. Anyway, Meredith has broken her arm and is in plaster, which is an issue for her because she's a novelist.'

'So, she's looking for someone to help her type?' I asked.

'Well, yes, but not only that, she's going to struggle with Gerald until her arm is healed.'

'You said they'd moved close to their daughter? Won't she help them?'

'They're flying out to New Zealand in a couple of days. Their son has been in a terrible car accident and they need to be with him as he comes out of hospital. They had someone lined up to help Meredith and Gerald, but he's let them down at the last minute and Meredith is very choosy.'

'Well, that does sound like a bit of a pickle,' I said, handing Dorothy her tea and sinking down onto the sofa next to her. I blew some of the steam from the top of mine and took a sip, then watched as Dorothy's eyes slid to mine and rested there for a moment longer than was comfortable. 'You're thinking of me, aren't you?'

'The thought did cross my mind, yes.'

'Well, I was looking at jobs, to be fair, especially as you're going to be away for three weeks, but I haven't found anything imminent.'

'This is pretty imminent.'

'I don't know much about dementia, to be honest.'

'You don't really need to. They just need someone to help them get used to being in a new town, do a bit of typing for Meredith, be a companion. We both know you're excellent at that.'

'Right,' I said slowly, feeling as if I was already on my way to the job. Dorothy could be very persuasive.

I watched Dorothy's face for a moment. She seemed more animated than I'd expect. After all, she was talking about one friend with dementia and the other with a broken arm.

'What's the real story?' I asked her, and watched as she picked her words carefully.

'Okay, the thing is, Meredith and I go back many years, have quite some history together and I've heard that she's writing her memoir.'

'Right, and?'

'Well, there are some things in our past that I'd rather not come out.'

'Ooh, Dorothy, you dark horse. Can't you just ask her not to put them in?'

'We haven't spoken in years, we fell out.'

'What? You just said you'd got off the phone from her.'

'No, I said I got off the phone with a friend. Actually, a mutual friend.'

'And what is it you're really asking me to do?' I said, feeling a little wary all of a sudden.

'Just to be a companion and to... well, find out what she writing.'

'Oh, Dorothy, I don't think I can do that.'

'Of course you can! You didn't think you could find a missing painting but you did.'

I narrowed my eyes at her and put my tea down on the table, suddenly losing my appetite for it.

'What makes you think I'd even get the job? She'd hardly choose me knowing that I know you.'

'Yes, well, that's why she won't know and the introduction will come through our mutual friend. You'd be brilliant, Gina, you *are* brilliant.'

There was no way I was going to take on another companion job under false pretences. Dorothy was definitely barking up the wrong tree.

'You haven't asked me where they live, it is relevant.'

I sighed and then decided to humour her.

'And where is it that Gerald and Meredith live?' I asked in a sing-song voice.

'Well, that's the most wonderful thing,' she said with a large smile. 'They live in a beautiful chateau in the South of France.'

Despite the fact I had no intention of taking on the role and that Dorothy was most definitely asking too much of me again, I couldn't help but suddenly find my interest piqued.

ABOUT THE AUTHOR

Kate Galley is the author of uplifting golden years fiction, including *The Second Chance Holiday Club*. She was previously published by Aria, and is a mobile hairdresser in her spare time.

Sign up to Kate Galley's mailing list for news, competitions and updates on future books.

Follow Kate on social media here:

facebook.com/Kate%20Galley%20Author

x.com/KateGalley1

instagram.com/kategalley1

Boldwᴓd

Boldwood Books is an award-winning fiction
publishing company seeking out the best
stories from around the world.

Find out more at www.boldwoodbooks.com

Join our reader community for brilliant books,
competitions and offers!

Follow us
@BoldwoodBooks
@TheBoldBookClub

Sign up to our weekly
deals newsletter

https://bit.ly/BoldwoodBNewsletter

Made in United States
Orlando, FL
15 January 2025

57325719R00153